M000031777

THE WIDOW'S HUSBAND

Sheila Evans

THE PERMANENT PRESS
4170 Noyac Road
Sag Harbor, NY 11963

Library of Congress Cataloging-in-Publication Data

Evans, Sheila.
The widows husband : a novel / by Sheila Evans
p. cm.
ISBN 1-57962-111-2 (alk. paper)
1. Widows- -Fiction. 2. Mistresses- -Fiction. 3. Loss (Psychology)- -Fiction. 4. Mothers and daughters- -Fiction. 5. Parent and adult child- -Fiction. I. Title

PS3555.V2598W53 2005
813'.54- -dc22

2004060246

Printed in The United States of America

THE PERMANENT PRESS
4170 Noyac Road
Sag Harbor, NY 11963

For Joel

Chapter 1

I'd fantasized leaving him. Not often, and not for long—and certainly not forever—but after a blowup, I'd drag out the idea and play with it, twist it this way and that way, a kaleidoscope of my anger. Savor it, my delicious anger: midnight ice cream sneaked behind the refrigerator door. Yeah, I'd leave him, clear out, slam doors, squeal tires, grind gears—I'd be gone. I'd show him.

I had left him, in the past. But now, at his funeral, such confusion in my mind, I can't remember what we fought about. I recall the delicious heat of battle—but over what?—followed by hours of blind driving, windows down, radio blaring out KROK, a station dedicated to the sort of middle-aged soft rock Emmett had scorned. He'd preferred Dixieland, which I despise. Okay, I've never been into the likes of Alice Cooper, Deep Purple, or Aretha Franklin either, but I blasted it out through opened windows in a spirit of rebellion, and to spite Emmett. It kept me going, my mood up.

The closest I came to really leaving him had been once after a fight when I stayed out all night. Slept, or tried to, in my VW behind the bank, the one where I keep my secret little account.

What had that fight been about? Emmett can't tell me anymore, lying there in his dark itchy suit on such a nice April afternoon, although the cloud-splattered sky has a tentative look: the weather could go either way. It's chilly here in the mortuary chapel. The reason for this floral scented, icy-edged air seems rather ghoulishly clear. Thoughts like these make me shiver even more. If I ever get out of here, I'm going to go somewhere and bake in the sun.

So much Emmett can't tell me now. How to light the pilot on the water heater. Where to recycle plastic. Who to see at City Hall about the utility bill. He'd always been there to sand down the rough edges of everyday life, although I'd accused him of ignoring my inner needs, my real needs. Of abandoning me. Now I *am* abandoned, and a prickle of raw fear, of incipient panic, surges from the backs of my hands into my hair.

I'd been afraid, too, that night behind the bank. But after my excitement about what I was doing to him died, after I'd gotten cold and cramped, when the sun was nowhere near to coming up and night seemed a permanent condition, well, even then I'd been loath to go home and face him. He could be so cold and punishing for such a long time. He hated what he called my hysterics, and I was sure he'd called that wild flight hysterical, and worse. How unfair he could be! Or rather *had been.* I have to learn to think in the past tense.

I have to learn to *think,* period. I've been lazy, true, I let him think for me. It'd just been easier. Easier to get along if I went along. Easier to cower there in the dark that night behind the bank than go home and thrash out our differences, even after I got over being angry. Even after rational (or irrational) thinking had kicked in and I imagined maniacal shapes in the dark, ominous noises filling the long black hours. Even then I wanted to stay there, hunker down in the VW, prolong my mutiny.

Amy still lived at home, a hell-bent teenager, at war with both her dad and me. I worried that night in the car behind the bank. I worried about Amy getting herself off to school in the morning. I thought Amy still needed me to dole out lunch money, check on getting a ride home and at what time, and if she had done her homework. Emmett didn't deal with what he called trifles—and I suppose he was right. But he wasn't right to ignore Amy. By then, he was angry with her, too. According to him, she'd grown (*regressed* he said) from cute toddler to troublesome teen. He was critical, when he was aware at all, of Amy's teenage traumas. In fact, *critical* or *oblivious* pretty much described his attitude toward any household management, and I much preferred the latter.

I chide myself for thinking such hateful thoughts and I glance over at Amy beside me here in the chapel. Is she grieving for her father? Is she afraid? That hardly seems likely—Amy's a strong independent girl, almost (I admit this to myself) a selfish girl. She is her own person, now that she's out of the house. She'll get along fine without her dad. After the service, which seems at once too long (we don't hold much belief in religion, nor do we know this minister provided by the mortuary), and too short (I dread the tangle of decisions and actions that awaits me at its close), I'll ask Amy about that fight. I'll say, "Remember that row your dad and I had, and I didn't come home all night? Remember that night I slept behind the bank? What had we been fighting about?" I'll say that with a sigh or with a rueful downturn of my mouth to show my consternation, my understanding of the futility of such questions now, when that part of our past is as dead as Emmett himself. Maybe Amy can recall the roots of that blowup.

All I see of Amy is the tip of her nose under her black straw hat. It's just the two of us here in this section reserved for family, an alcove screened from the chapel's main room, presumably so we can grieve in private. We can hear muffled sounds from the outer area, the kind of noises I associate with the threadbare rituals of churchiness: rustle of clothing as people fidget, faint coughs and throat clearings, a sob—someone out there is crying? Someone shushes a child, someone whispers. More people out there than I'd thought would show up, and I begin to worry about the impending funeral reception.

The minister says something about a loving and generous heart. That was true—just look at the turnout from his office, from the whole plant. I knew he'd been a different person there, a jovial, easy-going fellow with a sunny-side-up personality. Who wouldn't like him, like that?

Of course it had been a masquerade. Emmett admitted that, had once told me that I was the only person who really knew him. That had pleased me, had made me feel honored, *approved* of. To be his confidante. His intimate.

Besides, doesn't everyone wear a disguise? I myself put on an outward show of competence, of patience and reliability. The one who could be counted on to be room mother, to supply cakes for bake sales, to help with carpooling or chaperoning (which was how I found out about Amy and that kid, her pimply former boyfriend). I'm the one who volunteers for the diabetes Walkathon, the Cancer Prevention crusade, the March of Dimes collection drive. After the walk or the crusade or the drive, the organizers assign me to the back room to do filing or telephoning. This is a kindness, because they think they understand my diffident nature, my preference for low visibility. However, they, whoever "they" happen to be, know I'll come through, will murmur, "If there's anything I can do to help, please call me." Which is doubly ironic because half the time I don't care a fig for the cause itself—I can be, usually am, sly rather than shy—and because I feel that I need help myself. Emmett's help.

Abruptly I'm aware of the depth of my anger toward Emmett for going off and leaving me to muddle through this ordeal alone! To tend to this mob of his fellow workers when I barely know them. *He* should have to cope with *my* fellow workers, although how many of them would turn out for me is problematic. I tend to make few permanent connections, am something of a loner, which is why I like working temp. The gist of it is that Emmett is shirking his social responsibilities, something he'd rarely done in life. I have the illogical feeling that he's the host of this gathering, and he's not doing his part; he's in the other room telling off-color jokes, or serving drinks, or shooting the breeze with the boys. He's leaving it all to me, the fragile partner, the brittle, the less able member of the union.

He'd been the strong one, the sturdy one. So he'd had that one little attack—the doctor termed it a "wakeup call"—but he'd been following orders, he'd lost weight, quit smoking. Only forty-seven, two years older than I am, he was supposed to maintain, to prevail, to be my stalwart companion, my defense against the world. Husbands often die before their wives, due to job stress or life style choices—all that cigarette smoking, or drinking, or eating of red meat. But not Emmett, oh, no. Not him!

True, of late he'd seemed tired and listless, but I put it down to working all those extra hours. Why had he been working so hard? I vaguely recall some talk about deadlines, shortfalls, make-or-break projects with hair triggers. Meant nothing to me at the time, and I confess I listened to him the way he listened to me.

With scant attention. It was just Emmett again, the way he was, always putting pressure on himself. "Your dad, you know him," I'd say to Amy on the phone. Now Amy has her own condo across town, living with that fellow, what's his name? Again I shoot her a look, but she's bent under her hat, engaged in a study of her nails. They're painted an odd shade of lilac, hardly the thing for a funeral, but what is she supposed to do? Paint her nails black? Besides, since that awful morning, Amy has more or less moved back in with me and hasn't had time or inclination to tend to herself properly. I suppose that's it. Why else would she paint her nails lilac?

The minister's sonorous voice intones, "Unto the Lord, he was a faithful servant, working in the fields, bringing in the sheaves..."

No doubt about it, Emmett had been a worker, the engine, our power source. Last to turn in, first one up. Until that morning just a few days ago, although it seems years back now. The alarm went off and I climbed out of bed before him, which should have warned me something was wrong. I talked to him from our half-bath while he dozed, or I thought he was dozing. Then I yelled to him from the kitchen, "Come on, lazybones, better get up or you won't have time to look at the paper."

I went back to prod him, had actually shaken him rather roughly, a fact that later made me feel bad. "You have to get up. I'm filling in today at the library downtown, you have to give me a ride."

As I said earlier, I work as a temp, but only occasionally—not enough to warrant the expense of my own wheels. We'd been juggling around one car since giving Amy the old VW, the one I slept in behind the bank. At the time, Amy had just moved out and was borrowing it, borrowing and borrowing. Finally in a fit of exasperation, Emmett threw her the keys and said, "Here, take it, but when it needs tires or brakes, don't come to us." When I objected—after all, it was *my* car—he said, "Listen, it's going to need real money put in it soon, and I don't want to do it. Let her foot the bill."

"Well, how fair is that!" I said.

"Time she learned what real life is like. I know what I'm doing, and besides, this is between me and her."

I'd been bitter about the deal at the time, mad at both of them. But that was Emmett, the way he'd gotten with Amy, and with me, too. Besides, he'd usually been right about cars, although cars did not interest him. I respected his judgement, even when I didn't agree with it.

"You have to get up and give me a ride. You know I like the library gig, and it could last all week. I don't want to start out being late," I said, scolding him, shaking him. His form was inert, and his body moved easily under my touch, like a rag doll. From his mouth issued a thin trickle of blood, puddling on his pillow-case. My voice rising, "Emmett? What's wrong?"

His cheeks, usually ruddy, were chalk white. I suddenly realized his color, which I'd attributed to health and vigor, had come from a spider webbing of broken blood vessels. This webbing now formed a network of brownish-purple, making a pattern against the cold marble of his skin. It resembled a map of the freeway system into Sacramento, such a wild profane image for me to entertain, at this august moment of his death—I knew he was dead, even then—and I was ashamed. I put my hand on his forehead, found it, yes, cold. Cold as stone.

"Emmett!" I wailed as fear and shock took the place of reason. A part of my mind registered that he would not approve of my reaction. He would label this response "hysterical," lacking in qualities necessary for control. This made me even more tentative and clumsy, and I hated myself for it. Would I never achieve some authority, some resources of my own? My own self-doubt caused my hand to shake while turning back the covers—the Wedding Ring quilt, the white wool blanket, and the top sheet. As if by exposing him, I'd cause him to catch a chill. At the very least, I was infringing on his personal privacy.

Maybe I was. The last few years he'd slept nude. He said his pajamas bound up on him, whatever that meant. His exposed naked body looked weak and vulnerable. And small, much too small to contain the energy, the spirit of Emmett. He hadn't been large—five ten or so, one hundred sixty-five pounds, but he'd always given the impression of a lean and rangy fellow, wired with sinewy muscles.

His skin, ashy white, was almost a match for the sheets. Even then, at that point, I thought bitterly of the colored sheets I'd once bought that he refused to sleep on. (Had that been the cause of that out-all-night fight? No, I don't think so.)

"Emmett!" I shrieked and began to blubber. So deathly white, his only color that weird spider webbing, and a tattoo of an American flag on his shoulder he'd had done in Da Nang. Between his knees drawn up in a fetal curl, in the pocket of his crotch, lay his penis. It was gray, shriveled into a sort of ashy rosebud. A rosebud nestled in the misty baby's breath of his pubic hair, also gray. Why was he gray? Why was he chalky white? I covered him up again, tucking the blankets under his chin, as if he'd resurrect should I keep him wrapped up. I knew my actions were foolish, a way, really, to protect myself from the shocking sight of him.

I remember thinking: that is not my husband. That is not Emmett. Someone has substituted that dead thing for Emmett, who's alive at this moment, in another place. (I had the same reaction later in the mortuary, seeing him stretched out in his dark blue wool suit, that awful hairy thing, his hands folded across his chest, his cheeks rouged, his lashes beaded with mascara. I thought, That's not Emmett. They've substituted a mannequin for Emmett, a wax dummy with makeup and stiffly combed hair.)

Standing there in our bedroom, I began to keen, to cry open-mouthed, making a sound like an animal—I couldn't help it. My knees shook going down the hall to the kitchen phone, although there was a bedroom extension. As if I didn't want him to overhear me, didn't want to provide him the opportunity to criticize the way I gave directions, or details, or the way I communicated my information. Out of habit, I began dialing Amy's number, then hung up quickly and punched in 911.

I managed a disjointed description of the situation, and, no, Emmett would not have approved of the way I stuttered and stammered. But the competent woman understood, said help was on its way. Then I called Amy, managing a little better. After sobbing the news, I hung up, paced around, trying to make sense of Emmett's death. Yes, his *death.* Use the word. Get used to the word.

Emitting static, crackling with what I assumed was vital information received on its bristling antennae, a police cruiser arrived, and parked on the driveway. Then an ambulance pulled in. It didn't look like a proper ambulance, which I picture as a fancy station wagon. This thing was a truck, like the one that transports money from the bank. An armored car, yes, although a huge red ECNALUBMA blazed across the front in letters so garish I couldn't read them, even after I realized—and I already knew it, I *knew* that—the word was on there backward. Why backward! I am unaccountably angry at this nonsense why would they spell it backward? So you could read it in your rearview mirror, I seemed to hear Emmett's patient explanation. Still, it was a damn fool thing to do, because you automatically reversed the spelling. My mind played with this idea, fastened onto it, something to hang on to in the collapse of my world.

"Tough go, Mrs. Malone," said one of the young and hardy attendants, coming out of my house, breaking into my wild skein of thought. A mere kid with a ponytail and earring, he patted my shoulder in an avuncular manner. "Listen," he said, "it's a good way to go. He never knew what hit him, we should all be so lucky."

They were trundling Emmett off just as Amy careened up the driveway, slammed out of her lemon yellow Mustang, the same color as her workout suit. She stammered something about the morning commute holding her up, although she'd been going against the main stream rushing into the Bay Area. When I called, she'd been almost out the door, on her way to Fitness World where she teaches an early morning aerobics class.

There on the driveway, for all the neighbors to see, I clung to my daughter, inhaling Amy's strength and substance, and the faint lemon scent of her lotion. A part of me was shocked, even disturbed, at the feel of Amy's body, at its heat and firmness. We'd never been a family that touched much, so Amy's solidity and strength seemed foreign, disconcerting. As if by developing all that muscle tone Amy was betraying her femininity, becoming a stranger.

I blurted out the story of my tragedy. Amy patted me, as the ambulance attendant had done, then we repeated the story to a circle of sympathetic neighbors who'd been drawn to the driveway by the commotion. I lengthened the tale, embroidered emotions and medical facts and symptoms into its cloth, partly to postpone going back into the suddenly empty house, the house of death; and partly to refine the telling, to achieve a crisp grasp of my situation.

Which was that Emmett had died of a heart attack. Everyone's time comes, and that kid driving the ambulance had it right: we should all be so lucky as to go in our sleep.

Not that that's much comfort here, now, in the mortuary. I draw a deep ragged sigh, shuffle, dig for a tissue. I try to defeat a knot of tears about to dissolve in my head behind my eyes by paying closer attention to the minister. He's a nondescript fellow that I can't describe even while I'm looking at him. He's trying to prove something by telling us the Good Shepherd story. Out of habit, I scoff. After all, why was He so happy to find that lost lamb? Why, indeed! To increase His profit in the wool trade, and soon, in lamb chops. Sheer exploitation.

In tones heavy with certitude, finality, and power, the minister concludes his elastic one-size-fits-all sermon. He counterbalances the booming Shepherd story with a soft and pious benediction, and then retreats to sit in the shadows. Recorded organ music swells in the dim room, mingling with the scent of flowers. The sun breaks out from behind the clouds, beams through a stained glass window, and, as if on cue, tints our alcove with a rosy glow. Ah, well. Poor Emmett.

I experience a totally unexpected surge of peace. I unbend, unfold, flow formlessly within myself, like a strain of dye in water. I am weightless, light-headed; I'm in danger of wafting off in an out-of-body episode. Either that, or of dozing right here. So welcome, this sudden sense of futility, of soothing finality. Nothing matters. Something has ended; something else is about to begin. In either case, there's no help for it, nothing I can do. And I am here. It's Emmett up there in the box.

Soon enough, though—too soon—I jar back to reality. I have to face the rest of this barbaric ceremony. The beefy pallbearers carry Emmett out. They load him into a hearse the color of stainless steel, windows draped with velvet curtains, as if poor Emmett needs protection from prying eyes, or living people need to be protected from him. The hearse takes him away. Amy and I follow, rattling around in a huge limousine.

At the cemetery, the crowd, Emmett's crowd, gathers around the precisely hollowed-out rectangle, the dirt from which is piled nearby on a tarp, ready for replacement. The air smells of earth, of mold and compost, although this seems to be the only excavation. I wonder how they dig such square corners with such big machines—off in the distance is the back hoe, ready for reemployment as soon as we finish our chore here. My seldom-worn high heels dig more little holes in a crisply cut plot of grass, the sort of grass Emmett would have approved of. With a sense of rising panic, I watch the box disappear. The minister gives the "Earth to earth, ashes to ashes, dust to dust" finale. I bite my lip, sigh, and dig again for a tissue. I am going to cry. I can't help it. I am going to blubber in front of all these people.

I remember cozy times of lying in bed with Emmett, cuddling with him. In particular, I recall once when he reached for me, not for sex—that had happened rarely in the last few years—but to hold me because he knew I'd had a bad day. I'd been temping at a firm that makes dehydrating equipment, the kind people use in their homes for drying fruit. I mentioned to a coworker that I wanted one of the contraptions for myself; I wanted to dry apple slices, pears, cherries. Later I overheard the girl say to her friend, "Why bother? Just do whatever you do to your face." I had been hurt, and shocked at how hurt I was. I asked Emmett if I looked dried out. The remark had made me feel old and tired, too old and tired for temp work, which requires a young person's stamina. All that adjustment, readjustment every day, every day in a new place.

Emmett held me tenderly, said of course not. I was a fine looking woman, and he was proud of me. Oh, yes, Emmett had been my solace, my bulwark against the casual and random hurts of life.

He'd been a good man, a wonderful man. A joy to have around the house. The kind of man who could, who *did,* fix anything and everything. The kind who kept the lawn looking as good as this memorial park's. The kind who maintained the lawn mower, the sprinkler system, the weed eater, all things mechanical in good running condition. On that score alone, I am going to miss him sorely.

Amy begins to cry, too, letting her mascara run raccoon tracks down her cheeks. Next to Amy stands her current boyfriend, yes, I remember him now. This one is Larry, and he is, superficially, a nice kid, but he has a slick edge, and is too smoothly good-looking to make him the kind of guy I am comfortable with. He seems the sort who'll open doors and hold coats, but who will drive a vehicle from which issues a raucous stereo, the bumper pasted with a sticker reading, "IF IT'S TOO LOUD, YOU'RE TOO OLD!" (His sleek pickup has no such sticker—I already looked—but I maintain the unreasonable suspicion that he's just razored it off.) Larry is caressing the back of Amy's neck, murmuring in her ear, seemingly not to console her, assuage her sorrow, but…it looks like a seduction. Much too carnal for a graveside.

Then I remember what that fight had been about, the one that sent me careening off into the night to sleep behind the bank. Emmett had found out about me taking Amy to the doctor for birth control pills. Because on that long-ago field trip chaperoning Amy's class, I saw Amy necking with her then-boyfriend; I saw that she was on the verge. I watched a pimply kid fondle my daughter, and I knew it was time.

Emmett had blown up when I told him about the prescription we'd had the pharmacy fill. "No daughter of mine is going to screw around!" he'd shouted, his jaw set in that hard line I'd grown to dread. "No sirree!" So we had that fight and I roared away in the VW.

Eventually the story of my sleeping behind the bank passed into family mythology. "That crazy woman, once she slept all night behind the bank," Emmett liked to announce to a table of his company. Or to Amy, "Your crazy mother, remember that night she disappeared, didn't come home till dawn?" Sometimes I got a kick out of him telling it; sometimes it embarrassed me, or made me angry. It depended on how he told it: with stealthy admiration, or scorn, or quizzical amusement.

About those birth control pills—I tried to talk him down, get him to bend. All the girls, I told him, all the girls that Amy knew were on the Pill. After all, Amy was sixteen, kids develop rapidly, these are fast times. Parents are not in control anymore, what with their children being bombarded with outside influences. The growth and prevalence of the corrupting mass media, destruction of the ozone layer (global warming leading to wearing scanty clothing which arouses risky hormonal responses), the death of religion in the home, etc. I threw that last one in, my equivalent of a right jab to the solar plexus: Emmett had no interest in the spiritual realm, but he felt that he should have had. It was his deficit, his lack. Kids now, I told him in concluding wheedling tones, were not like we'd been when we were growing up.

But no, I couldn't wheedle him. Emmett had been too bullheaded. He'd been uncompromisingly rigid, he'd been so black and white! Of course it was no one's ideal situation to aid and abet a teenager in establishing a sex life, but the consequences of ignorance, of nonprotection, I told him, were absolutely dire, and life and times being what they were—

"No excuses!" he'd said flatly. "No fuzzy-headed rationalizations!"

But after the fight, the dust settled and the whole matter dropped, as if forgotten. I told Amy to keep her little disk of pills in her room, under some sanitary napkins that I knew Emmett would never touch. I told Amy not to bring it up, to leave her father alone. After all, Emmett was right, he'd always been right, and he thought his reaction and rejection were enough to thwart Amy's sexual drive.

He'd been that kind of a man. So moral, upright, virtuous—he thought everyone else should be, too.

In many ways I failed him miserably, as I had in giving in to Amy. I should have told Amy no, that she was too young for birth control. I should have sided with Emmett; I should have reinforced his rules regardless of the consequences.

If I could have him back, I'd make it up to him, I'd be a better person, more fair, more loving, more understanding. I'd live up to his standards, which I hadn't worked at hard enough while he was alive. But he is gone, and I let my hot tears fall.

CHAPTER 2

Not over yet, this ordeal of a send-off for Emmett. My street is, alarmingly, lined solid with cars, vans, and pickups; and we park in the last available space. I pause, steeling myself to go in my own house. The whole of Freeway Furniture must be here.

Among the vehicles, there's a Miata, bright red, with its top down, despite an increasing hint of rain in the air—someone's an optimist. Emmett had wanted a little sports car, talked of it often in the last year or so. Poor Emmett—now he'll never have one. I gulp for air, wonder when I'll be allowed to cry in peace.

We're the last to arrive because I stayed at the chapel to wind up my business. The director had presented me with a sheaf of paperwork, murmuring about last-minute expenses. I glanced through his figures, trying to look wise and businesslike, then said no, I didn't want any of the extras—tape of the service, mementos, etc. Wished I could get rid of the one memento I *did* have, the image of Emmett lying there in his scratchy wool suit. I should have buried him in something more spring-like, but hadn't figured out what. Shopping for clothes for a dead man seemed a waste, even ghoulish. So, with shaky fingers, I wrote that final check, wondering about my financial picture. But what a time to think of money! It was Emmett, dead. That was what counted.

Earlier, I'd had to go through Emmett's desk, his big oak rolltop, to locate the checkbook. He'd hated for me to rummage through it. What I found tucked away in drawers and pigeonholes bothered me. For one thing, I discovered he hadn't done the income tax, and it's due in a week. I've never done the taxes—that had been his job. He hadn't made even a start on the folders full of receipts and statements and bills. I berated myself for my lazy stupidity—I never so much as balanced the checkbook, let alone figured the state or federal income tax.

I didn't know what to make of the rest of his stuff. Travel brochures to Ireland-had he been considering a trip to the land of his ancestors? Emmett had been proud of his Irish roots; perhaps he'd planned a surprise for our twenty-fifth wedding anniversary coming up soon. Or would have come up soon, if his heart hadn't betrayed him. I think of his death in those terms: a traitorous heart let him down, let us both down. I needed him so badly, my rudder, my compass through life. But he'd allowed his heart to play him false.

Also in his desk, junk mail, odd bits of this or that. An envelope from an attorney, not the one we'd made a will with, but another one, its back covered with dates and figures. Had he been working on a new will?

A folder of poetry. Poetry! Later, I told myself, when I could think, I'd study his verses, after I went through the rest of his muddle.

Now, staring at all these vehicles, I tell Amy that we should have held the reception or the supper or the party—what does one call the gathering after a funeral?—in the mortuary's Hospitality Hall. But she'd objected, said Meadow Rest didn't allow alcohol, and some of the people from the plant would like a drink.

I snap, "So I'm to tend bar?"

"Oh, for Pete's sake, Larry will do it. After all, he is a bartender, on weekends. And the food's potluck, Mrs. Russell from across the way has seen to it. It's done—the supper, the tables, extra dishes, you don't have to think about a thing. Molly Maids have been in to clean. They do that, in situations like this."

"Well, of course, I know that." I am bone-tired. Talking seems such a bother, a drain on what little energy I have. "You forget I worked for them once." But that's not fair to Amy, because my stint as a maid had been a while back, a mere three weeks at that. Three weeks of dusting and pushing a vacuum, scrubbing floors and toilets for picky people with snotty kids. My back aching, my hands chapped, my stomach upset from eating on the run, I decided I better go back to school, at least long enough to get skills for temp work.

"I'm sorry, honey, I don't mean to be cross. I'm just frazzled." I hadn't slept since Emmett's death. I'm sleeping on the couch, or trying to. Haven't worked up enough nerve yet to use the bed, the bed Emmett died in. Amy is temporarily back in her old room, which is a comfort, but having her in the house requires a severe adjustment.

The real reason I haven't slept: I'm dreaming of Emmett as a young man, when I first met him. Emmett before he went to Vietnam, before he took on that hard edge, that moodiness, that exacting righteousness that exasperated me toward the end.

I really fell for him, right off. I think of it as a fall, going over a cliff in a speeding car. I'd been crazy for him, for his laughing blue eyes, the same blue as his embroidered denim shirts. I'd adored his blond hair curling over the tops of his ears, his strong chin, his dimples. In my dreams I feel his arms furred with fine golden hair, those strong arms holding me tight. I dream of kissing him, long deep kisses. All my senses collected on my lips, all my energy, and, in dreams, I give myself up to the assault of those kisses.

Kisses! I scoff on awakening, rolling over to find a better spot on the lumpy couch. A transitory pleasure, what's the saying, "A moment on the lips, a lifetime on the—"? No, that has to do with calories. When I broadened with a middle-aged spread, Emmett said that to me. "A moment on the lips, a lifetime on the hips," he said with a wry laugh, with that *look.* It had stricken me, made me feel I was letting him down. Also made me resentful of his restraint, especially in the last year or so when he'd watched his diet and weight like a marathoner.

Amy brushes at cat hair on my black dress, says soothingly, "I know you're tired, Mom, we're all tired. But everything's cool. All you have to do is...well, you don't have to do anything. Maybe enjoy yourself. Dad would want you to."

Amy has taken off her hat, and she leans into her reflection in the glass of a porch window, checking her hair. She tucks a long blond strand behind her ear, and I notice her turquoise earrings. Emmett bought her those earrings on a trip to Mexico, our last trip together, one of the few when it had been just the two of us. Had it been that much fun? He'd been preoccupied, distant, irritable. Well, of course it had been fun, I chide myself, we'd had a wonderful time.

Feeling ill with nerves, I follow Amy into my own house, into my new life. Without him, it's like going in naked. He'd always been there, my cover, my protection. Moreover, most of our social activities had been geared toward his interests. The Power Squadron; Emmett had been a whiz at boat handling, he could have docked the Queen Mary in a bathtub, which got him sent to Vietnam when most of his buddies managed to avoid active duty. The Marksman's Club; but Emmett sold his guns years ago after Amy toddled in clutching the barrel of a loaded .32. The Poker Club was his most recent interest, apart from an incipient fascination with fishing. It met every Wednesday night, at alternating houses. This Wednesday it was to have been here...I experience a shock...did I cancel it? Well, someone must have called it off. I'm not even sure who the members are anymore, but they must have been present for the funeral. I should know who they are.

But Emmett's friends have all begun to look alike. Paunchy and middle-aged, wearing glasses and old men's styles like Izod alligator shirts and pleated Dockers, the kind of pants for guys with big butts—that's how Amy puts it. And jogging shoes, for guys who don't jog, sneakers patterned with wild zigzags and lightning strikes of lurid colors. Most of these guys are cultivating a crop of gray in their hair, those lucky enough to have hair. A couple of them are bald. But not Emmett—he'd kept his thick hair, and what gray there was had been invisible. He'd never put on weight, not like the others.

His interest in clothes, which had seemed odd to me, intensified in the last few years. Wild dress shirts, and flashy ties. Regis Philbin, I teased him; a man who wouldn't sleep on colored sheets bought lavender button-downs and flamingo-colored ties. Dressy tailored natural fibers; he'd even gone back to denim. However, he depended on his specs, wire-rimmed half glasses that he peered over with *that look* I dreaded. A stern accusatory expression, the kind he gave me when I sneaked ice cream. I wonder if he used that look at the shop, on his fellow workers. I wonder who among my guests are his fellow workers.

No matter what was meeting, Power Squadron, Marksman Club, or the poker night bunch, I was merely the hostess in charge of providing refreshment. After pouring the first beers, putting out dishes of peanuts, bowls of chips and dips, I kept out of the way. I savored anonymity, bestowing, as it does, freedom, irresponsibility. I admit that I viewed his social life with a trace of contempt, secretly scoffed at his effusiveness, his hail fellow well met, his hearty glad-handedness that seemed to border on appeasement. Let him deal with those gullible idiots, I thought.

As somebody else has dealt with these people in my house. I follow Amy through the tiled entry, and turn into the dining room. Amy tells me that Mrs. Russell, Frieda, has been in charge of food. I know the woman only slightly, tend to steer clear of her. Her husband, Lyle Russell, is a silent hulk of a survivalist moron (in my opinion), who drives an aggressive looking four-wheel drive vehicle, with water cans strapped on its sides. He spends every weekend in the brushy hills above Ukiah, where he's building some kind of a fortress in which he'll survive the coming holocaust. Frieda, or someone, has rearranged the dining room, pushing the table, with all its leaves in it, against the wall, for the buffet.

A quarter of a century earlier, when Emmett and I were newlyweds, I'd bought that table at a specialty shop downtown. It's teak, a Scandinavian design. I'd planned to add matching chairs, but Emmett had been lukewarm and I never finished out the set. After all, he said, he worked with furniture. He should know the hot number, and it was oak. Oak was the thing. Besides, he could get seconds, at the employees' discount. I wanted to shout, "You're in charge of the shipping department of that furniture plant, not the design crew! Please don't tell me what I like." But I never said things like that to him. Moreover, to be honest, I'd grown to like the golden sturdy *practicality* of oak. A symbol of Emmett himself.

I met Emmett in junior college. One day in the cafeteria I

wandered around with my tray loaded, a square meal representing all four food groups. In the crush I couldn't find a place to sit, until Emmett got up and offered me his chair. Such manners, courtesy. A real gentleman, hard to come by in that tough new era. I was a raw freshman, too naïve to understand the fine points of college cuisine, that you don't eat a whole cafeteria lunch; you go for something from the machines, or coffee and donuts.

Emmett was a junior, an "older man," enrolled in deadbeat courses (I discovered later) to hide from the draft. But the army got him anyway, right after he dropped out to work in the furniture plant. While he was overseas, we stayed in touch through a lively correspondence. In letters we decided to pursue the relationship when his hitch was up.

Early on, his censuring of my taste seemed right—after all, he knew best, he was smart. I had no experience, no background, no innate knowledge or instincts to fall back on. Had gone straight from my parents' Depression-era brownstone to Emmett's apartment. I liked his apartment's eclectic furnishings, its board-and-brick bookcases, thrift shop knock-arounds; and posters everywhere, even on the refrigerator. I wanted to live with that kind of counter-culture ambiance, but Emmett decided the time for it was over. He was ready for a swing to the right. He became interested in security, in safe deposit boxes, retaining walls, steel belted radials. He was ready to take his place in life, and there was no room for decorating with posters.

Before Amy was born, we bought this house, the typical suburban American home, suitable for middle management personnel such as Emmett was getting to be. It's up a hill in what was then a new tract. All the houses are identical except for variations in trim—brick, or slump stone, or river rock. Ours is trimmed with brick, with a podocarpus-framed entry paved with more used brick, accented with long thin windows through which indoor plants get a peek of sun. From the front, these houses present impervious garage faces that stare at each other across suburban asphalt. They are, though, above the smog generated by the Interstate. A real plus, a selling point. Also, many of them are on cul-de-sacs. So good for kids, the circular streets branching from a thoroughfare, like grapes affixed to a stalk.

Homeowners around here tend toward identical landscaping. Retaining walls covered with English ivy, disguised with pampas grass. Aggregate cement decks trimmed with railroad ties, furnished with redwood tables, barbecues, and tiki lights. Some hot tubs, some swimming pools, but we never got that far. I sometimes railed at the assembly line atmosphere, but, as Emmett pointed out, it was a solid investment, you have to look at resale value. He'd usually been right, I had to admit that. So the tract house, the oak end tables, his roll-top desk, the tweed sofa, and Naugahyde La-Z-Boy recliner are what he, what *we,* settled on. Like everyone else.

And maybe the teak table isn't that nice anymore, I think, looking at it, really seeing it for the first time in years. It's scuffed and scarred, partly the result of those poker nights, and partly of my neglect—I've become an indifferent housekeeper. The table seems spindly, laden with a bountiful spread of food and serving dishes. Emmett had been right about the solidity of oak. He'd always been right.

At once my eyes fill, the lump behind them threatening to melt. I push hard, willing away an attack of blubbering. Look at the food, I tell myself, look at someone's good china and silver, the candles. Look at the irises, Dutch irises, clear deep purple, rich amethyst, delicate mauve, and pale blue, the same light clear blue that Emmett's eyes had been. I will not cry now. I cannot cry now, no, I will not permit it. Wait until later.

These irises have come from bulbs transplanted from my mother's yard to mine. This particular floral arrangement seems so special—my mother's irises—and again I fight tears. I cannot bear it. Think of something else. Anything.

My mother hadn't approved of Emmett, and I try to recall what she'd objected to. As with the fight that led me to sleep behind the bank, I can't remember any details. Is this to be my future? Go through the rest of life trying to piece together incidents that only the dead remember? Well, it doesn't matter, because by the time Amy was born, my mother had accepted Emmett. Or more likely, had decided to keep her objections to herself. Now both my parents are gone, as are Emmett's. Both of us were only children, so the family dwindles down to just Amy.

But Amy can carry on, even thrive. I watch her operate: Amy in a clingy black dress that makes her look lithe and sleek, not tough and meaty as in those sausage-casing workout suits. She effuses over the buffet, talking easily with neighbors she knows only slightly: she moved out two years ago, right after my mother died and left her a bit of money. PawPaw, Amy's six-toed Siamese, left with me because Amy's condo allows no pets, sidles forward, throws himself on his back for a belly rub. Amy obliges. She kneels, and the side slits of her skirt open, showing off her legs.

A thin woman in navy blue, her hair in a spun sugar poof, comes up to me. "Mrs. Malone, Peg, may I call you Peg? Here, let me fix you a plate." At my look, she adds, "I'm Irene, you know me? I live kitty-corner to Frieda? The whole neighborhood, we're so broken up, I can't tell you but time, you know what they say."

"Oh, well, thanks…yes, something about time. Uh, I guess I can help myself," I add stiffly as the woman starts to ladle food onto a plate for me. After all, it is my house, however alien it seems filled with these strangers. I assess my choices—scalloped potatoes and ham, fried chicken nuggets (KFC?), a Mexican casserole, an Irish stew. Rolls, biscuits, three-bean salad, a yellow Jell-O mold that's beginning to sit down in its own juice. Pickles, pies, cakes. The variety of serving dishes, from Tupperware to cut crystal, attests to the community effort behind this spread, and I am grateful. Such kind people—I'll have to reach out to them when this is over. But I am nervous, overcome, and the room seems overheated. Ah, Christ, I am going to have menopausal hot flashes on top of everything else.

Mingling with the smell of food is a cigarette. Someone is smoking…I haven't allowed smoking since Emmett was forced to quit a year ago. Who's smoking? I look around, see Larry, Amy's current swain, a cigarette dangling from his lip while he serves up drinks in the kitchen. Amy goes to talk to him, perhaps to caution him about the cigarette? She lays her hand with its lilac-painted nails on his bare arm—he's taken off his jacket and has rolled up his sleeves for the hard work of pouring drinks. And it is work: business is brisk. I am taken aback at the large collection of bottles he's amassed and is pouring from. Who's footing the bill for all this? The liquor will cost a fortune…maybe I should have Amy tell Larry to go light on the booze. Besides, Emmett wouldn't like it if his party got sloppy.

"I love your home, it's just made for entertaining," says Irene, still standing there, the hostess soothing the diffident guest.

I mutter something, yes, entertaining is easy, just the thing, some nonsense. As I turn away, I consider the stupidity of the woman's remark—the houses in this subdivision are almost clones. We all *entertain* the same way, no big deal. But then she's as nervous as I am, both of us clutching at the straws of small talk.

Through my own rooms, now filled with unfamiliar hazards, I weave like a pirogue through a bayou. I steer around old Mr. Purdy, mossy as an underwater snag. He lives next door, a cranky widower. I look away quickly after catching him stuff his pockets with cashews from a bowl on Amy's piano. I detour toward the den to avoid Frieda, whom I've known until now only as Mrs. Russell. The woman is painfully self-assured, frighteningly efficient. She organizes the Neighborhood Watch program, alerts people about invasions of noxious weeds (tansy ragwort, purple loosestrife, two-toed Pete), passes out homemade popcorn balls and candied apples on Halloween, although her own children are grown and gone.

I see her approach with another bowl of flowers, so I drift off trying to look casual. I speak to a few people, but sense that they yearn to keep their distance. After a well chosen word or two, they navigate away, as if death were contagious, or I'm about to do something loose and unseemly like blubber or talk philosophy or break into prayer. I see, as if for the first time in a long while, Emmett's big screen TV; I stare at his La-Z-Boy recliner. It seems to hold the shape of his body, and I visualize him in it, his long legs stretched out while he watches his baseball game, or football, or a *National Geographic* special. His presence is so immediate, I seem to smell his scent—soap, his after-shave, the fabric softener I used on his shirts.

I'd just done the laundry, put away his clean clothes. Before washing them, I held to my nose his soiled shirts, inhaling Emmett, his essence. Not just his essence, but the work he'd done while wearing these clothes. A faint aroma of wood, of cedar, like newly sharpened pencils; furniture finishing compounds and shipping containers; even a whiff of the hand soap in the dispenser at the plant. It was an odd scent, sort of greenish, like sage but spicier.

I have to get out of the den, away from the ghost of Emmett. Carrying my plate, I thread through the room, and go outside where the high cool cloud cover, now increasing into black storminess, has, thank goodness, discouraged the crowd. Someone has set up folding tables and chairs on the deck, and mowed the lawn. Such nice people, I should know who they are. I will go through the cards piled on the mantel, find their names. Emmett would have been so pleased.

Just as I breathe a sigh of relief at being alone, but worrying about it, too—I don't want to seem weird, or do anything untoward, memorable in any way, that they'll talk about in the office—a man opens the gate to the side yard and steps toward me.

"Just rolled up the windows on my truck, I think it's gonna rain. Besides, it's hot as a pistol in there."

"Oh, good, it's not just me. I think I'll sit down out here."

"Not in that one, it's wet. Someone just hosed off the deck. You know me? I'm Harold, from the plant." He's a pale man, perhaps also looking for solitude. He has washed-out blond hair, not burnished and bright as Emmett's had been. An old man, not like Emmett. "So sorry, Mrs. Malone," he says. "We're all just shook. Anything we can do to help you, let us know. Or let me know. Such as, well, clean out Emmett's desk, tie up loose ends."

"Clean out his desk? Yes, of course." I hadn't realized he'd have a desk at work to tidy up. What was I thinking! Of course he'd have a desk. "I will need someone to bring his things home. Yes, could you do that, please, uh, Harold?"

"Sure thing, Mrs. Malone."

"Peg. Call me Peg."

"Why, I thought your first name was Liz, Elizabeth."

I smile, shake my head, fork around a bite of the stew. The plate is white bone china with a circle of gold, ideal for a funeral supper. "No, I'm Peg, or Margaret. But nobody calls me Margaret." Hadn't Emmett ever mentioned my name? Hadn't he talked about his family? I used to attend the plant's social functions, the summer picnic, the Christmas party. Maybe the company no longer hosts such gatherings, what with the new concern for political correctness, for sobriety. "Tell me Harold, isn't that the boss, Mr. Hawley, in there talking to the woman in the green dress?" A discordant green dress with side slits, like Amy's. Surely it isn't right for this solemn gathering.

"Yeah, that's Chuck."

"And that woman? Is she new? She must be from the office. I don't think she's a neighbor."

"Maggie Quinn, or Margaret—another Margaret. She runs the front desk. Been there a couple of years." For a minute or two, we both watch the scene in the house. The woman, Maggie, has a spill of hair as red as an Irish setter's. I mentally sniff: no one has real hair that color. It's curly, not ripply, a mass of coils, like springs. Like the cascading arrangement on that stiff-armed step dancer in "Riverdance." Emmett had loved that program, even sent for the video.

In the den the man talks intently into the redhead's upturned face. But she's only half listening, has the pensive unfocused expression you sometimes see on models in underwear ads. Puffy areas around her eyes...has she been crying, mourning Emmett's death? I recall the muffled sob in the mortuary chapel. Could it have come from her? Such a pretty girl. I wonder uneasily why Emmett never mentioned her. That hair, so striking even if it's dyed. Emmett, awhile back, suggested I do something with my hair. A lot of gray in my dark brown now, giving me a sort of tweed effect I've begun to like. But Emmett hadn't liked it. Get a rinse, he urged, get a perm. I've worn my hair exactly the same way—straight and long, pulled back with barrettes—since the seventh grade.

I thought it odd at the time, Emmett's sudden interest in my hair, in my person. He'd also wanted me to add color to my wardrobe, wear high heels more often. Earrings and perfume. I'd scoffed, how ridiculous at my age, what frivolity. A waste of time and money. He knew who I was—his plain wife in flat shoes, with straight hair.

I stare at the woman in my house. She has pale skin, almost translucent, as if lit with an interior light bulb. And white, as waxy white as Emmett's had been in death. I have a wild image of the cover shot on a slick magazine touting tourism in Ireland. Maggie Quinn, yes, she's Irish. Emmett had developed an intense interest in things Irish the last few years—that "Riverdance" fixation, and shamrocks, Celtic crosses, dark beer and smoky pubs and fiddle music. Irish stew and soda biscuits, such as are on my plate now. I put down my knife, thinking that Maggie in there might have brought this very food into my house.

Those travel brochures in Emmett's desk. That brochure about Ireland…

The woman's dreamy expression, the slim but voluptuous figure, the rich colors—she could be one of the models in the brochure from Victoria's Secret, another piece of the junk mail in Emmett's desk.

Suddenly the parts all come together, and I know. Emmett's impatience, his indifference, yes, there's the cause, right in my den a mere ten feet away. I put a face on his restlessness, and it's that face. I tell myself that I'm being ridiculous. I tell myself that I'm surprised, and shocked, but on some subliminal level I'd known, at least I'd suspected that there had been another presence in Emmett's life. One of those foolish poems from Emmett's desk—I'd read it so many times it's engraved on my memory—chooses this moment to mock me:

Before you, my days were neutral shades—
Monday a blue, a pale but gloomy hue—
Tuesday off-white, the color of the hall, of flight—
Wednesday a faded gray, color of a rainy day—
Thursday a taupe, a nothing, a thing without hope—

Friday a blotch, a stew, cruel, before you—
Weekend dirt-colored, with calluses, wheelbarrows and shovels—
And then, without plan, again it began.
But now there's you, and my days are rainbow hues—
My purples, my yellows, my sapphire blues—
My Brilliance, my dear one, my darling—
Now there's you.

Emmett's handwiting, Emmett's mind behind the lines. After all, hadn't he insisted we paint the hall off-white? But doesn't everybody? At least everybody around here. And he'd done yard work on the weekends, had callused his hands with wheelbarrow and shovel. But that had been his choice.

I stare, openmouthed, at a loss. My skin prickles with electricity; I must be careful, or I'll do something foolish in front of these people that they'll discuss around the water cooler, e-mail each other about from their desks, laugh about at lunch time. I do so want to seem normal. But in what manner is a new widow "normal"?

Clearly uncomfortable, Harold shuffles, clears his throat, mumbles, "Say, maybe I should get Chuck out here, you can ask him about...well, you got anything you wanna ask about? Uh, death benefits, insurance...oh, forget it. What's the matter with me. Not now."

All those late hours, how tired Emmett had been, how indifferent he'd grown to anything around the house. The way he'd spruced up, had taken an interest in his clothes, his designer haircuts, his whole appearance. I thought he trimmed down and toned up for his health, but now I see the whole pattern of deception behind his self-improvement. My blood, under the electricity of my skin, runs to ice water; I can't eat this food, can't stand the way it smells. I think I'm going to be sick in the bushes.

"Liz, are you okay?"

"Peg, I'm Peg!"

"Peg, yeah, Peg. Short for Margaret. Like Maggie in there. The same name." When I glare at him, he adds quickly, "So, how about it?"

"How about what?"

"You wanna talk to Chuck?"

"No! Well, maybe later. I can't seem to think right now."

"You sure look white. Can I getcha a drink?"

I say yes, to get rid of him. I'm scaring him, at the very least making him uneasy. I'm probably making them all uneasy. Everyone in there from Emmett's office, from the whole plant, knows about that redhead and my husband. I am horribly embarrassed, ashamed; I grieve for Emmett, and I wish for him back so I could give him hell. I'd give him hell because he got away with it, he got away with it clean, he's beyond me. My anger boils over my grief; if I'm not careful, I'll make a mess; I'll make a scene.

I am angry at myself, too, for being blind and stupid. This is going to be painful, so painful I have no idea of the extent of the hurt I am going to have to live through. But that's the point, I think, almost gloating. I am going to live through it; Emmett is the one who's dead. I still have the gift of life.

I suddenly remember what turned my mother against Emmett. My mother thought Emmett had trouble with commitment. She saw the way Emmett treated me. Several times while we were dating, after Emmett came back from Vietnam and we were on the verge of seriously considering marriage, he'd deserted me, he'd left me to sit by the phone, pining for his call, waiting for some word from him. In those days, women didn't call men; at least, women like me didn't. Women like me sat by the silent phone and wondered what they'd done wrong.

At least I waited and worried and wondered. And walked miles around town looking for signs of Emmett or at least his car; losing weight and interest in life, crying myself to sleep every night. Then he'd turn up again, he'd call and ask me out, never giving an explanation for his absence, no reason offered for his silence. In this regard, my mother thought Emmett cruel. I would not allow that judgement. I told my mother that Emmett was going through a readjustment process. The war experience had changed him in some way, but he'd get over it. My own father had come back from Germany full of the glow of victory, but the guys from Vietnam were different. They tended to be a silent bunch, disillusioned, moody, bitter. I would change that in Emmett. I'd been that young, that naïve, back in those days. I should have known better.

Well, I know better now, I know what kind of man he'd been. I feel my anger flare even higher, I'll burn myself up if I'm not careful. I long to lunge into my own den, and right there in front of those people, pull out that woman's brilliant hair by the handfuls, snatch her bald-headed. Or maybe I'd read that expression somewhere, or perhaps my mother had said it. It sounds like something my mother would have said. I suddenly long for my mother, so I could tell her what Emmett has done. I also long to tear, rend, scream. Do something violent.

But I can't let those people know. I couldn't stand that. To be laughed at.

I do the next best thing. I fly out of my chair, clop across the deck, and fling open the sliding glass door, causing it to shriek on its metal track. But not before catching a glimpse of myself in the glass. A vulture, I've turned into a vulture. My black dress, bought for my mother's funeral two years earlier, flaps and swoops around me, accentuating shadows and hollows in my face, which looks folded and bleak and ashy. I look like Emmett, lying there dead in our bed.

I'm going to be ill, I think, stomping by the redheaded woman in green. I can't resist glaring into those glassy green eyes...surely the woman's wearing contacts. No one, outside of a Stephen King character, has eyes that eerie green color. And aren't her earrings identical to Amy's? Yes, they're dangly silver feathers studded with turquoise...why, Emmett had bought two sets of them in Cabo San Lucas! I gasp to myself, I feel dizzy...but there's the proof in clear view, beneath the masses of that snaky hair, so uncompromisingly, so preposterously colored.

I turn away, but not before catching a whiff of the woman's odd scent, a spicy green aroma. I must be imagining it, I must be delusional, I've lost my balance, my sanity. Nevertheless, with that odor in my nostrils, which I'm sure are flared and emitting smoke like a dragon's, I elbow through the kitchen, the dining room, the entry, race out the front door. Thank goodness I've left my car keys on the floor mat. Burning with adrenaline, I start the Bronco, throw it in gear, wishing, *longing* to peel out. Peel out as I wished I'd been able to do years earlier in the VW on my way to sleeping behind the bank. I have to put some decent distance, some clean air, some psychic space between myself and this hateful gathering that is celebrating, or mourning, I no longer know which, the death of Emmett.

CHAPTER 3

Amy stayed five days, then packed up for home. Before she left, she and Larry had a fight in Larry's pickup out front (I admit spying on them through the kitchen slats). At first I thought they were necking. *Necking.* That shows you where I am. What's the word for it now? Emmett would have known. I could have asked him.

A thousand times a day I think of things to ask him, or tell him. That the cherry tomatoes are the size of seed pearls; the dogwood's going to be beautiful. The hydrangea, the roses, the irises—they're bursting into glorious bloom. And the purple lilac that my mother gave us, it's gorgeous this year. I imagine its perfume filling the yard. That neither my mother nor Emmett will be there to share it with me causes me to weep right out in the open, where any of the neighbors could have seen me, had they looked.

After the spat with Larry, Amy bursts in red and angry, saying loud and bitter things about "control freak" and "pushing buttons." She says she'd planned to stay longer, but she can't. Larry's lonely. (Not lonely, I think: *horny.*) Ah, yes, because Amy adds that he's ready to go out and do some trolling. She says this with a wry twist to her mouth, but a pleased and satisfied glint in her eye. She holds sway over Larry, exercises the kind of sexual control I never dreamed of wielding over Emmett.

Amy dismisses Larry with a shrug. She says he's not the man she wants to marry, but she's not through with him yet. As if he were one of the leftovers in the fridge. Can't toss out the guacamole dip because avocados are so expensive, but one gets tired of it.

So I help her pack hot rollers, crème rinses and hair gels, foundation preparations, toners, spandex workout suits, sets of wispy underwear, the kind advertised in Emmett's Victoria's Secret, *secret,* catalogues. The kinds of bras and panties that require hand washing. For days, the bathroom has flapped and dripped with something hanging on the shower rod, which has, truth to tell, begun to annoy me considerably.

I help her box up nail polish, bottles and bottles of it. Her cuticle equipment alone overflows the shoebox her new Adidas, size 10, came in. The whole place has smelled of Amy, of lemon and lotion and shampoo and nail polish, or nail polish remover. So much gear, equipment, machinery. It's like moving a military unit into combat. I take another look at Larry, so sly and slippery, but he's no match for Amy. My respect for Amy increases. But it's respect tinged with contempt—for both of them. For her to think such subterfuge important; for him to fall for it. What do these kids know?

I also load her up with funeral supper leftovers. Neither of them really cooks anything. They live on takeout or microwave packaged goods, and oddities that Amy insists on like wheat germ, granola, soymilk from the health food section of the market. It's a relief to clean out the refrigerator. Feeding just myself, even with Amy here, I'm amazed at how long food lingers. I need Emmett's appetite; he would have polished off the chicken casserole, the beef stew which, yes, Maggie had brought—her name is on the bottom of the dish now washed and ready to return. He would have helped with the salads, but not with the cakes and pies. He'd cut sweets completely, in the last year.

Every time I consider his diet, his demand for low-fat, no-sugar this and that, and then finding out the reason for his interest in maintaining a svelte figure, a knot of cold rage unravels in my stomach. The result is I can't eat. I lose weight; I look gaunt and drawn, but this pleases me. At last, and at least, I'm into the thin end of my wardrobe, my jeans, my skinny pants, my size ten skirts. Take that, Emmett.

These early days are full of drama. On the surface, and during the daytime, I am able, sometimes, to wrap myself in a cloak of problem-solving efficiency that Amy wholeheartedly approves of. For example, I call the AAA guy down on the avenue to come see to the car when it won't start, and I find that Emmett let our membership lapse. I renew it, call again, and the guy comes out to give the Bronco a jump: its problem is merely a dead battery. But the battery's a ten-year-old antique that needs replacing. The Triple A guy looks at the tires and says uh-oh, in dire tones. The upshot: the Bronc goes in for battery, tires, and brakes. What had Emmett been thinking! I fume. He hadn't been the kind to let the car go. Unless he'd planned to get a new car—after all, there's that Mazda brochure in his desk. Or leave me with the old car while he gets a new wife who already has a red Mazda Miata.

Then too, there's the matter of the strange attorney whose empty envelope I find in Emmett's desk. Who is *he*? I look him up in the phone book, find that he specializes in "family law," which probably means a divorce specialist. I consider making an appointment to ask him what the hell he'd had to do with Emmett, but think better of it. He would, rightly, regard me as a nut case; at the very least he'd claim confidentiality.

Instead, I go to see the man who'd done a will for us years earlier. He helps me with various forms, the death certificate and paperwork the plant needs before I can file for Emmett's benefits and his insurance. The lawyer, Mr. Devlin, assures me that our affairs appear to be in order, I should be all right.

"I *should* be? What does that mean?"

"Well, when you made this will, Mrs. Malone, there were ample resources, a savings plan, and stock in Emmett's company. You still have all that, of course."

"Well, yes," I mumble, wondering where it is, and how much it's worth.

He says, dismissing me, that when the plant settles Emmett's account, I should make another appointment, for an update. In the meantime, he advises me to file for an extension on the income tax, which I do gratefully, feeling all the while like a grownup, a full-fledged adult dealing with real life for the first time.

Such a heady experience, especially at the bank, making out withdrawal slips with an authoritative hand. Really, I think smiling at the chirpy little teller, really, what is so hard about this? Anyone can do this. Emmett had me buffaloed, was all. Why had he done that? Why had he done anything? Who had he been?

I want him back. I want him seated stiffly upright at the kitchen table, not lounged comfortably in his La-Z-Boy; I want to fire a barrage of questions at him. What the hell had he been up to! What had he been thinking? planning? deciding? He owes me clear explanations. He owes me! Then too, I want him back so I can crow about my success at the bank, at the garage talking to the mechanic; I want to report my general progress in life itself.

Feeling unusually confident, I run errands around town. I pick up Emmett's dry cleaning: a burgundy cashmere jacket, wool slacks, his denim suit. I consider this suit. He'd loved it, the carefully cut and tailored denim, its slightly roguish style that established a fine balance between casual and dressy, a sassy cowboy chic. He once said it made a statement. I asked, "What does it say?" He'd continued knotting his paisley tie under his cerulean collar, said coolly, "If you have to ask, you wouldn't understand." How that had irked me! Now, looking at his denim suit in its plastic bag from the cleaners, I think with a prickle of guilt—and resentment—that I should have buried him in it, he would have liked that. But the idea hadn't occurred to me, and Emmett went into the ground in his fusty old wool.

I hang his clothes in his closet, then stand there considering his outrageous wardrobe. His bomber jacket from L.L.Bean's; his boots; his silk turtlenecks. His shirts…why, the man had become a walking fruit salad with these florid shirts—raspberry, lime, pumpkin. Once I told him he was Regis Philbin. He'd looked at me blankly, said, "Who's that?" I couldn't explain because "Regis and Cathy Lee" is a daytime show and he'd never seen it. Then Amy said that Regis is on at night, too, in some preposterous millionaire thing. Emmett and I had developed different TV habits, had watched our own sets in different parts of the house. I have no idea what he'd liked beyond sports and *National*

Geographic specials. Again I wonder who he's been, my husband.

Well, it doesn't matter now, and I briskly go about my routine. Today I'm functioning, a blessing I have to take advantage of. I clean house, a much lighter chore now without him, I admit to myself. I miss him, sure, Emmett in the shower singing "That's Amore," then stepping down the hall wrapped in a towel, filling my kitchen universe with the fragrant warmth of his pink skin. But tidying the bathroom's a snap without his residue of whiskers in the sink, tooth flossings on the mirror, foot powder on the floor around the toilet.

After a lunch of melted cheese sandwich, made with real cheddar, and an apple, but no milk—the half-gallon I bought had gone off and had to be dumped—I still feel strong, centered within myself, capable of paying utility bills. I park the Bronco in front of City Hall, and consider, smugly, that, according to the checkbook, this month's bills are less than last month's. I'll save money without Emmett; undoubtedly I'll have to. Finances are a fuzzy unknown; I don't know if I'm rich or poor...well, I know I'm not *rich,* but will I have to disconnect the cable? Sell the TV? Give up designer coffee beans?

The utilities cost less, without Emmett. But that's probably because the California Central Valley is now in that blessed time slot between hot and cold, between forced air heating and air-conditioning. On the whole, I think, briskly stepping along feeling as temperate as the weather, I'm doing well. I square my shoulders, hold up my head while slipping my bills into their proper slots.

But those are my good periods, and are overshadowed by my bad. Some days fill themselves with a sort of amnesia, of not remembering why I'm pacing from room to room, what I'm looking for. Or what day it is, what month. Or whether I've eaten yet; and if I have, what it had been. Some days I find myself waiting for Emmett to come home, listening for the sound of the car in the drive, the slamming of the door, his step into the kitchen. Even the cat, leaping out of Emmett's chair at five o'clock to curl on the mat by the door, seems to wait. The two of us, me and the cat, holding our breaths, suspended, waiting.

Even worse are spells of free-floating panic. Emmett is gone, the rock upon which I'd built my life. Some days I drift into the den and sit, not in Emmett's La-Z-Boy, but in my chair, an upright affair with brown plaid cushions in an oak frame. I watch the light, almost clutching at a pattern of light that flows across the room like a tide. As the day progresses the light lengthens to flood the beige Berber carpet, and then shadows appear in the texture of the rug, creating a pebble-like surface, a bog of quicksand. Before receding in late afternoon, it splashes onto a wall, changing it from gold to red, to brown, then to black.

Emmett paneled that wall in oak. It's a background upon which to display his achievements. Marksman and skeet shooting certificates, photos of himself with a trophy won in the South Tower race—he crewed on a friend's sailboat—commendations from the plant. He'd recently cleared space for a new passion. He'd taken up fishing, and dreamed of showing off a prize catch, either the fish itself, mounted; or a picture of himself, surrounded by an admiring crowd, congratulating him on the marlin or the swordfish or the shark dangling from a hoist at the pier. I study this empty space; I study the wall. I study the room itself, waiting for the abyss to open. My ability to fill time is gone. Futility overwhelms me.

On that sort of day, I can't open the blinds. I can't answer the door, or bring in the paper from the driveway. On trash day, getting the can out represents a major victory. Also a major victory: returning to the neighborhood, one by one, the dishes left from the reception. Most of them have their owners' names taped on the bottom; I have no excuse to put it off. And people are frighteningly nice.

Mrs. Russell, Frieda, urges me to stay for coffee, and I do it. I follow Frieda through the entry into the dining room—Frieda's floor plan is identical to mine, as is Irene's down the street, and Mr. Purdy's next door—and then into the kitchen. I perch on a kitchen barstool while Frieda grinds coffee beans. Frieda says she thinks French roast beans are the best. (I don't tell her I like Colombian.) She says she uses only bottled water, because city water is chlorinated. She instructs me on how to heat the water, gently, just to a boil. "If it's at a hard boil, it bruises the beans, brings out the tannins." She says that, with the air of imparting a state secret. No mass production here: coffee's made one precious cup at a time.

The aroma swells in Frieda's oak and gingham kitchen, and Frieda, with a gentle touch, propitiating her coffee god, reverently decants the rich dark brew into white mugs. Although I find it bitter, and thick as motor oil, I pay the expected compliments, which Freda accepts as her due. I admire the woman, her self-assurance, her confidence...her ability to live with that survivalist kook. I chide myself for incubating this negative aspect of Frieda, and of her husband, but I can avoid it no more than I can avoid the smell of coffee flooding me.

I smile, I sit up straight on her gingham cushion. I listen as Frieda's chiseled lips pour forth stories of good luck, auspicious beginnings, and happy endings. Frieda says she's been able to pay for her new kitchen décor—curtains, wallpaper, paint—with a run of luck at Tahoe. Frieda plays the slots, she has a foolproof system. She confides this information with a knowing look, a mental wink. Frieda likes to go up to the lake on a bus The Business and Professional Women's Club charters. Frieda is a member—she works part-time as a court reporter. She says the BPW does such fun things, the gambling trips merely one example. The club holds formal dances, the kind that the society section of the newspaper reports on, for which the group rents The Eagle's Hall. Women starved for a chance to dress up can shake out the tulle, the lace, the satin, and swish off for a romantic evening. I smile and nod, not able to imagine Mr. Russell in anything other than his camouflage suits.

The club members design a float for the New Year's Day parade downtown, spend whole weeks folding colored Kleenex into flowers to decorate a chicken-wired Jeep. They organize runs and rummage sales for charity. They put on a Home Tour, which allows ordinary people to inspect the homes of the town's élite, to wander through immaculate rooms done to a fare-thee-well, to meander along paths in designer gardens while sipping white wine. Frieda urges me to visit her group, to "network," to ratchet up to becoming a member. I say yes, no, maybe, my eyes darting away from Frieda's. Frieda's eyes are the same glassy blue you sometimes see in Alaskan huskies. An eerie lunatic blue. Frieda's hair is coiled into the shape of a hotdog bun, and is tinted the same color, too, what hairdressers call "champagne blond." When she lowers her head to glance into her coffee, I find myself staring at her pink scalp through gaps in the puff. She wears too much orangy-pink makeup, and I look for a line on her jaw where it stops, but she's too clever for that.

In consternation, as if I've tried to see something Frieda would rather not display, like her bank account, or her weight, I avert my eyes, gaze around the room. I focus briefly on those puffy blue curtains, knickknack shelves, a border print of geese wearing blue ribbons. I smile and smile and smile, stretching my mouth over my teeth, thinking the visit itself is stretching out like a string of Mozzarella cheese. Finally, I get to go home, shaking and sweaty, with pounding heart and queasy stomach. As if I've experienced a close call in the car.

"You're having a nervous breakdown," pronounces Amy firmly. "The thing to do is push yourself. Little by little, you'll get over it. Besides, you should listen to her, about getting out, I mean. You're going to have to do it sometime, to start your routine."

"I know," I mumble, feeling scolded and humble, but not resentful. After all, it's Amy, and Amy believes in action and direction. Amy believes in taking charge. In exercise.

"First, though, maybe you should see to the lawn, it's in a growing spurt. Don't let it get away from you." Amy fixes me with a steely look. "Another thing, Mom..."

"Yes, honey, what?" I begin to shake all over again.

"You've got to change the answering machine. It's weird to call up and get Dad. Put a new message on it."

"I don't know how."

So Amy takes me into the den, punches some buttons, and tells me when to talk. After a few tries, I achieve a sentence without a giggle or a sigh, or an "uh. " Another piece of Emmett erased, another part of him gone. But I am pleased, and after Amy leaves, I replay my message, relishing the sound of my own voice. As if I am a real person.

I suppose what Amy says about a breakdown is true. Eventually, I'll get over Emmett's death; I'll recover. And I do have to do the lawn. I will develop calluses, and a relationship with wheelbarrow and shovel, to paraphrase the line from Emmett's poem. I will become functional, able to cope. But for the present, I am relieved to have Amy gone so I can go back to the silence of the house and to my search for myself and for Emmett, the man to whom I'd been married for more than half my life.

I sift his belongings for clues. After rummaging through his desk, I go through his clothes, the pockets in his jackets, his pants. I find a theater ticket stub from a movie house I'm sure I've never been to. A single stub. If he'd gone with someone, wouldn't there be two stubs? I can't decide, can't tell. Otherwise, I find nothing incriminating, or enlightening. Just bits of debris, pocket fluff, shreds of paper, tag ends of this or that.

I try to reconstruct his evenings, his time at home. He'd been either out in the garage, or in his La-Z-Boy. I go through its cushions, find only odd change, hair from PawPaw—the cat has now adopted Emmett's chair—and lint. I push the cat out, sit down deep as Emmett had been wont to do, flop back, put my feet up, my arms out on its arms, where Emmett's arms had been. I smell it, the cold Naugahyde, catch a whiff of the stuff he'd used on his hair…and that odd greenish spicy scent that clung to the red-haired woman at the reception. I leap from the chair, from the room, thinking no, I'm imagining this, I'm farther gone that I'd thought. I have built a case against Emmett on pure air, on circumstantial evidence…but what about those earrings? That poetry? What about the travel brochure in his desk? What about the brochure from Mazda? The envelope from the attorney specializing in "family law"? The Victoria's Secret ad? What about…what about…

So I go around again. Until I investigate his nightstand.

I'd always respected his privacy; even now I'm suffused with a sense of prying as I slide open, quietly, as if he'll hear, the top drawer. I find a mishmash of his junk—belts, wallets, flashlights: Emmett had been a flashlight freak. I find clothes brushes, extra eyeglasses of an outdated prescription. His camera, obsolete, the kind that required operating a light meter. A framed photo of the three of us—me, Emmett, Amy—taken years earlier. Isn't this the picture he'd kept on his desk at the plant? I sit there, frozen, studying it.

It had been taken on Amy's fourteenth birthday. We were in the park, celebrating both the birthday and the removal of Amy's braces. Amy's smile is wide, challenging; she'd been almost belligerent with happiness. She's always dangerous when happy.

My own smile is tentative, shy. I'd been proud of the birthday cake, iced in pink and white swirls to resemble the petals of a rose. The idea had come from *Sunset,* a magazine I'd once read like a Bible. I'd been proud of Amy, too: my rose, my masterpiece. Emmett smiles as well. That is, his mouth stretches into a grin, but it doesn't reach his eyes. He's not enjoying, or perhaps not approving of the party. I sit between Amy and Emmett, stiff and tense. My posture, my expression pleads, "Please, my two dears, please be sweet to each other, at least for today." Because from the time Amy entered her teens, she'd taken Emmett on, had declared war on what she termed his rigidity, his dictatorship. I'd been caught in the middle, between these two strong people. Even now, looking at this picture, I fill with resentment. Why hadn't they been able to get along? Why, if I'm right and this is the photo from the plant, had Emmett chosen it to put on his desk? Maybe he'd suffered from some twisted sense of duty, of obligation, that forced him to stare at his two unsatisfactory women. Surely he hadn't enjoyed looking at it. Surely he hadn't wanted to remind himself in the workplace of his problem women at home. Perhaps there had been a darker motivation: he'd wanted to rationalize his misbehavior, if there had been misbehavior, which now seems likely.

If that is so, why, then, had he brought it home? Had he substituted a photo of someone else?

I wonder who snapped the picture, because the three of us are in it. Exasperated, I put it back and shut the drawer.

In the second drawer are stacks of monogrammed handkerchiefs, out-of-style ties, and his jewelry box. His jewelry box. It's a tri-fold affair, and tucked in one of the slots meant for cufflinks and tie tacks I find his wedding ring. It's a plain gold band, a twin to mine except mine is set with an emerald that had belonged to his family. Engraved inside his ring, and mine, are the letters EM and PM; around them twine the word *love.* A year or so earlier, he'd reported it lost after a repair job on the washer.

I ponder this discovery. If he'd intended to leave me, wouldn't he have in fact discarded his ring? Just as easy to toss it down the storm drain out front as to hide it in his nightstand. That he'd taken it off but kept it seems to point to an indecisiveness, a wavering of resolve. Had he thought he might "find" it again, and return to being a ring-wearing married man? I want him back, I'd grill him about so many things! What had he been about, that husband?

In our medicine cabinet, on his shelf, I find hidden in the dark back a hair preparation. A hair dye "especially formulated for blonds." Why, that ridiculous man, that jerk! I am amused, and irritated. He'd been engaged in a charade. I stand there staring at the bottle thinking that this proves something. Maybe I'll tell Amy; she'll have a good laugh. As yet I've not given Amy an opening, have said nothing about what are, after all, only suspicions about that woman in the green dress at the funeral and what she'd been to Emmett. That woman who smelled of the greenish scent, who'd worn earrings exactly like Amy's. Who drove a red Miata.

One morning I work up enough nerve to investigate the garage. Until now, I've gone in it only to get the car out, or put it away. The garage smells faintly of paint, glue, sawdust—the good and proper way Emmett himself had once smelled. It had been his exclusive territory, his domain, more sacrosanct than his shelves in the medicine cabinet, or his nightstand. He'd hated for me to touch anything in it. So I am tentative as I poke through shelves, boxes, his gardening gear, miscellaneous in his rollaway tool chest. Nothing. Well, just the usual. The most incriminating item is a flamboyant calendar featuring nudes of breathtaking unreal perfection. It came from a tool rental outlet on the frontage road, and that its page is still turned to January indicates he'd not taken a special or lewd interest in the photos.

Then I notice his cluttered workbench. So unlike Emmett, this jumble of unfinished projects. I see parts to a flagpole assembly, the brackets, bolts, the pole itself still raw wood, not yet sanded. Also, a half-constructed birdfeeder, the pieces scattered as if thrown down in a panic. In his vise, still clamped together, a right angle section of oak, the corner of what was to have been a picture frame. This, begun last August, was to display on his paneled wall a commendation from the local high school, a thank-you for his presentation at their Job Fair. He'd talked to the woodshop kids, showed them a video of employment opportunities at the plant. He'd gotten a good response.

Then it dawns on me: his electric drill is still out, still plugged in, the drill he cleaned, wiped, boxed after each use, his sacred drill. This neglect is evidence of a precipitous state of collapse that I'd been oblivious to. I survey the wreckage, the parts and pieces of what had been an orderly life, and think about midlife crises, middle-age angst, personality changes. He'd been undergoing turmoil, and I hadn't known, hadn't been aware enough to help him. Poor Emmett.

At the same time, a part of me shouts, So what! Women go through a lot worse with their hormone thing, and they live through it without making a mess. Why hadn't he? I'd thought of him as a solid man, a slab of granite; and he'd turned into sandstone; or rather into a glittery layered chunk of mica, fool's gold.

I see Emmett's weed eater and on a whim, and exercised enough, I decide I'll whack some weeds. The timing's perfect: I saw old Mr. Purdy from next door drive off in his pickup, and I can work without him witnessing my ineptitude. I am prejudiced against Mr. Purdy. His pie plate from the funeral supper had been the last in the neighborhood to go home. The old coot had brought over a cheap gooey store-bought pie but had transferred it to a ceramic dish, thinking that would fool people.

He'd been a hard guy to like. When Amy was growing up, he complained about her chalked hopscotch squares on the street, her Frisbee tossed in his yard, her bike trails through his grass. When Amy got older, he complained about loud music, about her boyfriends' cars. Then he went out and created a mound of earth on his side of the fence, a platform to stand on while he spied on her, bikini-clad, sunbathing. At least that's what *I* thought his mound was for. I told Emmett about it, but all he said was, "Let him be, he's old, he's lonely. Poor old guy." Emmett, so easy on everyone else, so hard on his family.

Yes, time to run the weed eater. After all, I conquered the bank and the intimidating little teller; I communicated with the garage mechanic, the Triple A guy, and the lawyer; the lawn equipment is my next victory. Emmett never allowed me to run the power tools, felt either that it was his job, or that I'm incapable. I don't know which. Something else I don't know.

I drag the weed eater out of the garage chaos. Timidly heft it, realize it's heavier, more awkward than I imagined. The pull cord, yes, the cord...tentatively, tug on it, pull it a few times. Nothing. More pulling, gently, then yanking with a firm hand, such a stiff balky machine needs a firm hand...savagely I yank the cord, sweating in the sudden heat. I pause for breath, push hair off my face, out of my eyes, away from my neck.

I hear Emmett's voice; he tells me in silky tones, with faux patience, "Here, here, not like that, like you're killing snakes. Gently but firmly, see? feel it catch? It's like this, it's all in the wrist just so..." His smooth-running commentary delivered in a monotone that is all sound and no sense. Blah, blah, blah. I hear his deceptively calm but scolding words in my mind, knowing I'm erecting a barrier between myself and the machine, between myself and the world Emmett created.

I concede that the damned thing isn't going to run for me, which is no big surprise. There's always the old way—the hand clippers. I fish the clippers out of the garden jumble, and head out to the back yard.

The lawn itself looks good, large swaths still smooth as paint. However, here and there tough "natives" are standing up, announcing their presence. I'll get to them, but first another area, one I have to look at from my cocoon in the den. It's a ragged edge around a bed of magenta petunias, under a vine maple where the unfinished birdfeeder was to have hung. I struggle with the clippers, can't get the blades apart due to a locking device. I push, pull, tug and tweak, to no avail.

The sun beats straight down, a palpable ball of fire, sledge hammer heat. Sweat trickles sticky tracks down my sides. I rake stray hairs from my face, from my eyes, out from under my collar, I reposition barrettes to hold it back. I twist the clippers, prod the locking mechanism. No dice. Finally, in frustration, I stride back into the garage, fling them back into Emmett's mess, then stomp into the house for my sewing scissors. This will not be good for them, but at least I understand how to make them work.

Then, clicking my pinking shears, I kneel on the grass and survey the bed of flowers. I begin trimming back the grass that is sprouting into the petunias, last year's petunias that have wintered over. More hair in my eyes, more sweat runs down my sides. More hair, more hair in my eyes, in my face…my damned hair…I pull out the barrettes, grab a handful of my hair, I scissor it off. I grab more hair, gather it off my neck, draw it forwards, I cut it with my pinking shears. I cut it, whack at it. So intoxicating, irresistible, the best thing I've ever done. Whack, whack, right there in the yard, I give myself a haircut, a wonderful, liberating haircut. Hair filters down in a fine rain onto the petunias, and I'm glad to be rid of it. I am sorry when there's no more hair to get hold of. I long for more hair to cut, more hair to cut away from my face, my neck, to cut away from my eyes. I shake my head, my light head, my cool unburdened head. Much better, so very much better.

At that precise moment, I see through the opened door into the garage that Harold's pickup has backed into my drive, Harold from the plant. YOU SHOULD SEE WHAT I SAW reads his bumper sticker. Oh, shit, I think, oh, holy smoking shit. What timing.

"Mrs. Malone," he calls, "I tried phoning, but first the line was busy and then no one answered. They cleaned out Emmett's stuff, getting ready for the new guy. Just thought I'd take a chance and come on out with these boxes. You want I should leave 'em in the garage? Or bring 'em in?"

"Well, I guess the garage would be fine. What is it?"

He puffs a bit, unloading cardboard boxes, stacking them in the hot garage. "I'll let you look through 'em, uh, Liz. Say, it's none of my business, but what're ya up to?" He steps into the yard, looks at the hairy petunias.

"Peg, I'm Peg, remember?"

"Oh, excuse me, Peg."

"What I'm up to is, well, I'm trimming grass. Couldn't get the clippers to work, so, uh, I'm using my sewing scissors. Never mind. I'm quitting anyway. Too hot."

"Yeah, it's a warm one today, heading into a hot summer. You got a weed eater…you want I should look at? The company, they don't expect me back right away."

I feel a thrill of alarm, throw him a look. But he seems innocent. And old, in the full merciless light beating down in the yard. He has that hollow-chested, potbellied build of an old guy, the kind who'd wear Sansabelt polyester pants, and wash-'n-wear rayon shirts. His face is jowls and bags, his high balding forehead sprinkled with freckles, the kind that look pre-cancerous. "No, that's all right," I say, and am ashamed of how rude I sound.

"Least lemme check the clippers. Where they at?"

As I've seen Amy do, I ruffle at my hair, trying to fluff it up, then brush grass and hair from the front my jeans. He's a nice person. Besides, why would anyone make a pass at me, for God's sake! "Yeah, okay. See? I can't get the blades to unlock."

He twists a gadget shaped like a figure 8, and the blades spring apart, ready to work. "It's a safety precaution, so you don't stab yourself unexpected. Nuthin' to it. You didn't do the lawn work, didja? I tell ya, it's tough takin' over when the man's gone. Otherwise, you look like you're doin' okay." He appraises me. "The family resemblance, I can see it now, 'tween you and your girl."

I say quickly, "Amy takes after her father, he had the looks."

"I don't know about that. Maybe it's your hair. It's different."

"Yes, I just cut it, right out there in the garden." I laugh nervously, then add, “But you’ve got to get on your way.”

“You want I should look at the weed eater?”

All I want is for him to go. “No, that’s okay, Harold. I’ll take it in for a tune-up, or whatever. Do they give weed eaters a tune-up? Is that the right word?”

He laughs as if I’ve said something funny. “You could run it on down to Bill’s Mowers on Main. Tell ‘em you want it serviced. Honest, I don’t mind lookin’ at it.” He reaches for the weed eater.

“Listen, I do need you to do something. Not with the weed eater. What I need is someone to take dishes back to the plant. To the people who brought food to the funeral supper. I don’t know how to get these dishes back. Could you do that for me?”

“Surely. Don’t mind a bit. Glad to help out.”

He follows me into the house, and in the service porch he hefts the box I’ve packed with plates and bowls from the office crowd. One is a green pottery that nestles in a wrought iron framework. MAGGIE QUINN reads the tape on the bottom. “Getting these back, it was awkward for me. I couldn’t make myself do it,” I mumble.

“Yes, I know. This is fine, you don’t have to face it.”

Face what, I wonder. But I do not want to question him, I want him gone. I want to be alone with Emmett’s stuff, to see what’s left of him. There must be clues in his paperwork, or whatever he’s left behind. I am barely able to smile and give a goodbye salute as Harold drives off with his cargo of kitchenware.

First, though, I have to see what I’ve done to my hair. I stare at myself in the bathroom mirror. I’ve cut what can pass as a fringe of bangs, and my face seems smaller, less horsy. Not bad, I don’t look bad. But not as good as Amy.

No, Amy’s the pretty one, with her smooth hair and skin, her deep-set hooded eyes shaped like triangles, like canoe paddles; her pointed little chin with Emmett’s dimple. Such looks made her popular with boys. Since grade school, she’s had them hanging around.

Then I remember who took that picture of the three of us in the park. Amy’s boyfriend, her callow pimpled swain, yeah, he’d come along with us to share the birthday cake. He’d been sixteen, two years older than Amy, and had his own car, which made him dangerous. Emmett had hated him on sight and never missed a chance to take pot-shots. His name was Matt Butterworth, which Emmett transposed into Butt Matterworth, sometimes Matterworthless. Emmett said the kid looked slick and greasy. Did he melt in the sun? Did he slide off the seat of his car? Did he rub off on Amy's hands? That kind of sly sexual insinuation had incensed Amy.

To be honest, I hadn't liked Matt, either, but my God, don't you have to be polite? Am I the only one burdened with politeness? Had Emmett cornered the market on rudeness? On bad manners? On the luxury of bluntly speaking one's mind?

No matter how Emmett had been at the plant, he'd been the stern old man at home. His instructions in sexual matters had consisted of shaken fists, dire warnings against "screwing around," and orders that I do something. Take charge. Well, I had, hadn't I? First with a talk about "saving herself," which got me nowhere. Then I'd embarrassed us both with a halting discussion of rubbers, with vague anxious advice, fumbling instructions.

"*Rubbers*!" Amy exclaimed. "Mom, they're condoms. I know all about them."

So the next step was the birth control pills. Emmett never came to terms with it. The trouble was that Emmett had been the old-fashioned parent, while Amy had grown into the New Woman. I'd tried to run interference between them. In the process, I'd been worn down, like a board under a planer. More than anything I'd wanted them to get along, to appreciate each other, to bend a little. To cooperate, at least on the damned birthday, for Christ's sake! If I could go back to that birthday in the park, I'd order, I'd command, I'd bellow at Emmett and Amy, I'd tell them in no uncertain terms to be nice, to behave, to be civil. If not for poor Matt, at least for me. Now, looking at my shorn self in the mirror, I think what a pleasure it's going to be to live without them and their backbiting kibitzing, their constant shooting gallery.

Then I stare into my own eyes, stung with guilt. But it's true, I am pleased now to have this chance to be on my own. Just because I've chosen, so far, to live my life without actively participating in it does not mean that there is not an active person in there. My first step in discovering that person will be to define the edges of Emmett. Just as an astronomer discovers objects in space not by seeing them, but by seeing where they are not.

Black holes, aren't they called black holes? Emmett would have known.

CHAPTER 4

I make a pot of tea and bring in Emmett's office boxes. I'll sort through them on my teak table. I've restored this table, rubbed it down with linseed oil and turpentine, bringing back its finish. It's my talisman. A wonderful table; it validates my taste, my judicious selection. I should have forced the issue, should have bought those matching chairs. Ah, well, next time, I tell myself ruefully.

The first box is crammed with incidentals: plastic raincoat, spare shirts and socks, a windbreaker. A fancy pen and pencil set I gave Emmett one Christmas, still new, still nestled in its box. Then I become exasperated: an electric shaver, an insistent after-shave, deodorant, hand mirror, clothes brush, hair dryer, tooth paste, a toothbrush, dental floss. Nail equipment, emery boards, nail clippers. Scissors with tiny curved blades, for those hard-to-reach nasal hairs? Why, the man had become a self-indulgent popinjay! My mother once called him that. Now I see why. He'd had more beautification *junk* at the plant than I do in the house, and I swell with disdain, disgust. On the bottom of the box, a rattling assortment of pills: aspirins, antacids, breath mints. A spare prescription of his blood pressure medication. A half-eaten bag of pork rinds, his favorite snack but absolutely forbidden since his attack. Also forbidden, also half-eaten, Reese's peanut butter cups, a bag of the snack size. So he hadn't been as pure as he'd let on, that sly dog, and I unwrap one for myself. It makes me thirsty, so I pour more tea.

The next box: another layer of Emmett, this one of the office-jokester ilk. Folders of cartoons and comic strips of the *Dilbert* sort, or clipped from slick magazines like *New Yorker,* or *Atlantic Monthly.* Despite my mood, which is growing irritation and scorn for the shallowness of the man, one makes me smile. The boss yells to his secretary in the next room, "That's okay, Mary, I only need one copy," while putting the document through a shredder. There's a computer-generated HAPPY BIRTHDAY banner, probably from a surprise party on Emmett's forty-sixth birthday, over a year ago. He'd been pleased. I'd been pleased for him, but would have hated it for myself. There's a foot-tall beer stein I don't recognize, emblazoned with MALONE and a supposed family crest. It's full of pencils, ballpoints, colored marking pens. A cigar box of miscellaneous, rubber bands, post-it-notes, labels, paper clips—the industrial kind shaped like clamps. A dictionary for poor spellers.

A large-scale map of Ireland, one he must have had on his wall because there are tack holes in the corners. Someone has marked out a route from Dublin to Galway to Limerick, then on to Cork. No doubt they'd planned, he and Maggie Quinn, to kiss the Blarney Stone, while some drunken Irishman held their ankles as they dangled over the pit. I am irate, I slurp my tea, but aren't I building on air again? I still have no real proof of wrongdoing. Not yet.

Also a large-scale joke labeled "The Chair." It's a series of pictures; the first shows the chair as designed, with three legs on the bottom, and one sticking straight up through the seat. The second as the chair as built, all four legs on one side. The third as shipped, now not a chair at all, but a table with legs of varying lengths. The fourth as viewed by the salesman, a splendid leather armchair, trimmed with brass studs. The last picture: what the customer had in mind—a plain straight-backed chair. Emmett had shown more sense of humor at work than he had at home. Had he ever been fun to have around? Well, of course...but when? I can't remember.

Feeling angry, betrayed, and deprived, I tackle the next box. It's a terrible assortment of heavy-going paperwork. His calendar, personalized memo pads, his blotter covered with doodles and misspelled words. He'd never been particularly literate. He'd been a mechanic, a technician; had, by choice, read little, other than the paper. That black hole business—he'd known that by way of TV, a PBS special viewed, probably, from his La-Z-Boy.

I glance through his appointment book, his time-line of pending job orders, an "at-a-glance" monthly layout. Lord, all these computer printouts, specification tables, books of regulations, order forms, invoices, graphs, diagrams—I'll have to return them.

Then, omit, a folder labeled STOCK OPTIONS. It, too, is full of printouts, columns of figures with dates going back twenty years and more. Down through time our assets had mounted steeply, into several hundred thousand dollars. Then a precipitous drop, with the most current date showing a balance of almost nothing. Well, a few hundred dollars. A few hundred dollars! That's all there is? This has to be a mistake. But I know it's no mistake. He'd been withdrawing funds. He'd been cashing in.

He'd been selling off behind my back. What for? But directly beneath the stock folder, as if in answer to my question: a clutch of real estate literature. Brochures, ads clipped from the paper, realtor-issued lists of properties for sale arranged from cheapest to most expensive. Emmett's left-handed check marks appear next to some in the middle-priced group, properties in the range of two to three hundred thousand dollars. Why, he'd bought a property, most likely a luxury condo, if the check marks mean anything.

And a Miata. Because under the real estate material is another Mazda brochure featuring a red sports car, with figures in the margin, in Emmett's draftsman hand. My stomach lurches. I stand, rotate my shoulders, pace into the den, and stare out at my back yard, at the magenta petunias under a thin film of my shorn hair. Such a long time ago that I'd cut my hair right out there under the vine maple, although it had been only this morning. But it's a lifetime, Emmett's lifetime. Going through those boxes has been like viewing a condensed version of his existence as he slogged along, day after day at the plant, consulting shipping schedules, packing up finished products, ordering supplies, routing mail orders. Poor Emmett. He'd been bored, and stressed. Bored and stressed. A deadly duo. I see that now.

But beneath my unsettling, surprisingly intimate look at his routine life, beneath my shock about the stock loss, there bubbles something else. Relief. Relief from nagging guilt. Because I'd formed the theory, in spite of myself, that his death had been my fault. I'd triggered the attack by being the kind of person I am—oblivious, self-involved, careless of his wellbeing.

I'd been laboring under the presumption that if I'd continuously monitored his emotions, I'd have kept his heart beating. If I'd straightened up his workbench, if I'd had the foresight to share the good news of the volunteer cherry tomato crop, or the petunias, if I'd cut my hair earlier…if, if, if…

If I'd gone back to work, full-time. Quit this hit-or-miss temp stuff. I told him I needed a steady job, but he said that starting out at my age, I wouldn't make enough to pay the taxes on the extra income. Better I should work for "pin money." He said that, *pin money*, and now I see it as disparaging, belittling of my abilities. I see it as hostile, as destructive. Because due to his sabotaging of our, of *my,* financial security, I'll have to get a job, I'll have to take what I can get. No, I need not trouble myself with guilt. Emmett sowed the seeds of his destruction by leading a double life.

I have to talk to someone. Amy. I rush to the phone and speed-dial her number. But all I get is Amy's purring message, "Talk to me."

Abruptly I hang up. What's the matter with me! This is the time of day that Amy's at the gym with her first after-work class of spreading secretaries. Besides, Amy has begun ennobling her father's memory, due to some late-arriving guilt trip of her own. Could I relate to her my mounting evidence of Emmett's treachery? No, it would not be well received; it would even be rejected. Even implied criticism, and mine is not that delicate anymore, might alienate the fragile armistice Amy's achieving. She'd turn on me.

Instead of Amy, I'll call the lawyer, I'll call Mr. Devlin who helped us make the will. Emmett had liked Mr. Devlin, a fellow

Irishman with whom he'd established a convivial rapport. Mr. Devlin will counsel me.

But Mr. Devlin, later that week, seems to have lost his joviality. "Mrs. Malone, come in, come in," he says. He smiles, but he also sighs, an impatient, put-upon sigh, as if I've been demanding too much of his attention, have become a problem, like a telephone marketer who calls during dinner, selling aluminum siding, or a new windshield for your car. Nevertheless, he attempts to be cheerful. "You've...done something...to your hair?" he says, twirling his fingers vaguely near his shoulders.

"Just a haircut," I mutter. At Amy's insistence, I'd gotten a trim at the Hairtage, Amy's favorite salon near Fitness World. The stylist had urged more drastic action: frosting, tint, or a perm. When I failed to enlist in the program, the woman had turned cool, just as Mr. Devlin seems to have done. I must be doing something to trigger this reaction.

For a few minutes he shuffles paperwork. "Yes, yes," he says curtly, snapping shut his glasses. He fixes his brown eyes on me, so brown I can't see the irises. He pushes the stock folder back across his desk. It's a black desk, smooth and shiny, as if carved of stone. "It would appear that these assets have been liquidated. Sold. These things happen, there is a communication gap, or breakdown, and whatever one spouse intended is not conveyed to the other. After all, Mrs. Malone, ownership was listed as 'either/or' so one spouse could sell without the other's signature. It's a wise move, in the case of a death, whereby a signature is not obtainable. Probate complications, endless delays. Sometimes years. He did the right thing, in that regard."

Despite myself, I shiver. His office is cold, all marble and stone, wall coverings in black overlain with a glittery gold design. This reflects some light, but several lamps are turned on to dispel the gloom. Outside the June afternoon sun blazes, with almost enough warmth to create heat waves off the parking lot asphalt. "But don't you see what this does to me?" I say, feeling absurdly on the edge of tears. "He never told me he was selling our assets."

Regally, he leans back in his chair, a leather chair trimmed with brass studs like the one the salesman visualized in Emmett's cartoon. He rubs at the dents his glasses leave in his fleshy nose, then says, "Yes, I see. But you might as well get hold of yourself, quit bleeding, climb down from that cross you've nailed yourself to." His tone is rough, and my cheeks burned—am I acting like a martyr? "Come on, Mrs. Malone, face facts. There's nothing you can do. Get a grip. After all, you're apparently healthy, you're a relatively young woman with a home of your own. Paid for, is it not? Yes, I see that it is. So you have to get a job. Most women work nowadays. The receptionist out there in the lobby? That's my wife. Women work. Nothing to be ashamed of."

I straighten up in my chair, a hard straight-backed chair, the one the customer wanted in the office joke. "I'm not ashamed. I'm shocked, and afraid. And I'm...unprepared." I regard him with new eyes. He's a tall massive man, and weighty—as if his own good self-opinion sits heavily on him, extra poundage. The only real fat is carried around his middle, a desk-jockey's belly, but his back and shoulders also bulge, and he looks soft and meaty in a dark jacket. He is wise to wear that jacket. I wish for my own coat. Excessive air-conditioning ices the air.

His legs are thick, as big around as my waist, requiring pants with pleats, knife-edged pleats, I noticed, when he stood to greet me. I can't quite make out his twinkling gold tie tack, possibly the emblem of some organization, Kiwanis, a fraternity, some good old boys' club that sends their brothers the best business by way of the two-martini lunch, or the golf course. I recall that Devlin's father had been a judge, the family an old one in the Valley, the kind that once owned extensive orchards and vineyards, now being paved over for shopping malls, housing tracts, and condo developments.

Solid family background, unlike Emmett's or mine. I think of that beer stein emblazoned with the MALONE coat-of-arms. As if Emmett's family had had a coat-of-arms! How presumptuous! Emmett's father had been a failed painter, a cubist long after cubism had run its course. He'd tried to support the family with odd jobs and casual labor. His mother, the main breadwinner, had worked in a school cafeteria. Family crest! My own father had been an accountant; my maiden name was Schneider. Combining my stout German stock with the Irish, maybe my mother had it right: Emmett and I had been star-crossed after all.

But haven't I got it backward? Regardless of our families and their bent, hadn't Emmett been the no-nonsense square headed burgher, while I butterflied around, the impractical romantic? Yes, in many ways we'd worked a role reversal, I can see that now. Stunned by this sudden revelation, I keep my unflinching look on Devlin, as if blinking would allow him to wriggle away. A staring contest with a reptile—a snake, or a lizard.

Devlin shifts his weight, causing his chair to creak in the uncomfortable silence. "Listen, I can do some research, but it'll cost you $150 an hour, and it won't take much to eat up a lot of capital. I'm telling you that right up front." He swings around a computer monitor, a flat one, very cutting edge, so I can view it with him. "Here's your account, itemized, the $1500 retainer to see the estate through probate, and a list of your assets. Now, I can go to the Courthouse, I can dig around in Records and sift through real estate transactions, I can go to San Francisco and search through stock records, but it will cost you, I guarantee, it'll cost you more than it's worth."

Satisfied, or at least I see him as exuding satisfaction like an extra sheen on his glossy skin, he leans back again, runs a smoothing hand over his hair. It's dark and wavy, not curly but sculpted into rolls that ripple back from a receding hairline shaped like a capital M. He, too, wafts the scent of some cologne, a heavy musk aroma. What is it with these men and their perfume, I wonder. My own father, the accountant with a green eye shade and plastic pocket protector, had worked hard; it had been his goal, pursued with honest unadorned soap and water, to smell of nothing at all.

By way of dismissal, Devlin turns the computer monitor back around so it faces him alone with its secrets—I'd been able to make nothing of the hieroglyphics on it. He hits a few keys, then squares his yellow pad in front of him. He'd been scribbling notes, and I strain to see what he'd written. As with the computer monitor, I can make out nothing, it's all gibberish, his penmanship as wild as a doctor's. Because I'd retrieved my stock folder, the only things on his black desk now are the yellow pad, his pen, and the monitor. He pushes his chair back and stands, pulling in his gut while adjusting his shirttail in his pants. In my head I hear Amy's voice, "Pleated pants are for guys with big butts," and I smirk.

"That's the ticket, chin up," he says.

"Yep," I say, which startles me. I never say *yep,* but he makes me want to regress into redneck-ism. I long to drop some g's, sprinkle around some *ain'ts*. "Chin up, shoulder to the wheel, nose to the grindstone." I rise to my feet.

He laughs. "Well, I don't know about all that."

"Me, neither. Sounds uncomfortable."

Now he replaces the laugh with an earnest frown. "Seriously, I know you're broken up, it's not a good time for you, but you've got to be sensible. Take my word for it, things will come out right in the end. My own philosophy is that we get to where we're going, despite road blocks." This he utters solemnly, as if giving me the key to life.

I mumble inanely, "Thanks for your time," as if he's done me a favor, but I know I've paid handsomely for my twenty minutes. He walks me to the door, treading heavily on oriental area rugs. Again I smell his after-shave. I feel my stomach lurch, I become light-headed, nauseated. In the outer office I ask to use the rest-room. The receptionist, Mrs. Devlin, points the way. The woman is icily perfect with frosted hair in artful curves around her face. No bangs. Amy told me in no uncertain terms that bangs are worn only by children, or retards. Or archaic remnants of the long gone '80s, which includes me. Mrs. Devlin's gray business suit is carefully tailored to disguise figure flaws. Even so, I note that under it lurks a body as shapeless as a sack of potatoes. Like her husband, she'll grow into a doughy fortress.

Matching the rest of the office, the bathroom is hard-edged, all tile and stone, which allows sounds to echo off mirrors and ceramic surfaces. Also, like the rest of the place, it's papered in black overlain with a gold design. There is scent, a potpourri of rose petals floating in a dish on the tile countertop. I turn on the gold-toned hot water tap—my hands are like ice—and stare into my own eyes, wondering aloud, "How much are they charging me to take a pee?"

The long and short of it is that Emmett is gone, and he's taken parts of me with him—my memories, my ability to cope, indeed, even to converse. He's taken my emotions—I feel numb half the time—and now I learn he's taken my money, too. But if he'd taken parts, he'd also left me with extra pieces. My too numerous and raw nerve endings thrum like power lines across the surface of my skin. My days have too many empty hours. My nights are long and restless, and when I do sleep, I dream of Emmett, young Emmett. Loving, cheerful, protective Emmett.

Emmett and I paddling a canoe across a pond that's pure and blue and still, mirror-like. He's in front of me, and I watch his paddle slice through the water; I see that paddle more clearly than I've ever seen any paddle, limned along its edge with silver droplets. I study Emmett, I can feel, I can *taste* the warm silk of his slightly salty skin, the smooth skin of his back under his jaunty denim shirt. I want to twine my fingers through the fringe of blond curls showing under his Aussie-style hat. I stare at his belt loops, because if anything happens—the canoe is as fragile as a willow leaf and the water beneath us has now turned an eerie black—I'll hold onto a belt loop and he'll save me; the water can't pull me down, if I have Emmett.

We did once rent a canoe to explore a Canadian pond. But Emmett, showing off, displaying his prowess, paddled his side so vigorously, I hadn't been able to counterbalance him and we'd progressed in erratic semi-circles. I'd smarted under his criticism, had been ashamed of my awkwardness. So the happiness of that preposterous dream is a lie.

Again: we're bicycling on a desert road. Infinity arches overhead so blue it makes me ache. It's wintertime, and the desert air is thin and sharp, almost painful to breathe. The canoe dream was silent, but this one has sound effects: birds chitter in the crystal air, wind soughs in gray-green foliage, bike tires whir over asphalt.

This ecstatic dream, well, it's another lie, the result of something I dredged up from my old uncontrollable lizard brain. We did once bicycle around some new subdivisions in Desert Hot Springs, because Emmett's parents wanted to move there. His mother had become arthritic from that cafeteria work; and back then, desert lots upon which to anchor a trailer were cheap, the ocean of land around Palm Springs inexhaustible. Emmett chose a route up a long steep incline, which his racy Peugeot had no trouble with. But I couldn't make it on my clunky old Schwinn. He had to walk both bikes up the hill. He was accommodating, he was nice about it; but I resented his big-hearted condescension.

Why did he have a racing bike when I made do with a sit-up-straight grandma variety? Well, because he did race it, occasionally; whereas I biked to the market, brought groceries home in a wire basket on the handlebars. Still, it wasn't fair! That old balloon-tired Schwinn—the deck had been stacked against me.

However—and here I stare at myself in the gold-framed mirror—what would I have had him do? Ride off and leave me? No, of course no; but I wanted him to falter, I wanted him to fail, just once. Just once I wanted him to be the one who couldn't make it, couldn't keep up, couldn't maintain. I wanted him weak, vulnerable. Well, now, in a sense, he is. Does this make me happy? Yes, I admit that it does.

I turn off the gold-toned faucet, dry my hands on a towel, a luxurious thick terrycloth, not a paper one. I resist the urge to wipe water spots out of the sink, because they'll leave spots on that black porcelain. Such impracticality. Such richness. Even the doorknob is gold.

Emmett had been the strong one, the enduring one, but I have survived him. Here I am, or there I am in the mirror, the proof. I am going to go on, and on, and on. *I* will become strong, I will grow, I will wise up. Just because I've lived my life on pause while he was alive doesn't mean I'll keep it there now that he's dead.

He *is* dead. At times I have to remind myself of that. He is gone, and the more I try to reach out to him, either awake or asleep, the farther he recedes. Sometimes I wonder if he'd ever *been.* One day I dug out photos to see how he looked. Had he parted his hair on the right or the left? How had his nose fit his face? The bridge of it, the bone, the flesh of his cheeks, his throat, his forehead…his teeth, had they been straight? On the small side, or large and square, like mine? Had he had a slight overbite? I can't tell from my most recent pictures, those taken in Cabo San Lucas. That day in the warm Mexican sun, the day he bought sandals soled with tire tread and a serape for the couch, the same day he bought turquoise-trimmed silver feather earrings for Amy—and Maggie, too?—that day he'd been disinclined to smile. In the photos he looked washed out, grim, and old. When had Emmett gotten old? It came as a shock to me, looking at those pictures. Because, after all, *I'm* not old. Not yet.

One more chore, one more lead to follow before closing the books on whatever Emmett had been up to before he died: the real estate listings. I get a new map—the area's growing so fast, maps are outdated almost before they roll off the press—a large-scale city map big enough to navigate by. I spread it out, I pore over a great colorful offering-up of the town.

The Interstate with its lining of motels and fast food outlets that advertise on billboards raised over the freeway like great square foreheads, a part of town I generally don't frequent. Then Main Street, downtown, or what used to be downtown. It's gradually dying, despite the efforts of various merchants, the ones stuck there, to resuscitate it. Then the malls, with their anchors of big box discount stores. Then houses, neighborhoods, parks, schools, all gradually becoming newer, more modern, as you travel into the foothills.

The farther into what had been the hinterland, areas once given over to orchards and vineyards, or pastures studded with oaks and cattle, the ritzier the developments, the more poetic the names. Mountain Oaks, a settlement bragging about hiking and biking trails. Broadmoor Terrace with tennis courts, saunas, and spas. Fairhaven Greens, a protective ring of houses around a golf course. Singing Waters, two-story condos hunched over a man-made lake, like animals at a waterhole. I know their general appearances, have driven by them, or seen their ads. I know how they'll be. White stucco boxes with red tile roofs, an army of these units marching along behind barricading serpentine slump stone walls.Landscaping: islands of Lily of the Nile, pampas grass, oleanders in churning seas of red bark; a gated decorative entryway, the tract's name on an overhead arch, written in wrought iron script as stylized, as delicate, as precise as Arabic, or calligraphy.

Apparently Emmett had looked at such developments. One in particular, Singing Waters, had interested him: on his printout, three addresses are check-marked, and one is circled. I take aim at it, I will follow his trail through Singing Waters, I will see what he looked at.

Saturday. People will be home on Saturday. Maggie Quinn, if she lives there, will be home. Her Miata, if she has one, will perhaps be visible. At any rate, it's a goal, something to aim at.

Saturday is recycling day in my part of town. I put out the newspapers—most of them unread since Emmett's death—but don't anchor them properly. A sudden gust out of the west sends sheets of newsprint blowing into the neighbors' yards. I charge out to corral papers. An unpromising start to the day. Then old Mr. Purdy appears to help, flapping out of his house next door in a bathrobe over a flannel shirt and faded jeans. Cross, mossy old Mr. Purdy.

"This recycling business, it's a bunch of hooey," he says, puffing from a sprint chasing down a brightly colored Sunday supplement section. "I read somewhere the garbage guys just throw it all out anyway. Like during the war, the Big One, there was all this hooey about saving bacon grease, tin cans and foil, newspapers. Ha! Useless. Just giving folks something to do, make them feel useful. Didn't amount to a hill of beans. Well, there, that's about it."

I thank him breathlessly. He goes on, "You're out early, all dressed up. Like maybe this is not the day to ask you for coffee...I've been thinking I'd have you in for a cuppa joe."

I mumble an excuse, a polite refusal, something, while turning away. Coffee with Mr. Purdy! I'm shocked, but also pleased. My day has gotten a lift; I am wrong about being off to a bad start. This connection with Mr. Purdy is auspicious; things are going my way. Backing out the Bronco, my maps, real estate printouts next to me, I feel...almost normal, special, even, in my dark pantsuit, white silk shirt, medium heels. Mr. Purdy thinks

I'm normal. He saw me as a whole person, making an effort and succeeding, living a life with shape and hope, like everyone else's life. Maybe I can pull this off after all.

I thread across town, then up into the hills. I find Singing Waters, park in a VISITOR space, lock up, and walk around feeling as conspicuous as a cat burglar caught in broad daylight, as welcome as a *Watchtower* peddler. People will suspect my motives. The proper people who belong here will ask to see my passport, my documentation. I expect to have to defend my presence.

I also expected some activity, people doing lawn work, washing cars or windows, or sweeping walks. But there's no life anywhere. Aha! I should have known. This is where other people do your work for you, little brown men in khaki work clothes and pith helmets; little brown women in uniforms, both men and women pinned with nametags, proof of their legitimacy.

Many cars in the assigned covered parking, but no red Miata. People are home, but not out and about because there's no reason to be out and about. Exterior chores involving leaf blowers, lawn mowers, weed eaters, even interior work with vacuum cleaners and dust mops, will be done during weekdays. The residents here don't want to put up with noise or inconvenience. Wouldn't this lack of activity make living here a pointless and sterile existence? What would Emmett have found to occupy him? No repairs to make, no weeds to eat, no cherry tomatoes to plant. He would have been lost.

But there was that literature about Ireland. He hadn't expected to be home.

With difficulty—the place is a maze—I find the manager's office, go in, introduce myself. She's a woman my age, and she believes—or doesn't care enough to question—my story that the real estate agent sent me to look at a unit. Two of the three listings on Emmett's printout have been sold, but one is still available. Sure, the woman says, she can show it to me. No problem.

Jingling keys, she leads me down an aggregate concrete walkway through sod so new the seams are still visible. Here and there, groupings of saplings with trunks the diameter of pencils lean against their stakes. Sycamores, the tree currently in vogue.

Their few pale green leaves are as pointed as a spread hand, and maple-like. London Plane trees, Emmett would have corrected. Emmett knew trees. Not just ordinary trees like maple or eucalyptus, but exotics not encountered in our city environment. "Oh, there's a bristle cone pine," he'd say, or "I didn't know Western Hemlock grew so far south." "A Pacific Yew, by golly, at this elevation." Emmett, the tree expert.

Emmett, Emmett, Emmett! Always Emmett! Emmett, the lawn man, the fixer, the complete house-husband. He'd taken care of the house and the car, or was supposed to have done so. He was the joiner, the joker, the canoe expert, the handsome one, the strong one. I am sick of him! Why had I let him dominate my life? Why am *I* not an expert on trees, weed eaters, investment portfolios? It's intolerable! I make a solemn vow to get better.

Singing Waters is built on gently rolling hills, and embankments are planted with English ivy, African daisies, verbena Peruviana. I tell the woman how much I admire the landscaping, so artistic, well planned. "Yard work," I say, "I'm no good at it. I'm doing it now because my husband passed away. He's been gone almost four months."

"Really. Must be hard."

"We had an embankment steeper than that, but Emmett, that was my husband, Emmett decided he didn't like it. So he leveled it, cut down the angle. One wheelbarrow full of dirt at a time. Took him weeks. Oh, he was a worker. Then to pack the earth after he got the slope the way he wanted it, he drove the car back and forth across it. This was the front yard next to the street."

"I'll be darned."

"Yes, he was clever. That man could do anything, build the Great Wall of China, the Transcontinental Railroad, the Panama Canal—if he had enough time."

"Why would he want to change the angle of the embankment?"

"He didn't like such a drop-off. Too hard to get anything to grow because we couldn't water it. It was hard pan, the water just ran off." Then I remember the rest of the story. Emmett ruptured the water main with the car; the broken line sent up a geyser thirty feet high. The City had to turn the water off; the whole neighborhood had been without water. A five-man work crew labored all afternoon to fix the main, on a Saturday. The neighbors, waiting to wash cars or clothes or the dishes, had been quite annoyed, especially Mr. Purdy. Then too, we'd been fined for the work crew and for the water we'd wasted. No point in telling this woman that; no point in telling her anything, really. But in spite of myself, I go on, "He planted the new flatter area with lantana, but it died. Then he went to low-growing cypresses, but it encouraged slugs. The neighbors said we were a slug farm." Abruptly I stop talking. This woman will think I'm crazy, or hard to get along with, an unwelcome addition to their roster. I remind myself that I'm not really planning to live here.

"Here's Number 17, a two-bedroom, two-bath model, about fifteen hundred square feet, appliances, drapes, carpets—all top of the line. European style cabinets. Nice view of the lake." We enter the condo by a side door, the woman turning on lights as we pass down a hall. "See? Here's what I mean." In the living room, she opens a drape, and there lies the man-made pond. A few Canada geese float desultorily in the distance; a few small boats, the kind you pedal, are drawn up on the grass in front of neighboring units. The wind that blew my recycling into the neighbors' yards is still at it, and the air is full of dust from nearby vineyards being cultivated, vineyards whose days are numbered. The choppy lake water reflects a dull blue-gray color, shadowed here and there with swaths of muddy brown. "The other two units on your printout were cheaper because they're not lake-front. That's them, over there." She points off to the next section. "Otherwise, these are all about the same."

"Oh, my…" I say, gazing around me.

"Yes, nice, isn't it? This townhouse'll go fast. The last one. If you want it, you should hurry."

I stare at the water, trying to imagine Emmett pedaling one of those silly little boats, and I can't. Nor can I see him rowing a canoe across this mud hole. Emmett had favored excursions with obstacles to overcome; he'd needed a steep hill to climb, a forty-knot wind in the Bay knocking down the *River Rat,* the sailboat he crewed on. He'd demanded exertion, difficulty, adventure. At least that's what he'd demanded when he'd been with me. But maybe with another woman, one who'd supply a challenge from another quarter—

I sigh, breathe in the newness emanating from carpet, drapes, paint. A heady aroma, indicating expense, luxury, ease. A fragrance such as the one you get in a new car, such as Maggie probably experiences with her Miata. The gray-blue of the carpet seems to extend into the lake, as if there's no separation between rug and water. A nice expanse, if one doesn't look too closely.

I like the décor, sleek and modern, no frills, no trim pieces, curlicues. Gray–blue starkness. But would Emmett have liked it? Would his fusty old La-Z-Boy fit here? His massive roll-top desk? His large-screen TV? No, they're too big and the wrong style. But he'd probably planned to leave his middle-aged over-stuffed shabby furniture with me, his middle-aged over-stuffed shabby wife. He'd begin again with everything new, everything sleek and toned. Now, when it's too late, I realize that Emmett, after his first attack and his brush with death, had been intent on a new life. He'd wanted all of life he could get. He'd wanted Youth. He'd wanted Maggie Quinn. At least I think now that that was what he wanted.

Upon which wall would he have displayed his trophy/clipping/testimonial collection? I see no suitable expanse. The design of the unit follows the modern plan of openness, leaving few interior walls for pictures or displays. There's no place for Emmett's real person, or the person I'd thought him to be. Then again, with Maggie Quinn by his side, he would have had no need for clippings, testimonials, thank-yous from the local high school. Maggie Quinn would have been trophy enough.

But *would* Maggie have been enough?

Here I go again, I think, exasperated. I am building a case against Emmett on pure speculation. On the basis of a printout with checkmarks that possibly are Emmett's, possibly are not. I have wasted my time, and the manager's. Emmett said I was like the man who got on a horse and rode off in all directions. He was right, as usual.

Briskly, as if to put distance between myself and my speculation, I turn away and step into the kitchen. The manager follows me, talking of flush mounted soffits, slate countertops, wall-hung cabinets with under-counter lighting, lazy susans, easy roll-out trays for pots, pans, roasters. She points out that no kitchen pulls and handles mar the purity of line, the classic simplicity of style, of function. Yes, I think, this is the kitchen I had in mind when Emmett remodeled. But Emmett wanted traditional styling, such as oak called for. He wanted trim pieces and knickknack shelves and turned dowelings. Gingerbread.

"Yes, very nice," I murmur. "Tell me, are there garages?" I'm looking out a non-lake window. "Or does everyone have to make do with covered parking? You see, I have a valuable car, oh, not the one I'm driving today, but a sports car. Well, it was my husband's, a Miata, but I'll want to keep it protected."

The woman frowns slightly. "Miata...I don't know what that is. But the parking for this unit is right there, facing east. Most of our worst weather comes from the west."

"Does anyone have a sports car here? Isn't there anyone I can talk to about it?"

"Gee, I don't know. Don't pay much attention to cars. All I know is security's real good, no break-ins, no car clouts. Of course that doesn't mean you can get silly about it. You still have to lock up." She jangles keys. Time to go.

Then she adds, "Well, now that I think about it, there is a gal here with a little red something-or-other. Maggie, a redhead, beautiful hair. Let's see, is she home? No, don't see her car and her drapes are pulled. She lives in that one over there, hasn't been here too long, but a nice person. You could talk to her. Let's go knock, just in case."

I lose my breath, can barely mutter about not having time, I am so busy, have an appointment, need to be on my way. But thanks, anyway. I'll think about the unit, talk to the realtor. I drive home shaking with nerves, sweating in my silk blouse, swimming in adrenalin.

Well, at least now I know. The immediate question is what can I do, I have to do something. Action is called for, exertion, to counter emotional and mental stress.

I stop at an up-scale produce market to buy apples, pie apples if such can be gotten—I have no sense of the season anymore, or of the year. My year has lost its grounding; I am adrift. But I am going to change that, I am going to get my bearings.

In the past, the kitchen was my refuge from Emmett's TV blaring a ballgame or a war or a special about some endangered animal. It was my refuge from Amy's teenage pouts and sulks, her endless stream of boyfriends and loud music and squealing cars. To escape the noise and confusion, I turned to baking bread, to putting up preserves, to the exotic terrain of calzones, frittatas, Indian curries. I will see if cooking still works. I will make an apple pie, a real apple pie involving apples, and not glue, for Mr. Purdy. To thank him for helping round up the errant newspaper recycling, and as an apology for the water shut-off so long ago. My family has put the poor man through enough.

CHAPTER 5

I drive home from Singing Waters and the grocery store in a puzzling state: half of me is numb, and the other half wants to do some violent cooking. Underneath it all, I yearn to crawl in a hole and brood, as if my discoveries about Emmett were a clutch of eggs. Although to be honest, I knew what I'd find in that condo development. Anybody with half a brain would have put it together long ago.

Then I turn the corner, and a stray shock of rage explodes behind my eyes: just what I need now—Amy's yellow Mustang's in the driveway. I park behind it—we'll have to do a car shuffle when she leaves—and sit there for a minute trying to calm down. Then it occurs to me that my anger, although misplaced, indicates a recovery of sorts going on. When I'd been down, really low and sad, feeling helpless and vulnerable, I hadn't allowed myself to experience anything but love and servile gratitude for Amy's presence. Amy had felt it, too, the cloying constraints of bereavement. Yes, a little ruffling is good, wholesome.

I stagger in under bags of food. Have bought groceries like a mad woman, shopping and spending as if to spite Emmett. Treat myself to all the things he'd disliked, disapproved of. Okay, a food rebellion. That's what I've engaged in.

In the dining room, Amy sits at my table, with the sympathy cards fanned in front of her. "Mom, where have you been? I've been waiting and waiting." She's still in her workout suit, a black body stocking, and I can smell that heated lemony scent—Amy's lotion, or shampoo. She slathers on so much, of so many items, and had told me once, in all seriousness, that lemon is her signature scent. I'd been impressed with such dedication and organization, and bemused that Amy would think such a thing important.

Her eyes are red and puffy, and I'm taken aback: she's been crying. "Oh, honey," I say, setting down my sacks. "What's the matter? Your dad again? I know, it's so sad—"

"It's not that. Well, yeah, it is. I never understood how great he was…and now he's gone. The kind of guy you could trust, you could count on, you know?"

"Uh, yeah, count. On. You could say that. I suppose."

"Not like Larry."

"Larry? What's going on? What's wrong?"

A loud wet snuff, then Amy wipes her nose on her hand. Her nails are painted dark blue. "Larry wants to split. While I was staying here with you, he met someone else, he wants to move in with her." Her eyes blaze with tears again, angry tears. "Not that I give a rat's ass, that jerk. It's just that, oh, I don't know what's the matter with me. What's the point, why am I here." It's not a question, but a flat statement of useless fact. "You wouldn't understand."

"Sure, I would. Uh, well, maybe not totally. But I know how it feels to get left."

"I'm not getting left! See? I knew you wouldn't understand. By the way, where have you been? I thought you were going to be here. I had to use my key to get in. I've been waiting at least forty-five minutes."

"I went out to look at a townhouse in Singing Waters. You

know where that is?" I stop unloading the groceries to watch Amy's reaction, although it's unlikely that Emmett confided in her.

"You're looking at townhouses? You're moving? What's going on! No one tells me anything, my own mother!" Amy's eyes flash. "And what's with all this food! You've been complaining about the refrigerator being too full."

"I'm not moving into a townhouse, at least not unless I have to. Certainly not the kind in Singing Waters, they're too expensive. *All* this food, really, I've just got the ingredients for, well, mainly, a pie. I've decided to do a pie, for Mr. Purdy."

"Mr. Purdy! You're making him a pie? You've got more than pie here. I see peanut butter, graham crackers, lemons, cheese, avocados, asparagus—"

"Yeah, I know. Never shop when you're hungry." I chuckle, hoping to jolly Amy, or at least defuse her. "I've been thinking about Mr. Purdy, he's been a good neighbor all these years. Time we were nicer to him." I add in a cajoling tone, "Amy, look at these apples. Aren't they a perfect color? Neon green, they glow. Did you ever see nicer Granny Smiths? They practically sing! And smell them, like perfume."

"Mom, they're just apples!"

"I know, just apples." I laugh, belittling myself. "I got the cheese to grate into the crust, and real butter, too. I'm tired of that pseudo stuff you dad tried to eat. Fresh cinnamon, cloves...an honest-to-God lemon. Amy, I used to make a good pie, time to see if I still remember how." I busy myself with paring the apples, determined to hold my own.

"Do you have to do that now?"

"It'll only take a minute."

"I should have known you'd be too busy for me."

"Amy! I'm not too busy for you. That's not fair! I'm right here, peeling apples. I want to get this in the oven tomorrow, and you have to let apple slices sit under the sugar overnight. That way they don't puff up big empty air pockets under the crust. Tell me about Larry, I can listen and peel at the same time."

"There's nothing to tell. Next week he's moving out. Period.

I was wondering if you wanted to go somewhere with me, for a day or two. I don't want to watch him pack."

"Maybe you should stay home and keep an eye on what he takes."

"Mot*her*! I trust him, he wouldn't take anything that didn't belong to him!"

I shoot her a look. Is it too early to tell Amy what I've found out? Instead I say, "I've been thinking about trees. You know how your dad knew trees? How he could name them off, pick them out? Remember that joke of his about the little sapling growing up in the forest, among birches and beeches? One of the big trees asked the little tree what kind he was, and he looked around and said, 'I'm either a son of a birch, or a son of a beech.' Your dad liked that joke. I remember once someone said cattails grew from sea-level to over five thousand feet, and your dad said, 'Wow, that's some cattail'."

Amy's lips twitch, she doesn't want to smile and ruin her rich purple pout. Instead, she bursts into real tears, as I'd been expecting. As a child, and as an adult, Amy cried rather than relinquish the leverage of a stony mood. "Really, Amy, what can I do? Just tell me." I keep on peeling apples on my side of the counter, determined not to be drawn into it. I have enough already.

"Do you want to go away with me for a day or two, or not? Probably next Saturday and Sunday, maybe Monday. Larry and I are both off then, I can be out of there when he comes for the rest of his stuff. Most of it's already gone. He says this is my fault, that I was over here too much."

I put down my knife. "Now, wait a minute, are you going to blame this on me? That's not fair."

"Oh, Mom, of course not. I didn't mean it that way. I need to get my head straight, breathe some air that's not poisoned. Besides, you're not doing anything."

"Not yet, but I may have to get a real job." I draw a deep breath, edge into telling her about Emmett. But the sight of her at the table, thumbing through the sympathy cards—I can't do it. Cannot form the words to say that her father had had a mistress, had ravaged our finances to support her. Not yet.

"Yeah, Mom, you might want a job. You'll get bored, without Dad to take care of."

Without Dad to take care of. I undergo a small shiver of expectation, of anticipation. Of satisfaction. Nothing as strong as *happiness,* not yet, but a brief flick of peace. Yes, a kind of peace, a mere blip, an inkling. I know I'm regressing into a puzzling state, a treacherous state. I'm waffling on the slippery edge of self-indulgence. Internal discipline, my sole restraint, is not strong. I am dangerous, fierce with freedom, giddy with it, able to wield authority over my time, now that Emmett's schedule and demands have been erased. The old order and rhythm are gone; I am on my own. It's possible that I'll go to pieces. It's possible that I will sit and stare at a wall all day. I can slop around in my bathrobe. I can, I *do,* skip dinner, a meal formerly planned around the Heart Association's pyramidal guidelines. I can eat popcorn with real butter for breakfast, ice cream right out of the carton at any time of the day. I can drink whole milk. Slice open an avocado and spoon up the entire fruit right out of the peel. Emmett had had a low opinion of avocados, said they were "slimy," but now avocados are mine, oh, the power and freedom! And asparagus, I can eat whole pounds of asparagus—Emmett hadn't liked asparagus, said it made his pee stink. "So who's going to smell it?" I said.

The joy of my new freedom can wane, I can put the brakes on it myself, out of guilt or self-spite, or even out of love. For I had loved Emmett, I had treasured him. He'd been my prize, awarded by some fortunate fluke of nature or fate or happenstance. My memories are pieces of gold, my treasures. I hoard them, shuffle them out one by one, burnish them with use.

Emmett bringing me a bouquet of sweet peas after Amy was born. Such fragrant flowers, they'd perfumed the entire semi-private ward I'd been assigned to after the difficult birth that made Amy an only child. Humble flowers from my mother's yard—so stony broke we'd been back then, every penny counted.

Emmett, one Mother's Day, making me a special breakfast, an offering of broiled tomatoes, eggs, and potatoes. How proud he'd been, bringing in a tray—breakfast in bed, a thing I secretly dislike, hinting of dissolution, terminal illness. Stained sheets. But I never would have said that to him, so overcome I'd been.

Emmett at the beach with tiny Amy, who toddled around with a pail and a spoon. Amy's hair had been long and silky, and white-blond, as Emmett's must have been as a child. Amy wearing a lemon yellow sundress I'd made her—so good with her sunshine complexion, so different from my own dark brunette. Emmett had been captivated, the proud indulgent father to the charming little daughter. Too bad that bond, that connection, hadn't held.

Most of all, meeting Emmett for the first time in that junior college cafeteria. Remembering it as if it were the opening shot of color in a black-and-white life. Wandering around and around, with that overloaded tray, the huge room echoing with high-strung jovial spirits, the edgy kind I feared could erupt in barbarism. It was early in the term; in-groups and cliques with exclusionary powers hadn't coalesced. Everyone was there, the smokers, the burn-outs who'd be gone by Veteran's Day, the cheerleaders, the Asians and the Mexicans and the Blacks, the grim and serious math and science people.

My tray balanced precariously, my mother's injunction to "eat a good lunch" in my ears; shy, awkward, embarrassed, I threaded my way through the mob, not knowing a soul. Emmett, lounging out his legs, so sexy—he'd always been the sexiest lounger—almost tripping me. He scrambled to his feet, he jostled close to me. Close enough for me to smell his scent, his Wildroot Cream Oil, his...something I couldn't place that seemed the essence of maleness. Gun oil, he told me later, it was gun oil. He'd just come from a meeting of the Rifle Club.

Emmett, shambling, shuffling—Emmett off-balance! Then offering me his chair. Such consideration and courtesy and manners...such superficiality! Nevertheless, my first impression had been of sensitivity and strength, not exactly a lie, but now that I think about it, not worth its weight in gold, either.

I had loved Emmett. But I wonder now if the reality of love has somehow not been satisfactory, not what it's cracked up to be. If love leaves you unprepared and vulnerable, if love does not contribute to feelings of self-worth, security, achievement, if love does not add to your happiness in any trustworthy way, what good is it?

Amy is now leaning on her elbows, on the dining room side of the counter. "Mom, what about that apple? Aren't you going to peel it, too?"

"I'm saving that one. Going to grate it into my pancakes tomorrow morning. Remember how your dad loved apple pancakes with ginger, and sour cream and honey? That was back when he could eat—"

And I'm weeping into the sink. The water in my head will drown me, it will dissolve my bones…it's too much. I am tired, stone tired. Amy comes around the counter, puts her strong lemon-scented arms around me. "There, there, I'm sorry. It's my fault, I'm bringing you down. Let's get out of here, I know where to go There's this neat town north of the Bay Area, in the redwoods. There's an Italian restaurant, and little cabins in the woods. I'll make a reservation. Come on, Mom, we used to be friends. We can be friends again."

"I didn't know we'd quit," I blubber.

"We didn't quit. It was just hard, around Dad."

"How did Dad stop us from being friends?" I wipe at my face, wait to hear her answer.

Amy bites her lip. "I don't know…I didn't mean that the way it sounded. Listen, let's just get away from here, take a couple of days off, okay? I'll treat you."

"I can't let you spend all your hard-earned money." But then I wonder how much *I* have to spend.

"So, let's split it, you pay for room, I pay for food. We can work out something." Amy digs in the mini-pack she carries instead of a purse, comes up with Kleenex, passes me one, too, and we both honk into them. "Oh, by the way, I almost forgot I picked this up for you, hope you don't mind. Just an idea."

It's a shampoo-in Lady Clairol application, a color called Burnt Almond. I frown, then mumble, "I dunno…you think my hair looks that bad?"

"Fer cryin' out loud! Not *bad*, you just need…oh, here,

gimme that back—"

"Not yet. Let me think about it." I'm reading the directions when Amy leaves, thinking it might be just the thing. After all, Emmett used something on his hair; why shouldn't I? In some perverse manner, this is another way to get back at him.

Cabinets of plywood showing raw wood here and there under a coat of general grime. Countertops of Formica scrubbed through the design, edged with aluminum stripping. Green and brown indoor-outdoor carpet, wrinkled, worn and dirty with deep traffic patterns. In the air a subtle odor of neglect and abuse: the odor of an old man living alone. Mr. Purdy's dark kitchen reminds me of my own before Emmett remodeled and took out a wall into the dining room. My solid oak cupboards, a couple of years old now, had cost an arm and a leg…that's what Emmett said. An arm and a leg. Which draws me up short. Had he borrowed against the stock to finish the kitchen project?And that trip to Baja, how much had it cost? We stayed at an El Presidente, a luxurious setting of splashing fountains, bougainvillea hedges, sunburst mosaics. True, it had been off-season, last September, but the expense must have been great.

All this runs through my mind while I watch Mr. Purdy carve the apple pie. "My Millie," he says getting down two Melmac plates, "she wasn't much of a cook, tell the truth. But I do admire a pie, yessir, or ma'am I should say. You whip this up yourself?"

"Well, sure, easy as pie, as they say. I used to bake for Emmett, before he, well, before—"

To my surprise, he reaches over and gives my shoulder a gentle touch. "You and me, we know what it's like getting left, having the one go on ahead of you. It's not easy. You want ice cream? Maybe I got some vanilla." He gets up to peer into a freezer compartment thick with frost. "Nope, just pistachio nut and peppermint."

"This is fine. I meant for you to have the pie, not me."

He's wearing a plaid shirt and khaki pants, and for the first time I notice how skinny and bent are his legs. Wishbone legs. (Later he tells me that he'd had rickets as a child.) "Good pie doesn't need any ice cream," he says. "It's better yet when there's someone to eat it with. Say, this's got real apples in it. Flaky crust, too. Nice of you, to do this."

"Well, I wanted to thank you for helping me corral the trash. And to ask a favor."

"Sure. What can I do?"

"Feed the cat for a couple of days while I'm gone. Going to take a break, go away for a change of scene. We used to have Amy come in and see to PawPaw, but she's going with me."

"No problem. Be glad to. Millie used to keep cats. Sorta miss 'em, but I can't get a cat, at my age. It'd outlive me."

"How long since your Millie, well, how long have you been alone?"

"Let's see, it's going on twenty-five years. Once thought I'd get hitched again, but that wouldn't a worked out." He fixes me with a look, holds his fork aloft. "When you had the best, you can't replace it. Better to be by yourself. 'Course for a woman...maybe it's different, maybe a woman's got to reconnect. For various reasons. Not you, on account of you had Emmett lookin' out for you, but some women—"

"Yes, some women," I echo vaguely. But I'm not thinking of Emmett savaging our stock plan. Instead, it's my lovely dream of getting the perfect job. I was hired by the dime store to sit in the window and create animals out of balloons. I inflated them with a canister of helium, then twisted, tied, and tweaked them into whimsical shapes. The audience on the sidewalk outside laughed and clapped, celebrating my creations that were rapidly filling up the display area. Their particular favorite was a hot pink poodle, complete with beribboned ears. It bumped along the ceiling of my cell-like work area, generating huge approval from the crowd. This was happening not in the new variety store in the mall, but in the old dime store downtown. The entrance was a bay-like space between angled sheets of glass, and the floor was paved with tiny hexagonal tiles. For some reason, these details had been important in my dream; and the whole of it so real I awoke with a sentence on my lips, about to say something important, illuminating, *cheerful*. I also awoke feeling rested, as if I'd escaped to a lovely place for a vacation, for a good long time.

Mr. Purdy smiles. "You're doing fine, look younger every day," he says, paying tribute to Miss Clairol. "You just hang in there. You want me to look at that weed eater? It don't seem to want to run right."

My first impulse is to deny the problem, reassure him that everything's fine, but instead, I say, "Would you, please? And I wanted to ask you about changing the filter in the furnace. Do you know someone I can call to check out the air-conditioning? I hate to spend the money, but it's going to start getting hot."

As ill luck would have it, Amy pulls in to pick me up just as Mr. Purdy is crossing the side yard from my house to his. She's early for our outing. *Outing.* I've begun to think of the trip as an *airing.* As you take out an old mattress or rug, give it some air. I need an airing, a dusting, something to shake out the cobwebs.

Amy flounces in and says, "What's *he* doing over here? That old guy, look at his posture, why doesn't he stand up straight!"

"Amy, he's seventy-eight years old! Mr. Purdy's going to feed the cat while we're gone. I was showing him the routine, giving him a key. While he was here, he shot some graphite into this mechanism on the door—remember how it stuck? See how easy it opens now? He's been a help to me, Amy." I hate the high wheedling tone in my voice, as if I have to get Amy's approval before establishing friends of my own. As if I need a replacement for the role of censurer. "Here, take this out for me," I say, changing the subject, handing over a suitcase, but Amy is staring.

"Mo..om!" Two syllables. "Look at you!" She laughs, rudely, I think. "Your hair!"

"So?"

More laughing. "I can't believe you did it!" Now a note of disapproval.

"You bought the stuff, it was your idea to color it." By now Amy and I are hooking up seatbelts.

"I know, I encouraged you. I just didn't... I thought…it looks good, really. Not quite right, not quite your real color, but never mind. Nobody else would know. I'll get used to it. Okay, there's the map, see where we're going? Out to 101, then north to this cut-off, then west. Not far." She adds bitterly, "Not far enough!" and hits the steering wheel with her fist. But I notice a good sign: her nails are painted a fiery red.

"Oh, honey, it's Larry, isn't it."

"I don't want to talk about it," she snaps, but then does. She describes how Larry came in smirking just as she was leaving, reeking of the other woman's perfume, a jasmine scent. He was wearing a shirt Amy'd given him, flaunting their former relationship (Amy thinks), taunting her. They'd immediately begun sparring over a division of the electronics they'd bought together, mainly a large screen TV and an "entertainment center" crammed with equipment, including CD and video collections. He wanted to trade the equipment for the collections, but Amy said what good would that be, having all those CDs and videos and no way to play them. They were at an impasse.

(An impasse solved by me giving Amy replacements for her relinquished TV—my little set from the bedroom—and my second-line VCR and a CD player. I tell myself I don't mind, I don't need two of those things. After all, now there's just me.)

Larry also wanted to trade a computer that neither of them knew how to run, that they were still making payments on, for the vacuum cleaner. His new girlfriend didn't have a vacuum, and her place was a sty. That was Larry's term, a sty.

"No argument over...over the rest of the stuff?" I'm at a loss. What else did they have? Their furniture was second-hand, shabby—a dirty orange velveteen sofa and two chairs, battered tables, a mattress on the floor. They kept their clothes, which are mostly the kind that you don't hang up—except Larry's bartending outfits—in cardboard storage boxes.

"Yeah, sure, I get the junk," Amy mutters.

I'm on the verge of saying something stupid about Amy going back to school to get a real job, one that pays well, but I stop in time. That won't go down well with her. I admit that I view her career at the Fitness Center as temporary, something she'll outgrow, as you outgrow Santa Claus, lollipops, Saturday matinees. In the beginning, Amy said it was a "fun job"; she could help her fatties lose weight, and keep herself in shape at the same time. Amy dismissed Emmett's outright criticism, his negative opinion that she'd get bored, fed up with the gymnasium atmosphere, reeking of hot foam rubber, sweat, and deodorant.

However, Emmett had to give Amy her due. She'd always been independent, emotionally secure, self-reliant. She could probably support herself, Emmett admitted, although he'd been forced to pay off her new car when she floundered in debt. Well, he'd told her not to buy a new car and dump the old VW we'd given her—he was quick to condemn the new car. He also told her to stay away from the Mustang—although he was a Ford man and disliked it less than her first choice of a Toyota Celica. "That piece of shit can't get out of its own way," he said. "It just looks sporty, but it's got no power package, it's all show and no go."

He told her not to buy on credit, to avoid payment situations, to keep the VW. So what, he said, if it didn't always run right, didn't have much "soul"—at least it was paid for. Emmett felt that if he were involved financially, he had the right to give advice. For her part, Amy felt that she had not only the right, she had the *duty* to turn a deaf ear. I watched the two of them, I tried to stay out of it. I'd never presumed so far as to give either of them any suggestions.

Emmett also paid Amy's and Larry's rent when Larry's hours were cut. Larry works days part-time as assistant manager at Circuit City, where he gets electronic stuff on employees' discount, and nights in a trendy pub downtown. The kind of place done in brass and brick décor, trailing plants, menus of beers on chalkboards, as if they're dinner entrees. Emmett had snorted at the prices, but he'd never been a beer drinker, said it was a waste of money.

I begin to wonder how much Emmett spent subsidizing Amy, then I suffer an unpleasant thought: without Larry, Amy might have to move back home again. It took both of them to pay the rent. Well, everyone's kids suffer fits and starts, advances and retreats. Still, the prospect alarms me. Those hot rollers in the bathroom, the smell of nail polish, dripping lingerie in the shower. I almost wish that Emmett were here now, because he'd take care of this for me; he'd tell her no way, Jose.

To cover my self-inflicted panic, I babble about trees again. "Look, eucalyptus, I know what those are. You can smell them, sort of like camphor. I read somewhere that Jack London—he lived in the area—Jack London imported fifty or sixty thousand eucalyptus, timber for railroad ties. Only it didn't work. The wood split too easily, or maybe not easily enough—I forget. He got them from Australia. Remember you dad's joke about pandas, they come from Australia, don't they?"

"China," says Amy.

"Anyway, this panda walks into a café, orders lunch, then pulls out a gun and shoots the waiter. One bystander says to another, 'Why'd he do that?' The other one says, 'I don't know. Let's look up *panda* in the dictionary, see what it tells us.' So they do, and they find the answer."

"I remember this one. *Panda: eats shoots and leaves.* Dad was so corny." Amy is impatient, exasperated, but she smiles.

We turn off 101 onto a series of progressively smaller roads, drive past a tiny settlement consisting of a derelict gas station, a deli-grocery and a bakery around which stand ranks of gleaming bicycles. Then pastures populated with sleek horses, cattle, llamas, even emus. Here and there a few redwoods, I think they're redwoods—needle-bearing trees that disappear into the sky above Amy's Mustang. Curves in the road become sharper, the sections in full sun are awash with lazy dust motes, and an earthy aroma. A warm soil and sawdust aroma, and I sigh with pleasure.

We arrive at the town. On our right an old-fashioned inn, such as you might find in a foreign country, Spain or Italy, commands a greensward. It's made of stone, with a deep porch behind rock pillars. Across the front stretches a brick walkway punctuated with redwood benches. On them sit a few people eating ice cream, reading the paper. On a grassy verge, couples walk hand-in-hand, kids play. A woman with long straight gray hair parted down the middle, wearing a patchwork vest and leather sandals, reads a paperback. A man hooked up to a headset keeps time to his private music. Helmeted bicyclists, in bright Spandex, weave through what little traffic there is, and bicycles, the kind that cost as much as Amy's car, are racked in front of an espresso stand. In the Inn's parking lot are Jaguars, Saabs, Mercedes, and a Lexus that gleams like pewter. "Amy," I breathe, alarmed. "This is too expensive!"

This damned new awareness of money! Of adding and subtracting prices in my head! Emmett always dealt with the finances. When he was alive I assumed that bills were paid, tips figured, credit cards dealt with. If he were alive, I wouldn't have to worry. On the other hand, if he were alive, I wouldn't be here. Because toward the end, he hadn't wanted to go anywhere.

If that were true, why had we gone to Mexico? It hadn't been my idea; it'd been his. Then in Cabo San Lucas, Emmett hadn't perked up from his funk. He hadn't enjoyed himself. He'd been bored, and out of sorts. Then why—

Why! Why! I'm sick of it. The bottom line is that I am here, and Emmett is not. I feel a wave of peace, of happiness, a weight lifting. Something that was there before is not there now, an ache, a longing, a sadness. For now, that's enough.

Amy turns left, away from the Inn. "No, we're not staying there. Our reservation's this way."

We drive a hundred yards or so on a gravel road that winds across an area of clipped grass—the whole place has the careful atmosphere of a park. She pulls up to a rustic cabin, one of a set. "This's where we're staying, see? Close to the restaurant over there in the Inn, so we can park and walk. No driving for a couple of days, unless we want to go to the coast, look at the ocean. Or there are trails everywhere. Or we can do nothing. Is this okay?"

I feel almost dizzy. Everything seems clear, easy, my life is as plain as a palm print. I can see from this new perspective, from this distance away from home, that I've been absorbed with putting one foot in front of the other, of getting from one room, one meal, one chore to another, to another, to another. And I've been calling it a day, a week, a life. But here, under these trees, in this light and air, I'll rediscover my purpose—if there is one. Surely there must be one.

“Is this okay!” I exclaim. “Is it okay! Do you suppose I could get work here? I know real estate’s been bought up by Bay Area folks. But I could rent, I could live on minimum wage. I could cook, clean—”

Amy gives a sardonic laugh. “Yeah, sure, you’d like that, all right.”

She opens the cabin door—it has been left unlocked against our arrival, the key inside on the table. The interior: just what I’d hoped for. Knotty pine, a low ceiling, a rock fireplace, braided rugs on wide board floors. One big room, with alcoves for kitchen and bath. A pair of double beds stretches out peacefully under quilted spreads. Small paned windows curtained with home-sewn red plaid material. A nest, a lair, a safe harbor. Yes, this will do, this is perfect. I inhale the room’s atmosphere, I breathe in a history of wood fires, coffee, damp wool; and something earthy, perhaps mildew, something that ought not to be good, but is. A musty smell, a good smell, as if from an older time when life was simple.

While Amy inspects the bathroom—she’s delighted that the toilet tank is overhead, operated by a pull chain—I wander around the main room, bewitched. My low-grade panic is at bay; the quiet in the room seems to hum, as if a cat purrs nearby. The real sounds are distant laughter, crunch of tires on gravel, creak of the old wood floor under my tread. And my stomach growling. I am hungry. How long since I’ve really looked forward to food?

To feel hunger, to feel anything—what a gift I’ve been given, and how I’ve wasted it.

CHAPTER 6

"Six dollars for a bowl of soup!" Amy and I are in the lobby of the Inn, reading a chalkboard of lunch specials.

"Shh, not so loud. But it's great soup, and comes with this cunning little loaf of bread, and herbed butter."

It's Amy's kind of menu, mostly vegetarian, except for a couple of hamburger items, a BLT—and a veal dish; I wince inwardly.

I stride into the dining room behind her, relishing but also disapproving of the stares she elicits from men diners. Amy does look spectacular in a tartish sort of way. She wears a tight yellow tee shirt, cropped so short it reveals a sliver of her toned belly, and black stretch pants that fit her like a second skin. Her long hair is in fetching disarray, piled up in a knot secured by a gadget like a bear trap. Wispy little tendrils frame her face and neck. It's a look carefully designed to convey a message—I'd watched her engineer it, tweaking at it—and that message is something about a roll in the hay. As if she'd just enjoyed one, and is willing to go for another.

She's wearing her silver feather earrings, like Maggie Quinn's at the funeral supper. But since then, I've noticed the feather design is common, and popular—every store sells, every woman wears, silver feather earrings.

Every woman, that is, but me. I've never had my ears pierced, obeying my mother's rule that one does not put holes in, or designs on, one's body. However, I've begun to consider pierced ears. I found, in a secondhand store where I was looking for chairs to match my table, a pair of earrings I want. They're also silver dangles, but pinecones, not feathers. Bits of glitter, like diamond chips, are tucked in the folds of the cones, so they're a tad on the flashy side, but I want them anyway (or maybe I want them *because* they're flashy). Would Emmett have approved of them? I don't know. Can no longer attest to his taste, what sort of style he'd favored. One thing for sure, though: he would have known what kind of tree the cones are from.

Amy heads toward a small table in the back, out in the open, not next to the wall. A good vantage point, she says, to "scope out the room." She flounces down, rattles her bracelets on the arms of an oak captain's chair. The room is rustic, suggests a hunting lodge. It's dominated by a huge stone fireplace, now full of what look like tumbleweeds; and a chandelier made of animal horns, with real candles, now unlit. I frown up at it, and Amy says flatly, "Elk lose their racks in autumn, Mother, they fall off. Don't worry about it." Then she adds, "At least there are no heads," and laughs in an edgy way I don't like. She's making fun of me, but she wouldn't like it either, if there were heads.

I pull my eyes away, then say, "A real tablecloth, Amy, that means we have to leave a twenty percent tip."

"Not if it's got a piece of glass over it. Dad told me that once."

Yeah, Emmett would have known a thing like that. The waiter arrives to take our order, and he stares at Amy. I clear my throat, then order quiche. Amy is having fish. She tries to be a vegetarian. Her rationale for eating fish: "At least they had a chance to be free, weren't raised in a crate, their feet never touching the ground." At this point, Emmett, ignoring logic, reason, the parameters of the argument, would have retorted, "Fish don't have feet." Amy would have replied, "No, and they don't need bicycles, either," and they'd be off, at each other, the dinner table not quite World War II, but not détente, either.

Amy whispers, "Mom, don't look now, but that guy over there, the one with the silver buzz cut, he's checking you out."

"Not me, Amy. You."

"No, Mom, definitely it's you. When you get a chance, glance that way…I'll signal you…okay, now, real casual like, he's looking down, take a peek."

"It's you he's looking at, Amy. If he's looking at all."

"You should get up and go to the restroom, walk by his table and make eye contact. Smile a little."

"I'll do no such thing. See, here comes his wife." We watch a woman shaped like a cello march toward the lone man. However, she passes him by, heads to the restroom. "Well, so that's not his wife. You can bet he's got one somewhere who wouldn't appreciate strange women ogling him."

"No, he looks single to me. He's on the prowl. He's done to the nines, the Silver Fox, very spiffy. Nice red shirt, I love that cranberry shade. It's his color, perfect on him. Now, that guy over there, he's married."

"How can you tell?"

"He's preoccupied, spaced out, almost harried. He's letting himself go, he's getting a potbelly. His shirt is rumpled, and it looks hard-finished, rayon or acrylic. His pants are too short. Sitting down, he shows too much bare leg, and trousers shouldn't be that green color, ever. His shoes are weird, off a bargain rack at Kmart or something. If he were single, he'd be more careful of details." Amy gestures at another man. "Now, he's a good bet. He's loose."

"Oh, come on. How can you tell that?"

"He's on the make, trust me."

The fellow she indicates is about thirty-five, thin and fit, nicely tanned. He wears a pale blue long-sleeved shirt with the cuffs turned back to show well-shaped forearms. His jeans are tailored, dressy. He wears boots, not flashy and new like a dude's, but well polished, expensive-looking. Draped on the back of his chair is a blue-gray tweed jacket. Jeans and tweed: my heart turns over—Emmett had worn such a combination, sexy, rakish.

"On second thought," says Amy, "he might be gay. Gay guys are the best dressers. If his jacket were leather, I'd know for sure."

"Amy, that's stereotyping. Besides, it's too hot for leather."

"Not if you're gay. Those guys love leather. Stereotyping, yes. So what's stereotyping? Just stating proven generalities in specific terms."

"I don't agree. Stereotypes are generalities we *want* to be true because we're lazy thinkers and can't be bothered with the facts. But to say that guys who wear leather—"

"Shh, Mom...here's our lunch."

The waiter arrives balancing a tray with one hand, wielding

a pepper mill two feet tall in the other. "Care for a grind?" He ogles the front of Amy's shirt.

We wave him off and begin to eat. I wonder if Amy and I had been on the verge of a quarrel, and would that have been good or bad? I think about Amy's analysis of the diners, how she'd focused on the men, whereas I'd seen only the couples. To me, on first glance, the room is populated with contented pairs, men and women, mates, so happy being partnered, eating together—which seems almost an act of sexual congress after almost three solid months of eating and sleeping alone. Men and women holding hands, laughing, talking, absorbed in and with each other. Me, I'm the odd one, the sole single woman, this eccentric who will never again be paired up. But Amy is here, I have Amy with me, and Amy is single, too. However, for Amy to be single is acceptable, even preferable. The single state fits her well; it fits me poorly.

I know I'm exaggerating, I am out of focus, out of whack, out of kilter; I am paranoid. But throughout lunch, the feeling persists: I am the only singleton on the face of the planet. The abyss yawns, it deepens; I am perilously close to toppling over when after lunch Amy murmurs, "Mom, I haven't slept for a week," and stumbles back to the cabin for a nap. So she leaves, and I find myself alone sitting outside on a bench in the sun, staring hungrily at happy couples, family groups.

Just as Amy predicted, the rumpled man from the dining room is married, because his wife, hauling along a bratty kid, had joined him halfway though the meal. The family has now finished its lunch, is sitting on a nearby bench. The child, a girl about four, whines for ice cream, which the father forbids because she hadn't eaten her food. But the permissive mother is ready to allow it. Just like we were, I think. I let Amy have her way, forcing Emmett to say no, no, no. Too many no's on his part; too many yes's on mine. How easy it is to see mistakes in the past, ten, twenty years beyond rectifying.

The pit yawns deeper, nearer. I get up and head toward a trail into the woods. As I walk, I resolve, again, not to stagger through the rest of my life having every single thing remind me of

Emmett, and what I now consider were my shortcomings as a wife. I take deep breaths, consciously pulling in pine-scented air, resolving not to think of complicated possibilities, dwindling prospects, my own tendency to fall off into down-heartedness. I take long strides, enjoying—in spite of myself—the soft duff of the trail under my feet, the border of ferns, the tall trees pressing in on either side of me. No, on a day like this, in a place like this, I'll not fall into the abyss.

Bridge Loop Trail is clearly marked, and promises to lead me to an overlook above the river in one point five miles. As if landscaped, the path is edged with trilliums, vines, ferns, nurse logs sprouting the next generation of forest. Beyond this richly textured undulating carpet is a hedge of shrubbery growing a crop of small purple berries. Then beyond that, dominating the forest, are the giants, the redwoods and other needle-bearers whose tops I cannot even see, their enormous trunks as big around as a telephone booth, as big around as Amy's car, as our cabin. Muscular trunks of shredded bark on these monsters, hairy, as if made of animal hide.

The green world breathes peace, a world of dappled sun; the warm and earthy smell of sawdust pulls me forward, farther into the woods. Such a palette of greens—pale yellowish green, emerald, aqua, green so deep it shades into purple. Here and there flowering shrubs with blooms like trumpets, like umbrellas, like stars, lilies. Most blossoms are miniatures, inconspicuous, giving way to leaves. Leaves as small as pennies, as big as plates. Leaves like feathers, hearts, swords, ruffled doilies, spread palms. And needles, some grouped into downward hanging bouquets, some arrowing into the sky; all sizes of needles. Enough needles to carpet this green world.

The trail circles by a meadow that tilts down into a bog. Patches of growth here resemble vegetables—artichokes, cabbage, asparagus, ribs of celery, some as delicate as chives thrusting from the soil. The trail now squishes under my shoes. Then it turns upward, and the earth becomes firm and allows the trees to regain their footing.

Other people are on the path. In some parts of the forest,

sounds carry as clearly as in an amphitheater, so clearly, I hear every word of conversations around me, every comment, sally, joke, laugh. I overtake and pass several groups who've stopped to admire scenery, take pictures. A breeze soughs in the trees; invisible birds caw, whistle, sing. I catch a flash of blue, and from somewhere overhead a jay scolds. In other places, the silence is palpable.

At last the promised bridge, a rustic structure designed to blend in with the environment. It stretches over a slow gurgle of river, now summer-drained to a mere creek that tumbles between rounded rocks. I lean on the railing, stare into transparent pools below, hoping to catch sight of...anything, really. What I see, instead, out of the corner of my eye, is a cranberry red shirt. The Silver Fox from lunch approaches on the trail, and will, in a moment, join me on the bridge.

Flustered, I try to concentrate on the pools below. I am embarrassed, and chide myself for this uncalled-for response. After all, this man, Amy's Silver Fox, has no way to know we'd discussed him. How absurd, how egotistical to think he'd even noticed me, *me,* in the dining room, how paranoid. He will walk across the bridge, he will pass me by and disappear into the forest. The path does continue into the woods beyond, although it's called Bridge Loop Trail, and here I am, on the bridge.

But he does not pass and disappear; he stops and leans on the railing next to me, and stares into the water below. "How was your lunch?" he says. "I saw you in the dining room with your friend."

I say quickly, "My daughter. She's my daughter."

He looks at me, honestly (honestly?) surprised. "Daughter? By Jove!"

"My lunch," I say quickly, "well, over-priced. Quiche, I always forget there're all those eggs, and three kinds of cheese. I ordered it out of curiosity, because my husband, he died two months ago, well, almost three months now, my husband had to watch his diet, he couldn't eat such stuff. Cholesterol, you know." I kick myself for babbling. Why am I telling him these things? I should have said, "Lunch was great." Period.

"Oh, heart attack. Sorry. The old ticker, it's modern life, the stress level, the frantic pace of how we live. We don't stop to smell the roses, spend enough time in places like this. You staying at the Inn?" He bestows on me the full effect of his eyes, which are a pretty blue. Nice with his sleek silver hair. He reminds me of some actor, James Brolin, yes, up close he's movie star handsome. His brows and lashes are black, startling with his hair and eyes. I see dark hairs on his arms, fine dark down on the backs of his hands. Not at all like Emmett's golden fuzz. I move away from him.

"No, not at the Inn. We've got one of the cabins across the way." I begin moving off.

"There's a nice little waterfall a little farther on—"

"No, no, my daughter's expecting me back." I rush off precipitously, as if being pursued, although he does not follow me, and I am soon alone on the path.

He must think I'm crazy, I scold myself. My cheeks burn with a sense of vulnerability, of ineptitude. To bring up Emmett's death! To wrap myself in it, my bulletproof cloak! To say I was curious about quiche…would he think I'm curious about other things I've been doing without? Men do hear those things, they think along those lines. Yeah, he'd hear that as an invitation, a come-on. Had it been an invitation? No, I don't think so. Besides, sex has nothing to do with me. Sex and Knott's Berry Farm: all false fronts and slick advertising. Another Mexico.

Then I'd compounded my miserable performance by running off as if he were Jack the Ripper, Freddy, and Jason all rolled into one, and this is a mews in London on Friday the 13th, in low swirling fog. Then I think, Do I care about any of this? I'll never see him again…and I'm surprised at the pain this gives me.

However, back at the Inn's sunny portico, I become diffused with a sense of victory. After all, I made myself walk the trail, I spoke to an attractive man, I offered to take a group photo for a bunch of people on the path, an offer they accepted. I joked with them about a "Kodak moment," one of Amy's lines. I'm functioning.

Then too, I have to allow for it being late afternoon, a time of falling off, when the light goes. A time when I still find myself waiting for Emmett to come home and share his day, his spirit, his mere presence. If I were at home now, I'd fix tea to go with the news, providing the news isn't too grim. If it's all destruction of the environment, wars breaking out, overpopulation, and grinding poverty, I'd switch over to AMC and watch Doris Day protect her virtue from Rock Hudson; or David Niven and Deborah Kerr circle each other in their sexless English way; or sleepy-eyed Robert Mitchum seduce Jane Greer in a wild caper across Mexico. I'll watch any movie from back when life, and the movie, was guaranteed to turn out okay. But here I am in this strange place, marooned without my safety net, a nice place, true...well, a very nice place. I square my shoulders, raise my eyes from the path, and tell myself I'm going to be fine. Just hunky-dory fine.

In a spirit of celebration, and in defiance, I march into the Inn's gift shop and buy a small tree-finder book. Then, remembering the whiny kid who'd bugged her folks for ice cream, I saunter up to the ice cream counter and order a double scoop, pistachio nut and peppermint, the two flavors in Mr. Purdy's freezer. Nice Mr. Purdy, a good neighbor. And Frieda, too, who'd asked me to Bingo Night at her BPW meeting—although I didn't go, hadn't wanted to go, would rather go in for a root canal or an IRS audit than attend such an event. Still, it's nice that she asked.

Outside on the porch, I sit in what's left of the sun and eat my ice cream. I think about Amy, my daughter, whom I love dearly. Poor dear Amy who is suffering in spite of her élan, her brave front—if that's what it is. I no longer know. I *do* know that if there's rejection, if anyone leaves, Amy prefers to do the rejecting, the leaving; she wants to deal out the punishment, and not suffer it—like all of us, I guess. Amy needs me right now, and I will do my best for her. I rotate my ice cream, licking drips from the sides of my waffle cone, and I realize that I am happy tonguing my pistachio nut into the peppermint. I am happy, right here, right now.

Just then, Amy appears. She looks cross and sleepy. "Mom! You're eating ice cream? You'll ruin your dinner!"

"No, it's okay. Good ice cream, Amy. You want one?" When

Amy shakes her head, I bite into the waffle cone, my favorite kind—the real reason I'd dropped a five-dollar bill on ice cream. The smell of baking waffles permeates the whole area, impossible to resist. "Even if I do ruin my dinner, it's worth it." But my defiant voice reminds of that bratty kid pleading for ice cream, and the parents who'd said no. Have Amy and I changed places? Have I become the spoilt child to Amy's responsible adult? My mood collapses. Now feeling nettled, I say, "Don't worry 'bout it, okay? I can eat what I want. And when."

"I know, Mom, I'm sorry. It's just that the food's great here. Family style. The antipasto—artichoke hearts, mushrooms, melon slices, pickled peppers, this yummy eggplant thing. I know you're not crazy about eggplant—"

"I like eggplant. It was your dad who didn't like it."

"Whatever. You're going to love the way they do it here. Then spaghetti, salad, garlic bread you can't believe. I'm looking forward to it. I wanted you to, too."

"I am, I am. I'll be ready."

But I'm not. There's a stomach-churning amount of food offered. The small tables from lunch are pushed together into seating for eight, and each table groans with heaping platters of chicken, and spaghetti, and a tomato something or other under a coating of melted cheese, and wooden bowls of mixed salad, and baskets of bread. The very air, lit now by the candles in the horn chandeliers, is caloric, freighted with tomato, garlic, and onion. And with the scent that the woman next to me wears, a sweet and heavy scent, like Cody's Emeraude.

Amy and I share our table with this heavily perfumed dowager (that's the only word for her), and her husband; and a husband and wife with their two teenage children. The eight of us work our way through the meal while playing a game assigned and explained by the dinner organizer. We are to tell four things about ourselves, only one of which is true. Table-mates are to guess the true from the false. Amy's "true" item: she'd once been a model, which makes my mouth drop open while she kicks me under the table. But what difference does it make? If a lie helps her enjoy herself, let her tell it. After my own embarrassing turn in the spotlight is over—they guessed quickly that I work as a temp—I find the game benign enough, even enjoyable. The older man is a retired minister; his wife, the one with the perfume, does needlepoint. The youngish couple had worked at home with their computers, a dot.com enterprise that they've converted to a lawn-mowing business. Their son is a skateboard enthusiast; their daughter collects Barbie dolls.

Seated at another table is the Silver Fox. His back is turned, but we see him talking with his companions. At yet another table is the good-looking guy who'd worn tweed with jeans at lunch. He's talking to a pretty girl with dark hair.

After the overload of food, the wine's glow wears off, the meal flattens, then becomes interminable. The congenial hubbub of small talk, plink of silver, clatter of dishes seem to falter, then die, as if the air is being sucked out of the room. Finally, small silver dishes of a yellowish ice cream appear, with almond-flavored cookies.

Sated, stuffed, struck dumb with food and drink, people begin yawning, gathering up possessions, leaving for their rooms. Amy becomes testy, just this side of rude. She rises, brushes crumbs from the red dress she changed into for dinner, and announces she needs a crème de menthe in the bar. At first I demur, but then I realize that Amy feels cheated, restless, annoyed at having wasted her presence, and her best outfit, on the likes of our table-mates—Amy is afraid of nothing happening.

I follow her into the bar, a paneled den-like room with a fireplace. We pick out a pair of barstools, and order drinks. Amy studies her red-painted nails for a second, then murmurs that she has to go to the john. When our drinks arrive, it's me who digs for the money, puts a couple of bills on the bar.

"I see you don't usually pay a bar tab," says a voice at my shoulder.

"What?" In spite of myself, I hope it's the Silver Fox. But no, it's just an ordinary guy, an anonymous fellow of an indeterminate age. He has a long thin face, red-veined nose, pale blue bloodshot eyes. He squints in such a way that I suspect he usually wears glasses. I imagine them on him, horn-rims, with clip-on shades, that flip up or down like sun visors. When he lowers his head, I see a bald spot as big as a saucer. What hair he does have is sparse and gray.

"Anyone who'd order two crème de menthes and put out two one dollar bills doesn't usually pay the bar bill."

"How much do these things cost?"

"Let me buy your drink."

"No, really...how much are these things?" I look around for a price list. After all, the ice cream shop had one.

"They don't post prices," he says.

"So how are you supposed to know...you could wander in here and not have enough money to pay your bill."

He laughs, showing white even teeth but too much of his gums. "An upscale place like this, price is not supposed to be a factor."

"How cozy. I'll remember that, for next time. You must think I'm out of it, don't you."

"Well, yeah. It's appealing, really."

"*This upscale place,*" I italicized the words, "you come here often?"

He laughs again. "Hey, I'm supposed to say that. Matter of fact, I do."

"My daughter—"

"If that's her, she may not be back for awhile." I glance in the direction he indicates, see Amy sitting in a booth with the tweed-and-jeans guy from lunch, the one who'd talked to the pretty dark-haired girl. "That's the way they are, these kids. They leave you. Is this a family affair? Your old man here with you?"

"No, I'm alone. Well, with my daughter. But I guess I'm...alone."

"Like I said, these kids leave you. Mind if I sit down?"

"Oh, why not. You have children?"

"Sure do. They're grown and gone, like yours over there." At that instant we hear Amy's theatrical laugh, a cascading tinkle of appreciation, of gratitude, and I know this fellow has it right: Amy's gone, at least for the evening. He holds out his hand. "Stan Ewing here."

I shake his hand, which seemed dry and rough, perhaps callused. I give my name and add, "Where's your wife?"

"Same as your husband—somewhere else. I have no idea where she is. Been divorced for, let's see, going on seven years now. I'm on my own, ma'am. Like you." At this, I feel a pang. Seven years, a long time. How does he exist? But he looks fine. He wears a summer-weight seersucker suit with thin ivory and olive drab stripes. His shirt's the same olive drab shade, and his tie picks up the ivory tone. Clearly, he'd put time and effort into mixing and matching. Would Amy say that paying so much attention to details indicates that he's on the make? I am afraid that she would, and she'd probably be right. This sends an icy chill through me, because I'm not ready, can't cope.

I look down to see what I'm wearing, a thing I have to do often. My dinner outfit is a beige linen dress, badly wrinkled from its trip in my suitcase. I knew this outfit didn't travel. Why did I bring it? I vow to do better, to smarten up.

"I come here when I can," says Stan, and I have to think what he's talking about. "I design automatic garage door openers for a firm in San Jose, well, tell the truth, mostly I install them, so I need a break, something to get the blood flowing. You see, what I do is...dry, mechanical...well, *bloodless* is the word. My passion is Jack London's work. His whole life, really. He lived near here, just over the ridge to the east. He loved this country. He was a real man, with real blood in his work. I commune with his spirit, that's why I come here."

"Jack London...something about building a fire in Alaska—"

"The Yukon."

"What I remember is personal stuff, a chaotic lifestyle. Didn't he leave his family, his wife—didn't he have daughters? He left them to marry some wild woman he'd fallen for. Wasn't there a scandal?"

"I suppose you'd call it that. He met Charmian Kittridge, she captivated him. He built Wolf House for her right over there in Glen Ellen, but it burned down just before they moved into it."

"Too bad."

"It was a tragedy. I can't begin to describe what it did to him, it…destroyed his life. There was a suspicion of arson, because he'd just fired a worker who was the type to bear a grudge. It was a horrible inferno. The redwood beams, heart wood, he'd had them cut from two thousand year-old trees felled on his own property, they burned so hot, they glowed blue in the night. He never recovered from the sight of his house being destroyed."

"Some things you never get over."

"Uh-oh, I don't like the sound of that. I hope that doesn't mean…well, I hope I didn't…ah, step on toes, open up old wounds. Your old man take off or something like that?"

"Something like that. So Jack London didn't desert his wife? Is that what you're saying? He wasn't cruel?" Immediately I regret the accusatory edge to my voice, and I worry about how it's going to affect him. But why am I trying to please or placate this nondescript man? Always the man, make yourself pleasant for the man, the man. I add defiantly, "If you ask me, there was a streak of cruelty there."

"You misunderstand him. See, he'd come back from the Yukon confused, adrift, he needed an anchor, a woman to keep his house, type his manuscripts. He needed to be above distractions like family, so he could do what he had to do, which was write. He needed a woman who wouldn't expect too much of him, be too demanding."

"Stay in the dark so he could shine."

"Yes, genius is always so." He says that firmly; I am not to argue with it.

"Seems to me I've read that his wife, the first one, did that."

"True, but he needed a woman with some fire, passion. He was highly sexed, and his mate had to keep up with him, in that regard."

"Is that so?"

"Yes. A man like Jack London is not going to put up with the dull convention of staying with a wife he didn't love, that he'd outgrown. Besides, with her he'd had only daughters, and he thought Charmian could give him sons—"

I interrupt him. "Not all men have to prove themselves through sons. Do you have sons?"

"Sure do, and men need sons. Especially a real man like Jack London. Daughters are fine, somebody's gotta have them, for the sons to marry. But they're not like sons. Jack wanted his line to go on, with male heirs. He was illegitimate, you see, he never knew who his own father was and that haunted him. It was a sort of death, and he was afraid of death." He bends in closer, and I catch a whiff of garlic, tobacco, and something stale—his clothes, despite his overall neatness, need an airing. "Jack London was a man among men," Stan confides. "He ate raw meat, he preferred it. During duck season, he ate two raw canvas-backs a day. He experimented with hashish, he drank, he brawled."

I shrug. I'm still put off by the allusion to sex, and the daughter put-down. Had Emmett needed a different kind of sex? Or more sex? Well, don't all men think that? Had he needed a son? What the hell had he needed? Was it something I could have provided, and hadn't? What nerve men have! But then again, Emmett might have resented the kind of competition a son would have presented. He'd had enough trouble dealing with Amy.

I sigh, lean back. Then I notice him looking at my breasts, so I lean forward again. "Jack London sounds like an animal."

Stan recoils. "No, he was a red-blooded hero. He was the great American writer, not properly understood or appreciated by ordinary people." He adds, "You want another couple of drinks? You've finished both of them. Be careful. Crème de menthe bites back."

"Why not. Where is the dang barkeep?" I notice that the room is quieter, emptier. Most people have drifted out, and I think that if I had any sense, I'd go, too. But Amy and her friend are still in their booth, heads together, deep in intimate conversation.

"He spends half his time out back having a cigarette. You can't smoke in here anymore. A new law." Stan scowls. "I mean, it's a bar, fer chrissake! Jack London wouldn't have put up with this shit."

"Cigarette smoke bothers people. My husband had to quit—"

The barkeep appears again. Trailing an odor of tobacco smoke, he brings our new drinks. Now that I look for it, I see his cigarette smoldering in an ashtray just beyond the doorway.

We're silent over our new bright green drinks. Now I've done it, I think. I've turned him off, and how. To bring up Emmett again. To argue about Jack London. To contradict him about smoking, and he's probably a smoker, too. I'll never get anywhere this way. But where do I want to get? I don't even like this guy. Idolizing Jack London! However, perhaps I haven't given his great American author proper due. I'll have to get his work from the library and give it a try.

I say that to Stan, that I'll read some Jack London, my peace offering.

"Yeah, do that, but don't stay with the kid stuff, the dog stories, *White Fang* and *Call of the Wild.* Reach out for his other works. Try *Voyage of the Snark*, or his Australian stories. My wife and I, when we were together, we traced some of his travels. The South Seas, Canada, Mexico."

"Mexico—is that where you got your watchband?"

"Yeah, in Baja." He straightens the band on his thin freckled wrist, holds it out so I can admire it. "You usually see these watchbands with turquoise, but these are pieces of carnelian, and onyx. I bought it because it was unique."

"You went to Baja to buy a watchband, or to follow in Jack London's footsteps?"

"Well, neither one, exactly. Me and Beth, my wife, we knew we were on thin ice, so we made that one last stab at it. You know, the rerun of a honeymoon, to see if we could make it work."

"And did it?"

"Christ, no, it was pure torture. See, I'd outgrown her, she bored me. That happens. One of you moves on, and the other one doesn't. You can't go back, even if you want to. So you go out there on the vacation, on the second honeymoon, or the third, in the heat and the light and the sun, and you give it your best shot, then you face facts. Mainly that it's over. We came home and got a divorce."

"Really. That's the way it was, huh?"

"Well, wasn't it? You been there. What did you think?"

"Yeah, I suppose that's how it is." I'm having trouble keeping my various personae straight. I drain my new drink, lean on the bar, and pull on my earlobes. As soon as Amy and I get home—where is Amy? she's disappeared—as soon as we get home, I'm going to buy those pinecone earrings. And a new dress to go with them, something that won't wrinkle. "We went to Baja once," I say, "me and Emmett. Our last vacation together." I add mentally, And we went for the same reason you did, although I didn't know it at the time. A last stab to keep it going. Of course it hadn't worked. Emmett found me spiritless and disappointing. I'd bored him, and he hadn't known what to do about it.

"Really? You went to Baja?"

"Yeah, Emmett, my husband, wanted to fish. See, he'd read about the fishing in the Sea of Cortez, or seen it on TV or something, and he wanted to give it a try." Wasn't that the truth? Yes, he'd run through his passion for sailing, wanted to take up something new. He wanted to land a marlin, or a tuna or something gigantic that he could have had mounted, or at least take a picture of, to hang on his trophy wall.

But there in Baja, after a couple of days of catching nothing, he'd given up. It was expensive to charter a boat and all that gear. Then too, he'd had the feeling the Mexicans were laughing at him, the gringo, the greenhorn, the ugly American. He'd caught nothing, except diarrhea, finally gave up in disgust.

None of that was my fault.

Nevertheless, Emmett had been disappointed. He'd been forced to spend a day with me, to tag along on my shopping trip instead of wresting from the azure sea that prize fish that the whole world, or at least the harbor folk, would admire. He'd moped through the plaza stalls, and yes, he shopped for silver feather earrings. That was the day I took pictures; no wonder he looked tired and disgusted. He *was* tired and disgusted. It wasn't my fault. None of it was my fault! I want to leap off my barstool and dance.

"Hey, you want to go over to Glen Ellen tomorrow? I could show you around."

"I don't think so. We're…well, we're doing something, I forget what." I giggle. Where is Amy?

"She's gone. They took off. You need help getting home?"

"God, no. There're lights along the path, no problem. And

Amy's a big girl, she can take care of herself. We can all take care of ourselves. We're adults." But I'm already feeling the beginning of a green headache and don't know how well I *am* taking care of myself.

Once on the path to the cabin, though, with cool air on my cheeks, damp breath of the forest in my face, I feel strong and sure. I still have tomorrow, I have tomorrow to walk the trail, to eat ice cream, and to dream in the sun. Emmett's tomorrows ran out, his heart had beat so many times, and then it beat no more.

My own heart will beat so many times, and then no more, but that number is still an unknown, and I step along the trail, relishing the beating of life, the beating of life in my body. I still have time, there is time. My heart is strong, and beats and beats and beats. As if it will go on forever.

CHAPTER 7

Painful, though, the beating. My heart is beating, *throbbing,* in unison with a surly green headache the next morning. I climb out of bed and stagger into the bathroom to slurp up handfuls of water, Indian style. In the wavy glass of the bathroom mirror, I see my tongue has a green crème de menthe coating. Amy, too, might wake up feeling ill. I glance back into the bedroom; she's still asleep, curled into a .loose knot under her quilt. She'd appeared sometime in the night—her bed had been empty when I turned in.

This can't be why people travel. To eat and drink too much, waste hours in a bar talking to a fool, and wake up feeling evilly out-of-sorts. My own house, where I feel physically well, if not emotionally gratified, shimmers in my memory, an oasis of sense and security. Moreover, my cozy nest, viewed from this alien place, seems a haven in which I can dream, meander through selected memories, enjoying the freedom of my own mind. A place where I can treasure my own silence, although lately I've been filling it with sighs and mutters, of talking to the cat or back at the TV like a crazy woman. Well, so what. I have the freedom now, at least at home, to furnish my solitary existence with such oddities as I alone deem appropriate. In this place, away from my refuge, I'm saddled with Amy, am somehow responsible to and for her. It seems an onerous weight after floating in free fall these last few months, and standing here in the bathroom, I let my shoulders sag under the burden. Suddenly my time alone becomes precious, and I yearn to get back to it. One more day, one more day in these environs, marooned.

But after I make coffee in our tiny kitchenette and drink a cup out on the porch, the fragrant forest again cast its spell. The quiet, the light and air, a hint of damp, of dew not yet disturbed—I'll be fine. While Amy sleeps, I should get the tree-finder booklet and explore, but recognizing varieties of trees no longer seems to matter.

Emmett's gone, and he took his knowledge with him. While Emmett studied trees, lawn care, use of equipment and machinery, household maintenance, joke-telling, income tax returns, how to make a living, routing schedules at the plant, and the details of his latest hobby (I now view his passionate submergence in hobbies as an escape from me), while he studied all that, I studied him. He'd been my discipline, my avocation, my major field of endeavor. I'd studied him as if my survival depended on grasping the subtleties of his persona. I wanted to please him. I ferreted out his tastes, discovered that he liked deviled eggs with dry mustard powder mixed with the mayonnaise. He preferred his meatloaf made with tomato sauce and cracker crumbs, not oatmeal and milk, my mother's recipe, which he said was blah. He liked his socks clipped together with a kind of clothespin contraption, not rolled together, which he said stretched out the tops. He liked his tee shirts folded in thirds, not halves, because that way they fit better in the drawer. He liked the sheets untucked because he couldn't sleep with hot feet. He slept hot; lying next to him, I felt that the bed contained an extra heating element, my own personal energy source.

He wanted to be the first to break open the Sunday paper—he hated for anyone else to take it apart. He read the sections in precise order: first sports, then commentary, then business and comics, and ending with the front page. All the while I cooed around him, bringing him his juice, his Sunday blueberry pancakes with orange syrup, keeping his coffee cup filled. I'd loved taking care of him. At least *that* part of him, I admit ruefully.

He'd come home from Vietnam, and that was it—I was lost to my previous existence. Vividly I remember the first time we reconnected after he mustered out of the Army. I opened the door of my parents' house, and there he was, shining on the step. So handsome in the yellow porch light, a blond god miraculously fallen to earth. For me.

He wore a suede jacket cut like a sport coat, and a denim shirt boiling with embroidery. And bellbottoms, not exactly the outrageous sort, but bellbottoms nevertheless. No bandanna, ponytail, or earring; but a blue beaded peace sign on a leather thong around his neck.

Of course it'd been the seventies, that gaudy decade. But my mother, the prim housewife, her print dress decorous and proper, my father, the accountant, his plastic pocket liner bristling with fine-point ballpoints, had gaped at Emmett. Later, my mother used *popinjay* to describe him. I can hear my mother's voice, "Well, he's a proper popinjay, isn't he." That archaic expression had filled me with indignation. At the same time, I was taken by the sound of it, the feel of it on my tongue, the slight sarsaparilla flavor. I was secretly impressed with my mother's tart, and correct, judgement. Emmett had looked a popinjay, whatever that meant. Then again, what did my mother know? To my meek and mild parents, hopelessly behind the times, anything untoward leaped out. But even if he had gone beyond colorful to flashy, even tawdry, in his personal taste and adornment, so what! Was that a crime?

I dedicated myself to him. I quit junior college and got on full-time at the phone company to support us when he thought he wanted to go back to school. I quit my friends, my habits and routines, and I embraced his. I became a part of Emmett, or tried to become a part, tried to graft myself onto him. And now here I am, struggling to find out who I have a chance of becoming, in the void that Emmett left.

So a woman who abdicates her own personality to adopt someone else's deserves to find herself in a fix, I scold, getting up and going into the cabin for more coffee. The coffee, at least I am sure of the coffee, will not equivocate about it: the coffee is delicious in the clear fresh air of the forest.

A hot shower further restores my spirits, and a good brushing restores my tongue to its natural color. I wipe mist off the mirror and study my reflection. I think about silver pinecone earrings. They'd match that gray silk dress I've been thinking about. The earrings will show off my new short hair, and the dress will show off my eyes, which are gray. Would Emmett approve of a gray dress? Well, not gray, *silver.* Silver is my color, I see that now. I will let this preposterous hair dye grow out, and put on a new shade, something to accentuate my multiplying gray, my *silver*. Silver, silver, silver, I'll go with silver. Shirley Jones, Elizabeth Taylor, James Brolin, Richard Gere, Michael Landon. They've all gone silver. Michael Landon is dead, true, but no matter, he belongs with those Silver Foxes. Briefly I think of the Silver Fox I'd met on the bridge, but push the memory down. Bad medicine that, finding a man attractive. The silk dress, though, is another matter. Even though silk requires dry cleaning—

"Mom, how long are you going be in there?" calls Amy through the bathroom door.

"Be right out," I say, chagrined. Caught mooning into my own eyes like a schoolgirl!

Wrapped in a skimpy motel-type towel, having forgotten to take my clothes in with me, I reenter the main room. How awkward! Amy, however, yawns, stretches, rolls casually out of bed in a short nightie.

Her near nudity reminds me of niggling concerns, makes me ask, "Amy, are you all right?"

"Of course. Why wouldn't I be?"

"You weren't here last night when I went to bed...I worried about you."

"Jeez, I can take care of myself. What do you think I do at home?"

"At home you've got your...equipment," I say, making a stab at delicacy. "Here, I don't know how prepared you are."

"Don't worry about it, okay?" Amy sighs, yawns, stretches again, and I look away but not before realizing she has a blurred, fuzzy, out-of-focus aura. It isn't just smeared makeup and mused hair, it's something else, a palpable presence of sex in the room. Oh, yeah, sex, *sex*, and I am on my guard, uneasy about it, although my mind stops short of defining, of accepting, of imagining what *it* is that I fear.

Later she continues to irritate me with unfocused attention while we eat a breakfast sandwich on the snack bar's porch—the Inn's dining room doesn't open until noon. She also irritates me by pulling the ham slice out of her sandwich and throwing it away. I want to snap, For God's sake! You're so damned pure—an unsullied vegetarian! That animal is dead, it gave up its life for you, and you're wasting it. But I can't say that. I can't, I *shouldn't,* comment on Amy's idealism, besmirch it with my pragmatism. That's what Emmett had done, and it had driven her wild.

As wild as I now feel burdened with Amy's befuddlement. Okay, she's love-struck. Wasn't I the same after my first date with Emmett? I must have been ecstatic, although I can't remember where we'd gone, what we'd done, how it ended. In fact, I feel some ancient unease around the subject. What had happened? Did I lose my purse? Stumble and fall? Expose an unacceptable opinion? I can't remember.

In glowing terms, Amy describes Jake, the handsome new guy. Gentle, soft-spoken, silky mannered: he's a glaring contrast to Larry, whom she now realizes is a jerk. Larry wouldn't do at all; she sees the error of her ways, her lack of perception, of judgement.

I'm only half-listening, my mind still occupied with Emmett. While he was in Vietnam, and we were corresponding, I'd had a couple of lukewarm boyfriends. But I rushed home from a coffee date, or a class at the junior college, or my part-time job at the telephone company, to check the mail for a letter from Emmett. A letter from him made my day, although it could be, usually was (I admitted to myself, but not to my mother), a boring missive, poorly written, sometimes carelessly scribbled in pencil.

He wrote too much about missing local social events that meant nothing to me—the Crawdad Festival in Isleton, the Pear Fair in Courtland. (I thought he wasn't missing crawdads and pears as much as the wild parties that went with them.) He missed sailing the South Tower Race, and, oh, the music scene. He bitterly resented being left out of the revival of Dixieland that was going on in Old Sacramento. He longed for a sweet combo—trumpet, trombone, clarinet, banjo, and tuba—guys in shiny suits and striped vests and top hats, swinging through the narrow streets of the historic district, wowing the crowd with "Mississippi Mud" or "When the Saints Come Marching In." He could practically *taste* the sweetness of a Jelly Roll Morton stomp, a Scott Joplin ragtime, "Chrysanthemum" or "Maple Leaf Rag" or "The Entertainer." In my return letters, I wrote about my music, Herb Alpert, the Doobie Brothers, Sergio Mendes, until Emmett let on that he considered them schlock; then I went hard-core: The Doors, Santana. He liked them almost as much as Dixieland. He grieved deeply over the deaths of Janis Joplin and Jimmy Hendricks, whom I considered no great loss.

Nevertheless, none of that mattered when I got a letter from him, when I first tore into it as if it were Christmas and I was five years old. A magic letter from Emmett, which I read greedily, rushing through the text looking for...what had I been looking for? What had I been expecting? Poetry? Like that doggerel in his desk folder?

I'd take one quick dash through his scribbles, scanning for that elusive something. Then I'd reread slowly, aware of vague disappointment, even anger. Was this facile document the return on the investment of my own careful prose, as full of grace and wit, as full of interesting news that I could make it? Then a third or a fourth reading...and I found hope, I found, I *created,* deep and passionate thoughts in his airy paragraphs, and I took up my pen again, reassured. Had he ever appreciated my efforts? He'd never said so, but he must have enjoyed my letters, because he came home to me; there he was, gleaming and golden in the porch light when I opened the door of my parents' house. If he hadn't enjoyed hearing from me, if my letters hadn't engaged him in some manner, he'd have appeared on someone else's step, wouldn't he? Wouldn't he?

New traitorous thought: could that misleading, perhaps empty, correspondence have been emblematic of our marriage? For years, Emmett did the best he could, he tried to please me, as I tried to please him. Had he sensed that I needed something more from him, something more than he was prepared or equipped to give? Impatient, demanding, I tore into the marriage as I'd torn into his letters, and found nothing there. In response, he tried to shield himself from my disappointment, but the lack of fusion between us had frustrated us both. Could that be true? Oh, yes, in some subtle manner, we'd let each other down.

By this time Amy and I have finished eating, and we stand, brush at crumbs, wad our trash into a barrel, and head down the path toward the cabin.

"Isn't it fascinating how people get together?" Amy says. "Whoever would have thought I'd come here to meet Jake? It's like fate. Do you believe in fate?"

"No."

"What do you believe in?"

"Willy-nilly circumstance, chance, the luck of the draw, balanced by a certain amount of control."

"Control!"

"Yeah, you've got to use your head. Find out if you're compatible with this person. Are your backgrounds the same? Your core values? You can't let your hormones run wild. You've got to use your brain, both sides of it. Learn about the person, see if he's someone you can live with."

"Like you did with Dad."

I'm appalled at what I'm telling her. I haven't a clue. What I am sure of is I thought I studied Emmett, knew him, his tastes, his needs, his desires. Now I realize I hadn't known anything about him except superficialities—how he liked his clothes folded, what to put in his meatloaf. The trouble was I'd been too infatuated with him from the start, and had never known him as a friend. If anything, he'd been an adversary I tried to overcome with distractions like blueberry pancakes, devilled eggs with mustard powder. I brought about my own downfall by never arguing, never contradicting, never ignoring him; by never showing any spirit. Emmett would have liked spirit, spunk, vivacity, such as Maggie Quinn in his office had no doubt provided.

I sigh, then kick at a weed growing up through the gravel on the trail. It's true, he wanted a display of grit, spirit, enough playful struggle to define himself against, and I hadn't given it to him. Against my will, in naked perversely, one of his damn poems surfaces in my traitor of a mind:

The work-week world, white noise—mere blips,
A brown-bag lunch, sandwich and chips.
The orders filled, the paycheck earned,
My time is bought, but nothing's learned.
Then home, a prison, more white noise,
Vanilla sweetness clogs, then cloys.
I'm trapped, I'm tamed, subdued, milk-mild,
I itch, I ache for something wild.

He'd wanted passion, adventure; he'd wanted drama, mystery; he'd even wanted fights. Like that night I careened off and slept behind the bank. He admired that, he'd tacitly approved, welcomed that contest of wills. Afterward he related the episode to his buddies, slyly adding his own details until the story took on a significance lacking in the real event. I became, in his telling of it, a headstrong wench, a hellion. I developed, in his wishful tale, the exact characteristics I am not only afraid of displaying, but am incapable of.

Suddenly my blood boils, I am overcome with anger. That damned man! What the hell had he wanted! Hadn't he known that he needed something I couldn't provide? Of course he'd known that; he'd been no dummy...but then, he'd been no genius, either. A middlin' guy, trudging along, running the shipping department in that furniture factory. Just an ordinary man, such as men are.

Then I consider another aspect of that sordid sleep-behind-the-bank caper. Would I have left him if I'd realized there were only so many nights left in his life span, or in mine, to sleep together? I wasted that night, used it up in plotting how to get him back for objecting to Amy's birth control pills.

Shit. Where *does* this sentimental claptrap come from! One less night of sleeping with him…out of over eight thousand…and I'm regretting *one*? Even when I *was* there, we rolled over, turned our backs to each other, we coiled into our separate dreams. The truth I'm avoiding is that we'd long ago finished each other off. We read while eating dinner, him a newspaper—his end of my table had been black with newsprint—me a novel. Watched TV on separate sets. But isn't that always the case? Does a long-term marriage always develop in lockstep? Isn't there always growth, change? Well, Emmett grew, he changed. Now it's my turn.

Amy yawns. I realize she'd gotten little sleep last night; plus, she retreats into pseudo boredom when I get too close, or become preachy.

"What do you want to do today, Mom? Any preference?" By this time, we'd reached the cabin, are sitting on the porch in a patch of sun.

"Let's drive over to the coast, see the ocean. Scout around for someplace else to grab a bite for dinner. That Inn, I'm not up for it again. Soggy pasta—did you notice how everything tasted the same under the tomato sauce and cheese? And those silly games."

"You don't want to meet Jake?" She adds slyly, "You don't want to meet your friend from the bar?"

"No on both counts."

Her grin is malicious. "You were hoping for the Silver Fox, weren't you?"

My face burns, but I say stiffly, "Let's go see the ocean, talk about dinner later."

Amy pulls out of the parking lot and points her Mustang toward the coast. The road is the sort AAA labels "Other, surface not known." It is, however, a fine road, a narrow black ribbon of asphalt twisting through the green blur of forest rushing by us on both sides. I think sadly that there are no real back roads left in California.

Nevertheless, I feel called upon to say, "Slow down. You can't see joggers around these curves. Or bicyclists."

"Don't worry about it." Her standard answer to any critique of her driving. But she does slow down, and then goes on with this tiresome rhapsody, this tedious description of her evening with her new friend. "...so we left because it got so smoky in there..." I hear her say.

"But Amy, no one was smoking—it's against the law. Besides, you used to smoke. And you lived with a smoker."

"Yeah, but I could smell it. I'm tired of cigarette smoke. Jake and I went for a walk. The woods, Mom, the fresh clear air in the woods, you wouldn't believe."

"Why wouldn't I believe it? Yesterday I went for a hike myself, while you took a nap. But you weren't out walking all night. What did you do then?" I glance at Amy to see if she'll accept this intrusion. If I push, Amy will bristle or turn silent. Just as her father had. But she is dreamy, beguiled, living her own fantasy. Poor girl. In her own tough modern way, Amy is as defenseless, as vulnerable and susceptible as I'd been.

But she answers blandly. "We got to talking, you know how it is. When it turned cold, we went back to his room in the Inn, no point in disturbing you." She swivels her sly blue gaze away from me.

"Are those rooms nice?"

"Um...no, they're not as good as our cabin. Clattery hardwood floors, high ceilings, drafty. Bathroom down the hall."

"At those prices, you don't get a private bath?"

"He's in an economy unit. He's going through a bad divorce, his ex is taking him to the cleaners."

"Oh, no, Amy—"

"I'm not going to marry him, fer chrissake! He's got kids! This is just for fun, no strings."

She goes on about what a controlling bitch the ex-wife is, how unfair and unjust the divorce laws. I bite back comments, tell myself to stay out of it, hold my tongue, let it pass.

The blue sky whitens, as if diluted with milk. Then it dissolves into a layer of fog that envelops the road. The edging of trees is replaced by low growth stunted and slanted by wind; then even small trees yield to scrub. The air, now chilled, holds a tang of salt, a cutting sharpness. I interrupt Amy's recital of Jake's ex-wife's contrary behaviors to say, "You're cold. I told you to dress warmer." Amy's bare legs are goose-bumped, and under her tan her skin has a reddish tinge.

"Mom, if I don't complain, why should you?" she snaps, looking pointedly at my jeans and sweater.

"I know," I say contritely, "I nag, don't I?"

"No, you're *right,* I'm cold, but I'll live."

By now we've dropped into a different climate zone. The white air contains a sharp mix of sea salt and seaweed, algae and chlorophyll. I can almost taste the extra ions in the atmosphere. The Mustang passes over the rolling crest of a hill and there lies the flat gray-white expanse of the Pacific Ocean, spread out like a sheet of crinkled aluminum foil. Amy turns south onto the main highway, saying, "I'll give you the ocean on your side." Then she adds, "Later we can grab a bowl of clam chowder in Bodega Bay, okay?"

I murmur something while staring out the window at the advance and retreat of white-edged rollers. The sea, I think, our picayune difficulties dissolve while contemplating the energy of the ocean. How insignificant, how puny—

"You want to walk on the beach?" her voice interrupts me. "Can those shoes take a little sand?"

"Yes, walk on the beach. Sand, no problem. How about you, are you going to be too cold?"

A three-syllable "*Mot th er*!" just as she'd done when she was five.

She pulls abruptly into a state beach lot, making the guy behind her honk. "How about this stretch? I think they're all pretty much alike."

We park, lock, and Amy stows the keys in her fanny pack. "You want to leave your purse?"

"Uh, car clouts? Amy, I read somewhere that guys watch you with binoculars, see where you stash your purse, then break in when you leave."

"*Mo th er*," again three syllables.

"I can't help it," I say, hooking my purse strap over a shoulder. "I never thought about money so much before, but—"

"I know what you're going to say. Don't worry, you won't have to front me a loan."

"Amy, no—"

She leads me down a gravel path through low rubbery shrubs, then out onto the shingle. "Tell me about your first date with Dad."

"I'm still trying remember it." I'm laboring ankle deep in dry sand.

The beach itself is not wide and flat, but narrowed by high tide, and haphazardly strewn with boulders, as if tossed about by a giant negligent hand. An interesting beach rather than a pleasant one. The going is tough, and I begin to have second thoughts about this particular expanse.

But Amy has no doubts, and pushes ahead. I follow her, picking my way through rocks now shell-encrusted, to a dark ribbon of hard-packed sand. Here, the walking is easier, and we edge along the surf, judging where to stay dry as lapping waves uncurl in a line of foam. Over the roar of water, I say loudly, "I suppose it doesn't matter where we went, but now that he's gone, I want to remember—"

"Like I want to remember everything about Jake." Over the noise of the sea, I hear, "...so what if Jake was late getting home that night...she'd changed the locks...threw his stuff out on the lawn...then attached his wages...never mind what he has to have to live on...court ordered by the judge..."

Then I hear, "...seen the writing on the wall and moved his assets..."

I interrupt, "He hid assets?"

"Mom, only things that were his, rightfully. A coin collection, a stamp album his father left him, stock in his company."

In my silence, in which Amy no doubt hears disapproval, she goes on, "Yeah, I know what you're thinking. Doesn't sound right to me, either. The kind of thing you can't imagine Dad doing.Dad was a straight shooter, you know?"

I make vague non-responses, then say, "This must be a common thing, hiding assets. So when it blows up, you can get out."

Never mind my own secret account at the sleep-behind bank. Nickels and dimes.

Amy rattles on, dissecting the male personality, and I listen with only half an ear, preoccupied, distracted, distressed. I am torn: I yearn to tell Amy about the missing stock, but I can't sour Emmett's memory for her. Isn't it my duty to keep it unsullied? At least for Amy? That's my best course; nothing would make any difference anyway.

Is it a rule or a law that all women, when they're alone, talk of men? Do men, by themselves, talk of women? From what I overheard of Emmett's conversations, I think not. He talked sports, weather, cars, road conditions, problems at work, what's on sale at Ace Hardware, the state budget, the national scene. However, Amy and I are discussing Jake, or Amy is discussing Jake, while I listen.

But then again, what could I, or *should* I, discuss with Amy? Pinecone earrings, silk dresses, silver highlights for my hair? No, and not because those things aren't important (and maybe they're not), but because they are simply beside the point.

We reach a small creek that bubbles through a great mass of boulders, braiding itself into a delta before twisting into the sea. It appears to be at least knee deep. To cross it, we'll have to get wet. We stand for a minute watching the ragged tumult of water. The sound of the surf, at this juncture of creek and sea, becomes a dull persistent roar, like a waterfall, or the stubborn rumble of traffic on the Interstate. Not hectic rush hour commuter traffic, but the continuous drone of early morning, or late evening vehicles traveling at a steady clip.

In silent agreement, we turn around and follow our own footprints back toward the car. Suddenly I turn to Amy. "Say, I just remembered."

"What?"

"That first date with your dad. What brought it back was that I was thinking the surf sounded like freeway traffic." She grimaces, but I go on, "This is important to me, Amy, hear me out. Well, that first date, I thought we'd go downtown, see a movie, then have a soda or a cup of coffee at Ernie's, which is what kids did then—"

"Still do, the young ones."

"Instead, he turned right to get on the freeway, not left on Main. So, I asked where we were going. Your dad says to Vallejo, to a club he knew about where they were playing Dixieland, this real hot music, or was it cool? I can't remember, but since we both liked the same stuff, we'd get a kick out of this group. Whoever they were. This guy played a banjo with real soul, you know, blah, blah, blah. Well, my heart sank."

"Because you really didn't like that kind of music?"

"Mainly because I knew I couldn't get in that place. See, I'd let on that I was twenty-one, but I was just nineteen."

"You shoulda just told him, why didn't you tell him?"

"Well, I had this fake ID, all the kids had them, we got them in Oakland, in a place that did passports. They took your picture, laminated it onto a thing that looked, at first glance, like a driver's license, and if you flashed it real quick when they carded you, it worked."

"Hokey."

"It was the best I could do. So, we went to Vallejo, all the time I'm worrying, wondering if I should tell him, or what. But your dad was full of talk, I could hardly get a word in edgewise. There was just no place in the conversation to tell him. And," I mumble, "I didn't want to lose him."

"All the way to Vallejo—"

"It's not *that* far," I say, nettled.

"So, you flashed this fake thing, and no dice."

"Exactly. Turned down flat. So embarrassing in front of all those people. Should have known. There was a line to get in, it snaked clear down the block...we could hear the noise all the way back to where he'd parked. This tuba thing, blatting away. Tuba music, imagine!"

"Better than accordion."

I laugh. "This oom pa, oom pa, oom pa. So...one-dimensional, mindless. As creative as a piston, up and down, up and down."

"Like a German making love."

I laugh again, turn self-conscious. "Hey, I resent that." I am abashed; we never discuss sex. "Remember, I used to be a

Schneider."

"Okay, a Schneider who didn't like Dixieland. I can just see it, I bet I know how Dad reacted."

"He went silent. Totally mute, with that expression around his mouth. We trudged back to his car—he'd parked way out, under a streetlight, and I was wearing some foolish sandals I could hardly walk in. I filled up the air with nervous chatter, chirping away about nothing, my heart pumping ice water, I remember it so clearly now. How could I have forgotten?"

"Because you didn't want to remember."

I shoot her a look. Amy is right, I didn't want to remember. Just talking about that horrible evening makes nerves twitch on the backs of my hands. "He unlocked my door, went around to his side, slid in, and I went on talking, talking. All the way back to town. He turned up the radio, I suppose to drown me out, so I raised *my* volume, went on with my noise, all the while absolutely sick to my stomach."

"Poor Mom. He was acting weird."

"Well, not really," I say quickly. "I should have leveled with him, about my age."

"An innocent mistake. He was being a jerk."

"Do you think so? Well, anyway, it got worse. While he was pouting, we passed a theater showing *The Sand Pebbles* with Steve McQueen, and I said why don't we go see it. Kind of an old movie, but your dad hadn't seen it."

I stop, sit on a piece of driftwood in a pretext of emptying and retying my shoes, but really to put energy into my story. "I should have known, yeah, I should have known."

"What?" Amy sits down next to me, brushes sand from her feet, and prepares to slip on her sandals—she'd been walking barefooted.

"How it would affect him. In the theater, in the dark, he sank down in his seat, got lower and lower, while up on the screen that Navy gunboat swarmed with little yellow people on that big yellow river. I don't know what happened in Vietnam, he never talked about it, but that movie brought it all back. It haunted him, the jungle, the muddy river, the Mekong Delta. His job had been to shuffle men and matériel from one swampy outpost to another, for no reason that he could imagine, except that he saw guys he knew getting blown up, or destroyed by drugs. The futility of the loss, the lack of purpose."

"I always thought that was why he didn't write you interesting letters. You know how you said his letters were boring? Well, life and death, the mortal combat. How could he polish his prose in the middle of that? Plus, maybe he was censored—"

"I never thought of that! Of course! The wonder was that he wrote anything at all, now that I think of it."

"And him not literary, anyway."

"Amy, people were horrible to those vets when they came back. Spit on them, mocked them. Your dad never volunteered that he'd been in Vietnam, if he could help it."

"You have to admit that some of those vets were really screwed up."

"Maybe through no fault of their own, either. Anyway, after the movie, he went silent again, didn't say six words on the way home. Later I told grandma that that was the last of him, he wouldn't call back."

"I bet she said good. Grandma was lukewarm about Dad."

"She thought...well, I don't know what she thought. Tell you one thing, she didn't like the way I hung there by the phone, pining for him to call. She thought I was trusting someone not...trustworthy. He didn't call for a month. Well, at least a couple of weeks. I just knew I'd ruined it."

Amy rubs her cold bare legs. "Still, I can't see that any of this was your fault, or Dad's, either."

"That first evening just didn't work out, although I wanted it to in the worst way." I sigh. "Then finally, *finally,* " I interpose a rueful laugh, to show my grown-up sense of proportion, "he called—I think it was a last-minute thing, someone else had stood him up—and we took it from there."

"Lived happily ever after," Amy says in a crisp, dismissive voice, wrapping things up tidily. She stands, swings her arms, seeking warmth. "It turned out fine, no regrets, huh, Mom?"

Now is when I should tell her. But I look into her round blue eyes, so like Emmett's, and I can't. She would label him a shit, and me a sap. Emmett cheated her, too, and she will be furious. I am not ready for her venting. "Regrets? Just the usual."

I get up, too, and walk back to the car with Amy, the daughter that Emmett had quit trying to understand, in a place he'd never wanted to visit—he'd disliked the north coast, had demanded seawater warm enough to swim in.

The truth of the matter: whatever had been bothering Emmett, perhaps triggering the sudden fatal heart attack, had little to do with me. It's hard to admit that I'd been an affectless element in his life.

Another of his poems intrudes, but one that had touched me, causing me to study it to a point of saturation:

He scrubs at the sink, half-numb, there he stands,
His hair brushed with paint, and paint on his hands.
His heart hears de Kooning, Picasso, and Klee;
His body betrays with an old trick knee.
His friends are a ladder, roller, a brush,
His orders are one coat pale gray, rush, rush.
My old man, broke when he died, not one thin dime—
My age exactly, do I still have time?

Emmett had been ashamed of his parents, his mother, the cafeteria drudge, his father, the laborer. Perhaps some sense of their failure had caused him to create his own competitive, even combative, nature. On top of that—his ills pile up like a clumsy stack of firewood—on top of that had been his Vietnam experience, his boring yet stressful job, his midlife crisis. But what could I have done about any of it?

We reach the car and get in; Amy points it toward Bodega Bay and the bowl of chowder. As we drive off, I feel almost lightheaded, as if I'm leaving a part of myself on the beach, a part I no longer have a use for.

CHAPTER 8

"Okay, we're ready." I stumble around a cardboard box of kitchen junk labeled FREE, Tupperwares, metal ice cube trays, parts for this and that. "Almost 8:30—few more minutes, I'll open the door and we'll spread camping on the grass, tools and hardware on the driveway."

That was Mr. Purdy's idea. A way, he said, to draw men into our garage sale. According to him, women nickel and dime you; they spend an hour haggling over a quarter's worth of goods, wear you out with their nit-picking.

Nit-picking. I'd smiled politely, hoped he wouldn't go on in that vein. It's exactly the kind of mean and belittling thing men say about women that drives me wild. What a shame to ruin our incipient friendship, nip it in the bud. It could happen: I could trigger it myself. Lately I'm irritable; I bubble with a snappy comeback to even the most innocent remarks. An outbreak of rudeness threatens to engulf me, like a case of the flu. My skin is a thin membrane stretched tight and bright, an over-inflated balloon within which I struggle for control. I am ready to snap, to rip, to attack at the drop of a hat. *Attack at the drop of a hat*—I like that, I could write some poetry of my own. But then again, I'm tired, not sleeping well, and I'm worn out prepping for this garage sale. I'll get over it. I have to because I'm about to go job-hunting, for a real job. No more play-acting with the temp stuff.

Now men, Mr. Purdy went on, *men* are a different story. Put your hardware out where a man driving by can see it, and he'll screech to a halt and buy big-ticket items, and pay with real folding money. No quibbling over prices, either. Display your hardware, he said, your driveway bait, your yard jewelry, and draw in the big bucks.

To get me started, he brought over some of his own stored treasures, among which was a camper shell. I had to help him with it, the two of us staggering along, a pair of ants transporting a fiberglass sugar cube. He added other odds and ends of car equipment—snow tires, air compressor, battery charger, timing light, a crawler with torn plastic padding, gas cans. He brought over a tow bar, a metal yoke contraption rattling with pieces of chain. I stared at this junk, puzzled. "Nobody's going to buy that," I hissed to Amy. Emmett wouldn't have; but then Emmett hadn't been interested in automotive stuff. But Mr. Purdy was, or had been, a car buff. And thank goodness: he'd tuned up the Bronco, changed its oil, and what with the AAA guy's tender loving care, it's running...not well, but better. For this I'm grateful, willing to overlook his crusty ways.

"Wow!" I'm peering through the garage window. "You should see them lined up at the curb, the street's packed. Are we ready?"

I'm talking to both Mr. Purdy and Amy, who are helping. To prepare for this Saturday extravaganza, we have spent a hot dirty week cleaning, sorting, pricing a garage full of junk. Mostly Emmett's stuff—tools and clothes.

In order to be here, Amy took some vacation days. "Oh, no, honey, not your vacation!" I said.

"Why not? You need me and nobody else does." Amy is suffering a letdown. Jake, her new guy, fizzled. I compounded the injury by spouting clichés about shipboard romances, cross-country love affairs, etc. I pointed out that Jake's life is too complicated for a long-distance connection, which by itself takes up a lot of time and energy. Not to mention the court battle over his kids, which is draining his finances. The fact remains: Amy is depressed without a man. She has painted her nails a startling chartreuse.

Feeling bad about my "negativity" (the label Amy pinned on me), I've taken her to lunch this week, to the Soup Kettle, Roy's Barbecue Pit, the Jade Garden, Antonio's Cocina.

Because I owe Amy, big time. That last night in the cabin, after Amy left with Jake, I'd felt bereft, abandoned, had settled in with my paperback—a self-help book about widowhood, *The Final Cycle*, which sounded like a tract about doing the wash—when Amy reappeared. Like a mirage, like a miracle, Amy sat down on the snack bar's redwood bench next to me. "I can't run off and leave you, Mom," she said. "I told Jake to go without me. Because you shouldn't be by yourself." So we ate together, not just mother and daughter, but two women alone in a time without men. I was overwhelmed with love and gratitude, because my world has become a slippery, dangerous and lonely place. So, at the moment, Amy can do no wrong. It's the rest of them I'm mad at. Well, not Mr. Purdy, of course. No, I'm not mad at him. Even Amy has warmed up to him, isn't near as rude to him these days.

What triggered this garage sale, for one thing, was getting home from the trip and finally understanding that Emmett is gone. He's not coming back from the plant at five o'clock, or six, or seven. Psychically I'd rejected the final acceptance of his death until Amy pulled into the drive, dropped me off, and Emmett wasn't here. Never would be here again—except in my dreams, which are still full of him.

Another thing urging me on: telephone calls from realtors wanting to list the house. They've probably gotten wind of my new status through the obituary, which finally appeared in the paper. If I have to sell, now's the time to lighten up.

Another bit of catastrophic news, one that gags me with nausea: I'll have to pay capital gains on the stock Emmett sold to support his mistress. However, the man I checked this out with said that due to the circumstances, I can work out a payment plan with the IRS. How nice of them! I rage, what a good bunch they are! How good of Emmett, too! Temporarily I considered burning down the damn house, and Emmett's stuff in it. Then I thought why not sell it for a nickel on the dollar? Beats nothing.

Then in the mail, a double whammy. One, a letter from a removal firm. On rich ivory paper, these people (vultures) promised a speedy and discreet removal of, as they put it, the deceased's effects. For this privilege, they'd pay a worthy lump sum, depending on what they could cull.

Whammy number two: a call from Mr. Hawley at Freeway Furniture to tell me that the beneficiary on Emmett's insurance is the plant, not me. I get nothing, while they collect. How can that be? Mr. Hawley explained, in embarrassed and halting language, that this is standard practice. Freeway Furniture paid the premiums. Therefore, it or they should collect the benefits. Emmett understood that. Why didn't I? I didn't know. I was aghast.

Too stunned to ask how they could do that, cut a worker's family out from the worker's insurance benefits, I stood there like a hammered sheep. Mr. Hawley saw his chance and took it (I thought), hanging up before I could collect my wits and become abrasive. I wandered around the house, dazed. Emmett's work gone up in smoke, gone to enrich the company. Had Emmett understood where this would leave me? He was smart; of course he'd known. The fault is mine. I should have been curious enough to get these details straight before he died. Nevertheless, I was furious. At Emmett, at Freeway Furniture, at myself, too.

I convinced myself that his plunge into an office romance with Maggie Quinn sapped his attention and his judgement. Became so convinced of it that *I* plunged into a purge of his things, his "effects". I'll show him, I'll extract revenge, retribution—at least enough to pay for that silver dress and the matching pinecone earrings.

"Quarter of nine, let's get this going." In the clutter, Amy trips over Emmett's fishing tackle. "I'll be glad to get rid of that," she mutters, rubbing her shin.

"Honey, don't hurt yourself. Yeah, fishing rods, reels, all that goes out on a tarp on the driveway. This stuff, too." I gesture at what I'd begun to think of as Emmett's boat shit: his all-weather waterproof clothing, which he'd needed for crewing on the *River Rat*, plus his duffel bags, and his sailor's technology—gauges, charts, compasses, whatever.

"Let's open for business," says Mr. Purdy. "Give 'em a thrill."

I hit the remote, the door whirs up and sunlight floods in. Mr. Purdy dashes out with Frieda's contributions: an old gas barbecue, a wheelbarrow minus its wheel, a collection of ceramic pots, gardening junk.

Earlier, when I got huffy over what I viewed as Frieda's piling on, Mr. Purdy smoothed me over, said it was okay, the more, the merrier. Garage sale etiquette allows neighbors to join in. A proper garage sale is a cleansing experience to be shared with the whole community, like a Baptist dunking down at the river. Nevertheless, I said—this time to Amy—"Nobody's going to buy that junk. The nerve, foisting it on us. Like throwing trash in an unguarded Dumpster." That's a capital crime in my neighborhood. A few cheapskates aren't above doing that to avoid expensive city dump fees. The real dump's miles out in the hinterland.

Dumpster: it reminds me of one of Emmett's capers. When he remodeled the kitchen, he rented a Dumpster for the debris, parked it out at the bottom of the driveway. It started filling up with alien trash, so Emmett dove in, sifted for clues. Finally found an envelope with an address of a neighbor a block over. Emmett boxed up as much of his rubbish as he could find, drove it over, left it on the guy's porch. I always wondered what he thought when he opened the door and found his trash returned to him.

That Emmett—he'd been one of a kind...but then my warm flare of pride in him is extinguished under a wave of anger. How dared that man do what he did! Take up with Maggie Quinn! Leave me with this mess!

However, now's not the time to waste energy in recrimination, because people are surging up the driveway and into the garage while Mr. Purdy arranges, according to his garage sale specs, the camping gear, sporting goods, the automotive. Amy takes her position at the card table near the front of the garage—she's cashier—and Mr. Purdy hovers around his big-ticket driveway jewelry. I wander around wringing my hands, smiling. In spite of my mood, I make myself smile; I smile, my face aches with forced smiling while I reshuffle piles of this and that, and answer questions. "Yes, size 12," I say of my jeans. "Oh, sure, it's washable," about a cotton sweater. Of some linen, "Queen bed size, with both pillowcases." I smile while a woman with orange hair, in a hot-pink stretch velour running suit, offers me a quarter for a vase priced at a dollar. I smile at a man who pays five dollars for the MALONE beer stein; at a woman who buys Emmett's whole collection of suspenders. I smile, pretending I haven't overheard Mr. Purdy, "...can't ever have too many rods and reels, or too big a pole, if you get my drift."

Smile while somebody buys Frieda's wheelless wheelbarrow, the rusty gas barbecue, some clay pots. Smile while someone else buys the gas cans, the camper shell, the snow tires. Smile bagging up Emmett's clothes, his salmon pink button-down, his matching paisley tie, his denim suit, oh, his denim suit! still in its plastic from the cleaner's. Smiling, although stricken, I turn away, don't want to watch his denim suit go home with someone else. However, I marked it at an exorbitant price, almost what the silver dress is going to cost. But not the pinecone earrings; I'm crazy if I pay what that antique shop is asking for them, but I think I'm going to do it.

A woman comes to me with his embroidered denim shirt, and I grab it away. "Sorry. That's not for sale."

"But it was over there on that table," she says. She's wearing a huge gray sweatshirt with cutoff sleeves. It spells out B.U.M. across breasts as big as bowling balls, and I wonder why anyone her age and shape would wear such a thing. "It's just what Brandon's been lookin' for, for Halloween," she says.

"Didn't you hear me? It's not for sale. Someone put it out by mistake. Go find something else, there's plenty of other stuff." Gripping the shirt, I slam into the house. Before the door closes, I hear, "Well, if she's not the rudest...come on, Betty Ann, put that back, these people are nuts..."

The kitchen seems dim and cool, and blessedly quiet, and I stand for a minute, remembering how I worked on this shirt, Emmett's embroidered denim shirt. We'd gone camping at Calaveras Big Trees, Emmett and Amy and I. While Emmett and Amy explored a tiny creek, so small it was merely a series of puddles upon which water spiders danced, I sat in the shade and stitched. I was happy that day, a pooling kind of happiness, thick and sweet as honey. For me, all the pieces came together that day, as I sat under that...what kind of tree was it? I can't remember, think maybe a sugar pine, the kind that sheds cones a foot long and the sun-baked bark smells sweet when you sniff deep in its ridges.

I watched them, my husband and daughter, while embroidering Emmett's denim shirt. It was the wildest design yet. It had to be wild to make it stand out because Pfaff had come out with a machine that did embroidery and I wanted to make sure everybody knew his shirt had been done by hand. I sewed him rows of mushrooms down the placket, and dotted them with rich red ladybugs, satin-stitched black spots on their backs. Ivy scrolled along the yoke; butterflies flitted along the ivy. I used threads of variegated shadings; and metallic threads, hard to work with, and expensive. I threw the book at this shirt, used French knots, featherstitches, snake and chain stitches, satin stitches, honeycomb stitches. I went all out. Maybe too far, because Emmett had rarely worn it. But then again, this was toward the end of the embroidered denim shirt craze, and he moved on to a western look. Still, I can't sell this shirt, and I drape it on the back of a chair to keep it from that weird cheapskate mob outside.

Back at my post, I notice the garage is heating up, but the crowd thins after ten-thirty. Most of the camping gear is gone, and the hardware, the garden tools. But not the stubborn weed eater. Why doesn't someone buy it? I've been kicking tires on a replacement, a user-friendly model, in a nursery out on the frontage road, The Garden Spot. "The G Spot—we know how to make you happy" reads its card in small print, with a wink and a nudge.

In the lull Mr. Purdy pulls up a chair beside me in the back of the garage. "See? I told ya," he says. "Lord, this is fun."

"Glad you think so."

"You don't?"

"It's embarrassing. Sitting out here surrounded by my own hoarded goods, my lapses in judgement, my discards in full view, in daylight. Like sitting in my underwear, I'm exposed. I keep thinking, am I doing the right thing? Wholesaling Emmett out like this? Maybe I should wait."

"He's not coming back."

"I know that. Well, part of me knows it. The other part of me wants to protect his belongings, keep them safe. Make a shrine of them." That denim shirt in the house...but that's a shrine to me, not him.

I find myself resenting how he spent our money. His collection of cashmere, the MALONE beer stein. His dress-up junk, and his assortments of flashlights, wallets, and Dixieland records and tapes. Nobody bought any of the Dixieland. Someone did spring for the *Riverdance* videos. I put out the pen and pencil set from his desk at work, then took it in again. My gift to myself. The kind of thing people give at graduation. I'm the one graduating.

"I went through the same thing when my Millie died."

"Did you have a garage sale?"

"No, I was too worn out to deal with it right then. She'd been sick a long time, and I'd been, how do they put it? main caregiver. Plum tuckered, I was. Donated everything to the church. Anyway, she woulda liked that, she was a church person. My Millie, she taught me everything I know about garage sales. She could sell a coffee can full of bent nails for a buck. Tie a ribbon around a pile of rags, call 'em 'treated polish cloths' or some damn fool thing, and get three dollars for it. She was queen of the rummage sale. Usually held 'em in the basement of the church. The ladies would serve up lunch or tea and coffee and pie, charge for that, too. Fundraiser. My Millie'd organize the whole shootin' match, she was never nuthin' but a housewife, no fancy education, but she shoulda been in business, in sales or promotion or whatever. Yeah, she was the best." He draws a sigh. "How 'bout you?"

"Oh, my Emmett—" I blush. He'd never been "my" Emmett. He'd been his own person, had belonged to no one but himself. "My Emmett, he worked in business but he wasn't a businessman, didn't enjoy it. He should have been an architect. He wanted to study it; closest he got was a design class in junior college, a glorified woodshop class where most of the guys were hiding from the draft. His folks pushed him into this work-with-your-hands stuff, they wanted him to have something practical, a sure skill he could count on, make a living with. See, his dad was a failed painter, didn't want that to happen to Emmett. But Emmett did okay with what he learned in woodshop. Over there on the workbench? The projects he was working on. A bird feeder, a picture frame, flagpole assembly."

"No, I meant *you.* What were your goals, your dreams?"

I try to think what I'd ever wanted, besides Emmett. Early on, though, I knew he was the withholding sort; so hadn't I set myself up, right off the bat? I see that that's true. All those years I concentrated on Emmett, trying to take him over, make him over, when I should have been working on myself. "Me? Oh, I suppose I'd have liked more children." That's a lie, but I have to say something.

I glance over at Amy at her card table, which she's moved so she can sit in the sun under a coating of lemon-scented sun block. She's reading a paperback from my twenty-five cent table: Margaret Atwood's *Edible Woman.* She probably picked it up thinking it a diet book—I once used to read such things. Amy worried all week about putting on weight because of the lunches I bought us. To compound it, she hasn't worked out with her "fatties," and misses them and her routines. I told her she looked good with a little extra padding, which was a mistake, because she turned her mouth down in a sour grimace, the same kind I used to get from Emmett. Well, at least I won't have to look at him wearing *that* expression anymore!

"Do you have children?" I'd never heard a word about his family.

"Nope. No kids. No tragedy, that. See, Millie was the oldest of twelve, she'd had enough of kids, she didn't care. Besides, like I said, she wasn't your typical happy homemaker. Shoulda been in business. She kept the books for people, worked on their income tax, did other stuff like organize the church bazaar, the bake sales. Had the parking lot at the church set up for folks to sell produce. Used to be a lot of little farms around, couple of acres that people'd plant to crops like pears, cherries, walnuts, and of course corn, melons, and tomatoes. Oh, and they sold fresh eggs, herbs, cut flowers, crafts stuff—potholders, planters, decorations. My Millie had everybody signed up, plots marked out."

"I can't imagine this area being agricultural."

Just then a battered car swoops up. All four doors open and what looks like a dozen people spill out and troop up the driveway. “Hola, senora,” calls the driver. “Como esta? Esta bien?”

“Si, muy bien,” I answer. “Que tal?”

When he answers back with a barrage of Spanish, I throw up my hands and laugh.

He laughs, too. “Is okay. We learn the English at night school. Everything cool.”

Mr. Purdy steps forward, points out to the men what bargains, what splendid possibilities are being offered, what adventures to be had with…a bench grinder? a vise? an extension cord? He’s taken the measure of these folks, and he knows. He’s pushing tools, camping gear, the last of the tarps. The women move into my territory and sift through and buy clothes, mostly Emmett’s—shirts, ties, a paisley vest, shoes, jackets. “Is good stuff,” says a woman juggling a baby. They buy Amy’s discarded make-up, nail polish, and workout suits. They buy Frieda’s ceramic pots, kitchen goods, my jeans.

“Is best sale yet,” says a man, smiling, showing white teeth in his dark face.

Amy takes their money, and helps carry out goods to a car already packed with other garage sale buys. After these people leave, there’s another lull, a deeper one. A few neighborhood snoops stop in to size up the extent of my tragedy. Garage sales are signs of tragedy, Mr. Purdy says. Either that or of a shifting of the ground. He gives these casual pedestrians a once-over, then doesn’t bother going out to talk to them. Finally, around 11:30, the three of us, Mr. Purdy, Amy, and I, retreat to the deep cool of the garage. PawPaw reappears—he’d run off when strangers started arriving—and jumps up on Mr. Purdy’s lap. He’d become his friend while Amy and I were gone. This annoys Amy, but she’s nice about it.

“Well, this is dead,” says Amy. “What are we going to do for four more hours?”

“It’ll pick up after lunch,” Mr. Purdy says. “It’s always like this. After lunch, the Seventh Day Adventists come around, and the folks tied up with chores this morning.” He talks about other garage sales he’d either been to or his Millie had put on. In reminiscence, or fatigue—he’d probably gotten up as early as I had, and maybe he hadn't been able to sleep, either—his voice drops until he's murmuring as if only to himself. Air tankers from Travis drone overhead, drowning him out. I lose the thread of his conversation, fall to reminiscing…how Emmett used to drive out to Suisun City to watch the Air Force's Big Birds practice take-offs and landings, aluminum giants floating through the air like feathers. I thought it was boring, sitting there on the edge of the airfield, but put it down to some lack on my part. Now I think it *was* boring.

At noon Frieda halloos across the street, asks if we can stop for lunch. Clutching a bag lunch and a six-pack of Cokes, she clumps up the driveway in platform sandals—just looking at them makes my feet hurt. She's wearing a yellow knit top and white shorts. Amy exclaims over the top, which surprises me. It's just a tee shirt. Frieda chirps that Splurge, the shop where I found that silver dress, has tees on sale, summer clearance. I'll have to check it out on Monday. Maybe my silver dress is on sale, too. My fairytale silver dress, although it's not fancy; it's plain in design, bordering on severe. A sort of sheath dress, cut on the bias, so it doesn't hang, but drapes the body. Very good on me, I think, with my new flat belly. A deceptively simple dress that begs for pinecone earrings.

Frieda presents lunch—ham and turkey sandwiches, and a tuna for Amy. She hands out Cokes, and gingerbread squares with a lemon glaze. A thank-you for letting her piggyback into our garage sale. She sits with us while we eat, the four of us pulling chairs deeper into the garage.

Mr. Purdy comes to life, with Frieda. He sparkles, his voice takes on a fresh timbre; he's jokey, jovial. As if he's never before eaten lunch with a yellow top and white shorts. Never had such a feast packed for him. He pushes PawPaw off his lap so he can engage fully with his food. Frieda lavishes compliments for his success—he's sold all her stuff—and he expounds on his garage sale philosophy. The perfect time of year, he says. The fruit pickers are in town; people are back from vacation waiting for school to start. Everyone's bored and lazy, stricken with summertime doldrums. Yeah, yeah, I think sourly. Tell me something else I don't know: he'd already said the same things to me.

He exclaims continually over his turkey sandwich, as earlier he'd exclaimed over my apple pie. It's the perfect turkey sandwich, with mayo, lettuce, pepper. How had Frieda known to put mayo, lettuce, pepper on a turkey sandwich, he asks. Because, I think, you always put mayo, lettuce, and pepper on turkey sandwiches, to cover up how dry they are otherwise.

He effuses over the gingerbread—his favorite, he says; he loves gingerbread. I think that he has no judgement, either. It's obviously from a package mix because there's a chemical undertaste. If he wants gingerbread, I fume, if he's so hot for gingerbread, why hadn't he said something? I'd have made him a shitload of gingerbread, the old coot, the old geezer.

I boil with jealousy as Mr. Purdy effervesces into Frieda's face, which is turned toward his like a flower to the sun. Then I am struck by my own neediness, to react like this! What is the matter with me! But I continue to suffer waves of envy and possessiveness. Frieda is going to take Mr. Purdy away from me, and I have just discovered him for myself. It's Providence that sent him, and I don't want it messed with. But what's the use? There will always be a Frieda, and I'll never catch up at this rate, never be able to transmit creamy looks such as Frieda gives Mr. Purdy; it's all over, there's no hope. Anyway, I'm tired of this whole thing. That's it in a nutshell, I'm tired. All the while I think this, my balloon face is painted with a smile.

Lunch over, Frieda collects the trash and stuffs it in a bag by the door. She stretches in what I consider a provocative manner, then says she has to get home. She minces down the driveway, balancing on her platforms. On the backs of her legs are impressions of the chair's plastic webbing. I wonder if Mr. Purdy is watching her, too; I throw him a look, and see that he is. At least his face is pointed that way. He's thinking she's better looking than I am, I muse, and I set to work gathering the beginning of a sticky gray funk around me, like a collapsed parachute.

Then Mr. Purdy says, "Those last guys wanted to buy the tow bar, and maybe I should 'a sold it to them."

"Why didn't you?" So he wasn't thinking about Frieda!

“Because earlier a fellow said he wanted it, he’d be back this afternoon with the money. I said I’d save it for him.”

“Did he put anything down, to hold it?”

“No, he didn’t. He told me a sob story, his wife’s got cancer and he needs the tow bar to get them back to Missouri, where they got family to help out. Shoot! I almost gave him the tow bar. It was probably all lies.”

“It’s early yet. Maybe he’ll be back.”

“Well, if he don’t show, I’m out a hundred bucks. But cancer, see, I know cancer. It’s what got my Millie. I know what it’s like watching your wife fail.”

He describes Millie’s slow descent, a once vigorous and energetic woman reduced to using a cane, then a walker, finally a wheelchair, before being bedridden. Along the way she’d been subjected to various surgeries, unspeakable dismemberments—she’d had cancer of the uterus that spread to her breasts, her lungs, her spine, finally settling in her brain. Towards the end, not knowing who he was, she lay there in the hospital full of wires and tubes; bald of any hair including eyebrows and lashes, dried out as a bundle of sticks, no better than a living—if you call that *living*—skeleton. I mumble sympathetic comments. I consider this opening up to be his gift to me. To be worthy of it, I put aside my pique.

I’d like to tell him about the shock of finding Emmett dead in our bed, his skin that odd gray color, the blood dark on the pillowcase. Cordovan brown blood, dead; menstrual blood. I threw out the linen. The rest—blankets, pillows, spread—was in this sale, and the Mexicans bought it. I want to tell Mr. Purdy how glad I was to see it go away. I can’t tell him, or anyone, about that ashy little rosebud nestled in the gray of Emmett’s pubic hair, an image that still haunts me. I’ll say nothing; in spite of the shock, horror, and disbelief that Emmett’s death left me with, my ordeal had been quick and merciful compared to his Millie’s lingering misery.

The mailman jeeps around the corner. He stops and has to get out to stuff mail in our cluster of boxes—I’d parked the Bronco on the street, to free up the driveway. “Oh, sorry about that,” I call, getting up to collect my delivery.

"Good day for a garage sale," he says, smiling, holding out my mail. He's wearing summer issue shorts, blue-gray, with a stripe up the sides, and I stare at his legs. Nice legs; curvy, good color, not too hairy.

"Yeah, we've had a real turnout."

I never paid much attention to him before; imagined, for some reason, his name was Vern or Ernie, something anonymous for an anonymous guy. But I see now that he's pleasant looking—tall, thin, with a long, thin face. A beaky nose, but I like it. A no-nonsense nose, one you wouldn't mistake for a turnip or a door-knob or an elbow. I smile at him, a real smile, it washes over my face like the tide coming in…then I catch myself…what am I doing! Flirting with the mailman! Ogling his legs! Another sign of my neediness. What the hell do I need! Not sex, surely not sex. Well, for starters, I need a man to smile back at me, to approve of me, to like me. Just as I am, no holding back. But it's not that simple—if that's simple. I need to be important to a man, to *count,* to come first. Had I come first, with Emmett? Maybe in some ways, but he'd been inaccessible; the part of him I'd wanted and needed had been off-limits. He'd denied me what would have made him "my" Emmett, the way Mr. Purdy's Millie had been "his" Millie. Now, it's too late, I'll never have that fundamental piece I'd needed so badly.

The mail is another form letter from a realtor; a slick flyer from a chichi department store; and the water bill, which isn't so high now that I'm living alone. I put the water bill in my pocket, the realtor's letter in the recycling, then flip through the flier. It's the biannual white sale, clearances on bedding—and here it is, a bedspread I must have. White and black and yellow, a pulsing display of daisies, fantasy daisies, perfect. I hear Emmett's voice, something about bumblebee colors, but *this* is the bedspread. I'll buy it for myself out of the proceeds from Emmett's stuff. I collapse in my chair, peaceful with the afternoon, with the time.

A couple of kids wearing huge baggy pants and turned-around baseball caps carry their skateboards up the driveway. "You got any Nintendo games, or videos?" asks one of them. They're of "minority" extraction, Filipino, South East Asian...Salvadorian?

When I say no, they jump on their boards and zip down the drive in a heart-stopping display of agility, athleticism, and foolhardy disregard for traffic, even though the street's a cul-de-sac and ends just above my house.

"They're going to break their necks," I say.

"Kids! Well, bless 'em. I tell you, it's their turn, these young people coming on. We had our chance, now let's see what they make of it. Can't create a bigger mess than we done."

The afternoon doesn't drag, it stops dead in its tracks. The sun freezes at an odd angle overhead and glares down, seeking us out even in the back of the garage. Only a few customers break the monotony. A guy with a silver buzz-cut stops by, asks about vacuum cleaners. No vacuums. I tell him, as a joke, that I'm looking for a vacuum, too, and if he finds a good one, let me know—I'll arm-wrestle him for it...and this last part makes both of us blush. What is the matter with me! I want him to leave and take my embarrassment with him. But he lingers to poke through the household stuff, makes a little pile of miscellaneous this and that. He circles through gardening equipment, which is almost gone. Clutching the weed eater, he comes up to me. "I had one just like this. Did a dandy job, but the dickens to get started."

I laugh. "Yeah, well, just between you and me, that's why it's out here. It works okay, but I've got my eye on a new one. Although I'm job-hunting...gotta watch my pennies."

"Looking for a job? We're hiring, or I should say, *they* are. Mountain Valley Cable. We're swamped on account of this new digital system they're introducing. Office's down in the Fremont complex off Main. Why don't you put in an application?"

I look in my pockets, pull out the water bill, write on the back of it. "Mountain Valley Cable, you say? Thanks for the tip. Tell you what, I'll knock half off the weed eater." It wasn't selling anyway.

His turn to laugh. "I don't have a yard anymore. Otherwise, that would be a deal."

"No yard...what a blessing. This one's getting away from

me. But I do the best I can," I add hastily.

"It looks okay. Just water it real good, then spread some weed 'n seed—it kills broadleaf stuff like dandelions and oxalis. Use a drop spreader and not one of those whirlybird things. You wouldn't want to get it on your nice shrubs."

"Oh, sure, of course not." I frown. What is he talking about?

"A lot of gardeners just bite the bullet and dig out dandelions—they're easy with one of those grabber things. Then too, there's a big negative in using chemicals, poisons, especially if you've got kids."

"Well, I have kids, or one. But she's not about to get down and play on the grass anymore. That's her over there." I indicate Amy, who's sending over a smirk.

"You're kidding! You're not old enough—well, excuse me, I don't want to sound like, well, I don't want to sound like I'm sounding."

I curl my lip. "That's perfectly okay. You sound fine. When I show up at..." I look at the water bill envelope, "...Mountain Valley Cable TV, who should I say sent me?"

"I'm Bruce, Bruce McDermott." He sticks out a hand and we shake.

"Uh, Peg Malone."

"Another Irisher."

"No, but my husband is, or was...he died last spring." I busy myself bagging his pick of the litter.

"Sorry." He hands over a five-dollar bill.

"No problem. Getting along fine," I say, making change. "Thanks for stopping. And for admitting it's the weed eater's fault, and not mine."

As soon as he drives off, Amy hurries over. "So?"

"So *what?*"

"What did he buy?"

"Exciting stuff. A spatula, bowls, mixing spoons, bread knife...let's see, what else."

"That's enough to tell me he's a throw-out."

"What?"

"His wife threw him out, he's setting up his own kitchen."

“The way you jump to conclusions! Ridiculous!” I frown, am about to embark on a lecture, but Amy flounces back to her card table. I settle into my thoughts, delivering to myself a lecture: no more Silver Foxes. Absolutely not. I’m glad to be alone for a bit. Mr. Purdy has taken a break, I have the garage to myself.

Then a surprising thing happens. The man with the sick wife comes back for the tow bar, but with only half the money. Mr. Purdy reappears, they talk over a deal, walking around the contraption, now on the lawn. Finally I see the buyer hand over some bills, the two men shake hands, and load the thing into a rattly pickup. Mr. Purdy watches it depart, shambles up the driveway on his wishbone legs, and shrugs. “What the hell.”

Mr. Purdy is a good person, better than I am. He’s kind and tolerant, and understanding. I could tell him about Emmett, but why would I want to do that? Mr. Purdy has had enough troubles of his own. What I will do, I will make him some real gingerbread, serve it with applesauce and whipped cream.

Only a smattering of people for a long time; then there’s a final rush. Among the newcomers is the manager from Singing Waters, who’d showed me the condo unit. She recognizes me, too. “Don’t I know you? Something about a sports car?”

“Uh, well, actually—“

“Yeah, it was you. Your husband just died? The one who smoothed out an embankment with the car and broke a water main?” She looks pointedly at Mr. Purdy who’s demonstrating a paint sprayer, kneeling before it as if it’s an idol, or a pet dog.

“Oh,” I say hurriedly, “*he’s* not my husband, he’s a neighbor helping out.”

“Cute man.”

Cute? I am struck: men aren’t cute. Babies and puppies and knit tops are cute. Men are …intriguing (like that Bruce fellow), or rugged, distinguished, attractive, personable, interesting, maybe even handsome. Emmett had been handsome. But Mr. Purdy *cute?* His jowls hang down like turkey wattles, and his nose and ears sprout too many wayward hairs. He’s wearing brown polyester pants, and a green and brown plaid shirt, but the brown isn’t the same brown as the one in the pants. They’re both permanent press, and have seen better days. But he *is* cute, by damn, and I should come first with him, not Frieda.

"A neighbor, huh?" The woman steps closer. "That makes me think, well, I want to tell you that you'd be a fool to leave this nice neighborhood. Singing Waters, it's okay, but you never get to know anybody. The people leave in the morning, they come home at night, they go in their condos and shut the door. No sense of community. There's nothing for them to do around the place on account of they got Miguel and Jesus and Jorge, and me and the maids, doing it all for them. I been there two years, and I don't know a soul. Well, that's just between you and me. A word to the wise. Don't tell them I said that."

"Thank you, I appreciate it. I'm not going to move anyway. It was just a thought."

"That's good. Don't do anything you'll regret later. How much you want for this?" She holds out one of Emmett's belts.

"How about a buck."

"Wow. A bargain. I better look around some more." She wanders off, then returns with a scarlet watered silk vest. Emmett wore it with a dark blue shirt. "How much?"

"Uh, two-fifty."

"Can I have a bag? We came in the pickup, I don't want it to get dirty."

Mr. Purdy sells the woman's husband the paint sprayer, a set of jackstands, and portable ramps. After they leave he rubs his hands together, satisfied. "See? I told you there would be a spurt toward the end, a last gasp. Well, almost time to fold our tent and close down."

"Now I have to take in all this stuff, after all that work of getting it out here." I want him to tell me not to bother, that he'll take care of it for me. Load it into his pickup and make it disappear. As if he's the father, telling the child it's all right, go on to bed, I'll clean up. He could be my father; he's old enough. Then too, he doesn't have anything else to do because most of what he brought over, and all of Frieda's, has been sold, but only half of mine is gone.

Then I think, *half of it is gone, HALF!* And I feel an upwelling of spirits, a relaxing of something that has been constraining me. Like taking off a tight bra, or shoes that pinch. Room! Freedom! Release! I feel too good to feel bad; maybe later, yes, I'll work on a guilt trip later. But why should I? I no longer, nor did I ever, owe Emmett anything.

Mr. Purdy surveys the leftovers, says with a shrug, "Sometimes what you think is your best stuff doesn't move. Garage sales can fool ya. If I was you, I'd make a list, haul it down to the Humane Society's Thrift Shop, then take it off your income tax, a deduction." Then he says how much he'd enjoyed the day, what a treat to feel useful again. I smile, I smile a real smile. I say, me, too, I had a great day. A lovely time.

Just as he's leaving, I call out, "Mr. Purdy? Mr. Purdy, I don't even know your first name."

"It's Edwin. Or Millie called me Ed." He comes back to me, holds out his hand. "Edwin, here, glad to meet you."

I laugh, shake his hand. "I'm Peg. Thanks, Edwin. Thanks, again for your help."

"My pleasure," he says, and leaves.

After counting the money, I tell Amy that despite slow sales, my share is enough for the dress, the earrings, and the bedspread. Then Amy goes home, too. I am glad to be alone. Before closing the door of the garage, now filled with leftovers, I glance at Emmett's workbench. I'd cleared it off by sweeping the mess into one corner. It's still there, but now takes up less room. One of Emmett's poems...I go in the house to chase it down in that folder. Something about his workbench, about his ability to fix things. Yes. I read it again:

> I am a work of art; I am what God intended—
> All but my injured heart that must quite soon be mended.
> I'll take myself apart, I'll see what makes me tick—
> Unfolding life's green chart—this ought to do the trick.
> My workbench boils with gear and wheel and sprockets,
> My soul struck dumb with fear, my brain with hands in pockets—
> Beyond me, I confess, this troubled bloodless gadget.
> A fixer once, now less—I'm tired, I'm sick, I've had it.

He'd crossed out "broken" and put in "injured" so I'm not sure what he was getting at, but the rest of it's pretty plain. Doggerel, really, because I understand that poetry, if it's any good, shouldn't rhyme. All his stuff's heavy on rhyme. And heavy with the depression that gripped him toward the end. Ah, well. I'm tired; it's late. Time to call it a day.

When the garage sale dust cleared, when I got my wits about me again, I decided against that silk dress—what had I been thinking! But later that next week, to celebrate my new job, I did buy that bedspread and those pinecone earrings; after all, earrings like that will go anywhere, with anything. I'll get my money's worth out of them.

To celebrate the earrings, to accommodate them, I had my ears pierced in a jewelry store in the mall. Amy said she'd do it with a needle and an ice cube, but the store was offering a special: if you bought gold studs, you got the piercing free.

(Who the hell am I kidding…of course I'll buy that dress. I can hardly wait to go down and try it on again. Then I'll have the nice little clerk, a sweet thing done to the nines, wrap it in tissue, tuck it into one of those elegant Splurge bags. After all, I'm working hard honing an edge on my self-esteem: I deserve that dress.)

(Plus, I deserve to be seen carrying that glorious bag—stiff silver metallic paper, with a crimson SPLURGE across its front, and cunning padded handles—I'll treasure it, too, a memento. I'll find a use for it.)

CHAPTER 9

About that new job, well, I go down to Mountain Valley Cable TV for an application, and they hire me on the spot. I tell Amy—this is that night, after my first day at work—that I got hired because of Emmett. The manager, Vi Corbet, had known Emmett, or actually her husband Ed had known him. So it's due to Emmett's influence that I succeed; but if he hadn't sabotaged me, I wouldn't have had to apply in the first place. Of course I don't say this to Amy. Instead, I tell her about Tiffany. "If it'd been up to this little bitch Tiffany—"

Amy laughs a bit snidely, "Mom, you're so dramatic. You don't even know this woman."

"Are you telling me not to validate the evidence that my own senses provide? Are you questioning my judgement?"

She draws back. "No, of course not. Well, maybe a little. You're not yourself lately."

"Why should I be? Where did *being myself* get me?" I take a breath. "By the way, would you please use a coaster under that glass? All the work I put into this table, I don't want rings on it." I know I'm pushing her, but I also know I can get away with it because her nails are painted rosy pink.

"Oops, sorry. Go on, tell me the rest."

We're having a quick pick-up supper of tuna salad, and I lay down my fork to better focus on my story. How I go up to the Customer Service desk and a girl (Tiffany) greets me, if you can call it that.

"Help you?" she says around her gum, flicking a flat glance over my looking-at-condos dark suit, white blouse.

"I heard you were hiring? I want to apply?"

Without a word, but with a pained expression, she gets up, rifles through a file drawer. I'm thinking, oh, poor thing, she's been ill.

A thin girl, sallow, pasty skin, long stringy blond hair. Her part shows an inch of black roots; her eyebrows are plucked or shaved, and redrawn with harsh pencilled lines. Cancer? Chemotherapy, radiation? Later, that afternoon, Helen—the other clerk who works in the back—tells me it's a practiced look, the punk thing.

Amy rubs at the circle left by her glass, forks at her salad. "Punk! That is so over, so…juvenile. In the corporate world—" But she trails off, either because she can't focus her thought, or she's gotten a look at my expression, which must be war-like. I've had a hell of a day.

I've got this job, yeah, and now I don't want it. I long to go back to moping around the house, which seems, in retrospect, an enchanted existence. I feel my life taking a deep breath, about to speak, and I don't want to hear what it has to say. No more than Amy wants to hear what I could say. *In the corporate world... What could you possibly know about the corporate world? You spend your life in a Spandex workout suit.*

Anyway, Amy isn't really paying attention to me. She has that muzzy expression—I know it well—indicating…a new love interest? How can that be? She was man-less at the garage sale only a Saturday ago. She hasn't had time to reconnect, has she? This look, plus the nail polish, annoys me; I undergo a prickly shock, as if a part of me that had gone to sleep is waking up, getting the circulation back.

"Okay, okay, Mom, go on with your story."

My *story* is that as Tiffany is about to hand over, reluctantly, an application, a woman more my age than Tiffany's comes in the rear door and calls, "Everything okay, Tiff?"

"She's asking about a job."

"I'll take care of it, Tiff, hon. You're busy with that inventory."

"Yeah, sure, Vi." More gum snapping.

At this point, Amy pushes her plate away, props her pointed chin on a nail-polished hand. "Snaps her gum! Gross!"

"Yeah, well, they're not formal at that place. I was overdressed. The code's sweatshirts and jeans and running shoes."

"Sweatshirts! Too hot!"

"Not in there. It's like a cave. On account of these old computers. Amy, the system they use, it's those of F-stops across the top. No mouse."

At Amy's blank look, I say, "Back to how your dad plays into this. Vi, her name is Vi Corbet, well, she takes one look at my résumé, says, oh, *Malone,* any relation to Emmett Malone? I say yes, and she says how sorry they were to read the obit. She comes around the counter, holds out her hand. I give her mine, by now I'm so nervous, it's like offering her a dead fish. And...I got the job."

"I don't understand the connection."

"Amy, her husband and your dad had been buddies in junior college."

"Great. Lucky for you."

"I don't know how *great.* I mean, who is this Ed Corbet? I never heard your dad mention him. *Lucky* for me to get hired...I dunno. Vi goes on about how she wants someone mature, sensible. Does that sound like me?"

"Sure does."

"She says she's sick of these kids who think in ones and zeros, hardwired, like machines. Dyeing their hair green, covered with tattoos, piercings. Did I know, she says, that these kids can't give blood on account of what they've done to their bodies? Who's going to give blood when the whole generation has gone crazy?"

"I don't know how you'd answer that."

"Especially with Tiffany sitting there, glaring from behind the bull's-eye makeup. I said I had a daughter who'd not done those things, who could give blood." I laugh, to show Amy it's a joke, but she just stares. "Then she said this odd thing."

"Well, what! Don't leave me hanging."

"She says my daughter, Emmett's daughter, must take after me. If she's that sensible and level-headed."

Amy sits up straight. "See! I told you Dad was weird."

"*Weird.* Just exactly what does that mean? Covers a lot of territory, if you ask me," I snap. I clatter off with our plates. I want Amy to go. Nevertheless, I give her a chance. "What's going on with you?"

“Nothing,” she says, with that sly look. “You’ve had a hard day. I’m clearing out.”

Hard day—Amy has no idea.

Vi’s intent on the paperwork; otherwise, I’d ask her about the connection to Emmett. But I’ll have time later—there will be a later, as I seem to be getting hired.

Vi awes me. She’s a no-nonsense executive type. Her short dark hair frames her face like a pair of parentheses; her makeup is understated, her earrings small pearls (in contrast to Tiffany, who wears what appear to be safety pins); neat figure in a dark sweatshirt and pants. Dressed up, she’d be the picture of self-assured success, like a model in an ad for a luxury car, a Lexus or Mercedes, on her way to preside over a board meeting.

Vi shows me around. She points out my workstation, a side-car thing next to Tiff’s desk. Then I follow her down a long dark hall to the conference room. Vi says, “I’ll get you started, the training session stuff, you know. But first, here’s the washroom, unisex, so lock up. The storeroom, a locker, place to keep your things.” Sotto voce, “Don’t carry cash, and watch your purse—Tiff and I have both been ripped off.” In a normal tone, “The warehouse.” She pushes on a pressure bar, we step into a large room, blessedly warm, the walls lined with boxed equipment, the receivers and parts for their new digital system.

Above a hum of activity, Vi calls out, her voice echoing off high walls, “This is Peg Malone, people, new office person. Peg, Eugene and Al, installers. And Bruce, our chief troubleshooter.” Hard-hatted, safety goggled—I stifle the imagery around the word *nerd*—he’s barely recognizable as the guy at my garage sale. He gives me a grin and a thumb’s up. “And Helen, our all-around Girl Friday. That’s Zack back there on the ladder. Zack, king of the stacks, huh, Zack?” she sings out to a kid who looks like he ought to be in junior high. Her condescension surprises me. I wonder if Zack is aware of it, but all I can make out in the distance is the turned-around baseball cap, the big clothes. I smile and nod, offer to shake hands with one of the installers—Al? Eugene? but pull back and laugh self-consciously when I note his leather gloves. Then Vi closes the door, shutting out the noise, but the warmth, too.

Back down the hall to the glassed-in cubicle, the conference room. "Coffee?" says Vi. "No? I don't blame you. By this time in the morning, it's vile." She clears a place for me at a battered table, sweeping into a pile some papers, tucking in the top of a half-empty box of donuts, pushing it to one side; brushes crumbs into the trashcan, empties ashtrays. On a counter simmers the poisonous coffee, condensing into syrupy acid. "Moon River" plays softly through overhead speakers. "Just got time to get you started before I leave."

"You don't work here?

"No, I'm from the district office in Oakland. I come in once in a while to give Tiff a hand. Traffic was murder this morning."

"When you're not here, she's the boss?"

"Yes, she's a whiz. You'll love her."

The flat green eyes, the makeup, the black outfit. Yeah, right, I'm going to love her.

The *training*: I read through a loose-leafed binder, fill in an answer sheet like a junior high school worksheet. The section about company policy and/or philosophy is numbingly dull but understandable. The rest of it—graphs, circuitry diagrams, the specs, jargon, lingo, model numbers, charts of plug-ins, add-ons, modules, clock set-ups—might as well be in Urdu or Sanskrit, and runs together in a mishmash of confusion. I tell myself it's not that bad, just hang tight—but I'm on the verge of despair. Then like an intervening miracle—the cavalry riding over the hill, the FBI cracking the code, the fairy godmother waving her magic wand—Vi sticks her head in and says go to lunch, an hour break.

There's a parking ticket on my car. I stuff it in the glove box, drive down to a Subway, collapse in a plastic booth with a BLT and a Dr. Pepper, trying to ignore a thin panic, a bubble of hysteria. Not the right job; I'm not right for it. But I always told myself I could do anything I wanted to, if I set my mind to it...although I haven't done much.

But that's not true. Temp work is tough, demands adaptability and a range of skills. I'd been a success, had even liked some jobs. Working in the library, and at the main office of the school district. In the photo booth at Mountain View Mall. A blast, a kick, really. During slack times ungumming envelopes of developed pictures, seeing what people take shots of. Flower gardens, children, lofty scenery. And nudes and sex parties, drunken brawls—I stared at *those* people when they picked up their photos.

Bad jobs, too. A stint at the VA office in the Mission District. On the sidewalk outside, stepping around pools of piss and puke; in the lobby over bundles of drunks and bums, some of them Vietnam vets. There, but for the grace of God, lay Emmett, and I puff up a bit thinking that I'd influenced him, kept him steady and centered. I give myself credit for that.

At the beginning, sure, I wanted to do the hippie bit, decorate with beads and cushions on the floor, hang a huge poster of Richard Nixon on the bathroom door, the one of him saying, "I am not a crook." But Emmett had shown deeper flaws. He was the one who lied to the property assessor, lied on our income tax. Lied to Amy, told her a bunch of bull about his parents, how gifted, cultured, discriminating they were (they died before Amy got to know them).

I was the one with common sense, including a sense of what was right. He'd latched onto me, he'd installed me in his life as you'd install a stabilizer on a boat. I kept him level. I've shortchanged my impact on him.

I've got a certain amount of steel in my backbone. Whatever the job, if I set my mind to it, I could see it out.

And that's the answer. Of course! Hold out until 5 o'clock, then go home and live my real life. I can do this, I feel determination developing in me, around me—like a hardening shell. Properly armored, I can get through a day at Mountain Valley Cable, one hour at a time, as Emmett had gotten through one hour at a time at Freeway Furniture. I recall one of his poems—and remark to myself how I'm carrying around his menopausal hogwash, when I can't even remember my grocery list! It's...infuriating, a curse, something I've got to get over, like a case of the flu:

Here I am, Fortune's pawn. I stand, then sit and wait.
Blue with doze, I yawn. Stillborn at ten of eight
As t'was before gray dawn. Where *is* the fucking freight?

And then too much it comes,
There's never enough time.
My shop runs red, it hums…
And so I pass my prime?
To stack and pack and strap,
To ship and sort and send
This crap all o'er the map?
My labor will not end.

It's not so bad, I say,
Onward I will fight
To end this goddamned day
March forward into night.

For all's in icy vain, Mammon's wood will be done—
My home I will attain, and then I'll call *this* fun.

He'd been caught between not enough to do, and too much. So what! Besides, what the hell could I have done about it? Jump out of a cake in the lunchroom at noon? Meet him at night by the garage door wrapped in Saran Wrap, a rose between my teeth, a cold beer in one hand, *TV Guide* in the other? The man pissed me off! What had gone on at Freeway Furniture was out of my control…besides, it must have been a romp compared to what I'm up against.

Freeway Furniture has a showroom, but their main business is supplier to other outlets around the country, around the world, and this burden of shipping had been Emmett's. Lately, though, more comes into the States from the Philippines, China, Indonesia, than goes out. Emmett had felt this narrowing, another vise grip—too much production for too few consumers. But the global marketplace was out of his control.

Then onto his parched stressed landscape Maggie Quinn had

sashayed, willing, ripe, ready, and he'd fallen. But I will not dwell on this, I will not. I give my Dr. Pepper a vicious slurp, then switch over to a new line of thinking that's helping me these days. I am creating a new Emmett, adding parts, discarding others, making him into such a man as he'd never been. A new improved version, this numinous presence, my own private cheerleader, one I can turn to, confide in, depend on. The mental health of this maneuver I will not examine, not yet. I will, as soon as I'm able. Something has to happen first, and I'm not sure what it is.

I glance at my watch...holy cow, I'm late. I grab my jacket and purse and drive back to Mountain Valley Cable. I pull into their lot, which is down an alley and behind the warehouse. I park in an EMPLOYEES ONLY slot. I am an employee, I belong. Take that, Emmett Malone!

The first clue that things have changed: the music's no longer mainstream; now it's rap, Snoop Doggy Dogg or some such rot. It plays softly, a throb, like a low-grade fever, the words not quite comprehensible.

"You're late," says Tiffany. "Lunch *hour,* get it?"

"I know, I'm sorry. It won't happen again. I'll explain to Vi—"

"Vi's gone back to Oakland. I'm the boss now. Finish that manual, then get started."

I put my coat back on, take up my chore in the icy conference room, hunch over the loose-leaf spiral-bound notebook. More diagrams, charts, parts, tables of serial numbers. Undergo an almost fatal attack of sleepiness, take off my coat, am about to go for the poisonous coffee when there's a stir in the outer office.

"Who's parked in my spot? A beige Ford Bronco?"

I leap up, scramble out into the hall. "Sorry...I didn't realize..."

"Oh, it's you, I should have known," says Bruce, blushing.

He *blushes*, mottled red creeps into his cheeks. I am alarmed. "That's okay, sorry, I didn't mean to jump."

"I'll move my car."

"Oh, no, please. Sorry."

I notice Tiffany watching our exchange. The smile she'd incubated for Bruce is stillborn and the cold dead look comes back into her eyes. "You know Peg, our new clerk?" she says.

"Yeah, well, no," he says. "Just met her at a garage sale. Told her about the job. Glad you're aboard, Peg. My fault, the parking. Spaces are not assigned. We're just in a rut here, it's me, not you."

"Well, don't just stand there." Tiff snaps her words, and her gum. "Finish that manual, get going."

"Oh, sure, sorry." I retreat, gladly. Don't want any part of office politics. She can have him; I don't want him.

I finish the blasted training manual, with no idea how it's supposed to help me. Thus *trained,* I am theoretically able to take my place under the headset, which frees up Tiffany. With a sigh of relief, she goes back to staring into her computer. Despite Vi's apparent disapproval, Tiff does think in ones and zeros, and a clone of her is what Vi should have hired.

My main job, now, is to troubleshoot, over the phone, the new digital systems. People call in with questions. "What's this OK stand for, this button in the middle?" "What happened to STRZ? It used to be right next to ENC, but now it's gone." "If the clock doesn't work in that black box, will the programs be on at the right time?"

At first I don't have a clue. I hiss at Tiffany, "He says there's nothing but static on HBO. What should I tell him?"

"Really, you read the manual. Figure it out. Use your head."

Then again, "This woman says the sound keeps fading. What should I tell her?"

A loud put-upon sigh. "You still don't get it! No one's going to do your job for you. Use some logic! What's with you any-way!"

So I'm on my own, or it's me and the useless manual. The two of us, getting used to digital. But I learn to cope. Many eld-erly, not able to think in ones and zeros, have problems, and I can untangle their snafus by tracing which buttons they've pushed on their remotes. I flip through the manual to "cause and effect," find the column labeled PROBLEM, then read across to SOLUTION. At first I'm just one step ahead of them, which is nerve-wracking. Then things ease up: I parry their thrusts with increasing comfort, and bullshit. In fact, I sort of like it, especially helping the older ones. "And then you go to the Main Menu...see if it reads AM or PM."

"Push the OK button every time, except after three digits. That's right, not anything over Channel 100."

"Did you push both CABLE and TV buttons? Did you push POWER each time?"

But some customers want their old systems back, with the simple components. Frustrated and impatient, they scold me. I sweet-talk, wheedle; I cajole. "Give it one more chance; this is no problem. Yes, I know you're eighty-two years old, and you're missing *All My Children...Guiding Light...The 700 Club*...this will be fine, and you'll catch up. With the plot, or whatever."

It's my job to wait on walk-ins, people who don't trust the mail, or who want to complain. I know some of them. Larry comes in with his new girlfriend, guiding her with a proprietary hand on her back. In spite of myself, I stare. Amy will want to know. The girl is petite, a froth of a blonde with round blue eyes—Amy will not be pleased, and maybe I won't tell her. "Mrs. Malone," exclaims Larry. "Hi! Remember me?"

"Oh, sure, uh—"

"Larry Sturdevant, Amy's ...friend. How's Amy doing? This is Amber? We want to sign up for cable, the deluxe package. Got a new place, new big screen TV, way better than that old one. We're doing so good. Amber's got a great job, she's a photographer's model, just got back from a shoot at Pebble Beach."

I smile, nod at Amber. I think this Kewpie doll will not willingly push the Hoover that Larry swapped Amy for the computer. I'd objected at the time because I knew my own vacuum would go AWOL, which it has. But Amy said she wanted to keep the computer and learn it, so, I give in, like always. The result is I'm continually loading my Hoover into Amy's Mustang. Emmett would be having a fit, which somehow makes it easier for me to loan the vacuum. I am getting contrary, as difficult to get along with as...Tiffany.

Larry rattles on about financial successes, both his and Amber's. I know I'm supposed to carry this information back to Amy. I think, smiling into Larry's sly brown eyes, into Amber's empty blue ones, you can both go to hell.

It's also my job to deal with delivery people, to sign for whatever comes. Jerry, the UPS driver, stops every morning. I've seen him across the street delivering survival gear to Lyle, Frieda's husband. Jerry takes to hanging around, shooting the breeze. A short jolly Santa Claus of a guy, I think he's okay until one day he starts making passes. I *think* that's what he's doing. "I love your hair, it's spectacular," he mutters while I sign his clipboard. At Amy's salon, I had it trimmed into a new asymmetrical shape, with a bleached foxtail in the front. "It's dynamite with those earrings," he says, complimenting the dangly pinecones.

Another time Jerry leans in and breathes, "Oh, babe, you smell good enough to eat." He's complimenting the Bluegrass cologne I unearthed in the back of the bathroom cabinet, a bottle of scent I'm sure is older than he is.

Again, "That color on you, it oughta be illegal, man, that shade of red." It's a new crimson sweatshirt with a hokey poodle on the front, bought because it reminded me of that sweet dream of creating balloon animals in the dime store window.

I don't know what to do with Jerry. I can't deal with his slippery compliments. I'd like to run and hide when I see him coming, but I have to sign his clipboard. I'm used to doing without, or with very little. Just a pat, a kind word, a smile—or not even a smile, just the absence of a frown, and I react naturally. But I'm helpless with Jerry. Vi or Amy or any experienced woman would know what to do. Just whisper, "Sexual harassment," and that would settle him down, put out his fire. But I can't do that. Why not? Because I was raised to be polite. Of course I know it goes deeper than that. I was raised to avoid giving injury, which means that I am self-effacing and submissive, especially with men, to the point of assuming blame whether it is mine or not. I was raised to protect men from themselves. This is an attitude I failed to instill in Amy, thank goodness.

Tiffany watches these exchanges; she watches and listens. If she wants to flirt with him, why did she give me the chore of dealing with the delivery people? But maybe it's the dog in the manger bit—she doesn't want Jerry, until he goes for someone else. Nevertheless, I'm on guard, as uneasy with her attention as I am with his.

Tiff watches me with the FedEx guy, Raoul. He appears in the afternoon, backs up his van, *beep, beep, beep,* and dollies case lots through the double glass doors, down the hall, into the warehouse. Raoul's manner is polite but remote. His black eyes droop, his mustache droops, his whole face droops, as if he's experiencing some terrific sadness, a tragedy that has knocked him for a loop. I imagine disappearances, border shootings, Green Card problems; I am intrigued, I'd like to crack him open like a clam, a nut, a jar of salsa. I make friendly small talk. "Hey, Raoul, you're early (late, right on time)." "What's going on (coming down, the good word)?" "You seen the price of gas (the game last night, the weather report)?" A glance from down-tilted obsidian eyes, a glimmer of white teeth under the Poncho Villa mustache; that's all I get. It isn't nothing, but it's not much, either.

Because he's impossible, the project seduces me. I ache to get under his terra cotta exterior. He's as beautiful and remote as an Aztec god, and I have a weakness for guys who withhold, are inaccessible. It, he, becomes a challenge, a game; and he wins, as I know he will—anything else would scare me, to tell the truth. He leaves with his secrets intact, his tragedies, his dreams, his dramas. Every day I watch him escape, swinging lithely into his door-less van. I imagine him swinging up the stone face of a jungle-shrouded ziggurat, a dagger between his teeth. But, I tell myself, he's on his way to sacrifice a virgin, so get over it. I wonder if Tiffany ever had any luck.

Between the humidity of Jerry and the ice of Raoul, there's Sid, the mailman. He's not *my* mailman, the neighborhood guy with nice legs, but a commercial deliverer. He's friendly and harmless as a puppy, and (sometimes) as annoying as one that jumps up on you with muddy paws, insistently sniffing your crotch. But he brings with him an aura of leather, newly cut grass, and gasoline; he brings into the cold office the warm outside that I miss badly, now that autumn's hard on us.

Sid tells jokes, cable TV jokes. "These two cable guys were flying to Hawaii on a four-engine plane, and one of the engines conks out. The captain comes back and says, 'Don't worry, we'll make it, but we'll be an hour late.'

"Then the second engine goes, and the captain says, 'Don't worry, we'll be three hours late, is all.' Then the third engine conks and the captain says, 'We'll be six hours late, but everything's okay.' Then the fourth engine quits and one cable guys says to the other, 'Shit, we're going to be up here all day.'"

Dutifully, I laugh, thankful that he doesn't tell dirty jokes. I am as defenseless against dirty jokes as I am against flirtiness. Almost light-headed with the realization that he'll soon be gone, I initial his clipboard, then take on my natural coloration, my camouflage—which is to disappear under my headset. As a temp, I learned to do that. Temps are invisible. Once I worked in an insurance office for a couple of weeks. Came back from lunch one day and the guy who sat at the next desk got up and came to the counter to wait on me. "Help you?" Customer-polite. Temps have no presence.

For Tiffany, I have presence. She watches and waits, and I am worn out with it. I don't know what she wants, or what she's got against me. But there is something electric in the air when one of the men talks to me—it hisses and hums with hostility, as if a downed power line were writhing loose on the floor. Tiffany of the green eye shadow and black clothes, who slams and sulks and skulks, who watches for Vi to head back for Oakland so she can switch the FM from E-Z Listenin' to K-Porn. Tiffany has it in for me. She waits, hard-edged with resentment.

It's not because Sid tells me jokes. I have heard the men—Al or Eugene or one of the vendors—tell her a joke or two. These, apparently, also involve cable installers. I overheard one about installers going into a whorehouse, because one of the girls...and the teller's voice drops so I can't make it out. Because one of the girls...what? Is getting poor reception? Has her wires crossed?

Needs new plug-ins? What's the punch line, I want to shout. I'll hide my embarrassment, I promise.

I see Zack, the warehouse gofer, come up behind Tiff and touch her shoulder, smile into her face, murmur into her ear. But Tiff likes Zack—they are of the same generation, and certainly of the same psychic bent—so this titillation is allowed. Tiff flirts with Zack, although she lives with someone. Despite the punk look, which I associate with rebellious freethinking, I have overheard Tiff on the phone giving orders to Someone. "At Albertson's, buy milk, bread—not that seedy kind, but plain white bread—bananas—not too green, but not too ripe, either—and coffee. Now," commands Tiff, "read back to me what I said. What kind of bread? And the milk, tell me again, is it skim, 1%, 2% or whole?" I long to get in it, mix it up, say to Tiffany, "The coffee, is it regular or decaf? Thirty-two ounce can or forty-eight? Colombian or French Roast?"

I wonder what Bruce, blushing Bruce from my garage sale, thinks of Tiffany. But Bruce is the exact opposite of Raoul: I sense that he's available, he's even eager. This makes me avoid him, as I do Jerry and Sid. I can't win. No one needs to tell me that I have issues around men. I know that.

So I am alarmed when Bruce from the warehouse appears with his own bagged lunch (I'd started bringing mine, an economy measure), settles with me to eat in the conference room. Amy was right about him: he's a throw-out. His wife evicted him, and he lives with his grown daughter, Isabel, in an apartment out near the freeway. He's adrift, and I am uneasily aware of his dependence, his neediness, his tendency to grasp at straws. He's attractive enough, a tall guy with a lean runner's body. He wears his iron filings hair in an old-fashioned flattop that reminds me of my father, a style uncool, yet cool at the same time. I like his gray eyes. But they're full of vulnerability, susceptibility; I'm afraid he'll latch onto me and sink us both. I'm not that strong. He should know that.

I'm relieved when Helen, also from the warehouse, begins to pack her lunch, too. At noon we unwrap our sandwiches together. Ham and cheese for me, something extravagant for Helen (she lives to eat), peanut butter and jelly for Bruce—he confides that Izzie is no cook, their kitchen is disorganized, ill-equipped. The three of us: are we kooks? Is that our bond? Are we affording each other cover? I accept that Helen will eat with me—two single women…but what's with Bruce? I have suspicions about his motives, consider him unmanly, to choose the company of women over the men available—Eugene and Al also bring bag lunches and eat in the warehouse. Is Bruce gay? Is he looking for someone to do his ironing?

I welcome Helen wholeheartedly—I see clearly now that I need more people, more women, in my life. Helen is a jolly short plump woman a bit younger than I, the kind you'd call a "gal," a career single who keeps busy on the weekends. She drives one of the new Beetles, a convertible, and she talks of spinning along with the top down on the Silverado Trail to the Wine Country, or out to the Mother Lode, or into San Francisco for a shopping spree. Listening to her stories, I begin to long for a new car, too—as if that will fill up some of the holes in my life. A new VW, like Helen's, to replace my clunky Bronco—well, I'll never get that far. But I enjoy the fantasy, and I recall with pleasure that night of sleeping in my little old VW behind the bank, the nascence of myself as a real person, separate and apart from Emmett.

On the whole, though, I'm glad of my lunch company, because Amy and I have fallen apart. When Emmett had been alive, Amy and I had practiced a stealth alliance, had established a conspiratorial understanding. Without him providing an adversarial backdrop, our relationship breaks down. Amy becomes preoccupied; I grow testy, and I blame myself for alienating her with attacks of insensitivity, of rudeness such as I displayed that night of the tuna salad. In short, we're operating at crosscurrents. I suggest we meet for lunch; but Amy is busy. I mention shopping, but no, there's that thing she has to do. Come for dinner—same excuse (I see it as an excuse), too much to do.

So despite my tendency to be a loner, I welcome my lunch companions and I begin to open up to them. At first it's superficial nonevents—how Amy borrows the vacuum cleaner just when I'm ready to use it; how hard the Bronco is on gas; how easy to save money on groceries when you're shopping for one. By now I've told them about Emmett's shocking death, and how it had thrown me for a loop. Helen, who urges me to get out and get on with it, says not to tell people—men—that I'm a widow. Men don't cotton to widows. Just say I'm alone, no reason given—which is what Bruce does. He admits his ex-wife filed first, then evicted him from their house with a court order. He does not elaborate on the cause.

While we eat, Tiffany stomps by in the hall, glaring in at us. I wonder why she doesn't go somewhere and scarf up some bolts, nails, and batwings. Despite that grocery list she gave Someone, I've never seen her eat anything. Finally she can't stand it, she interrupts, "Peg, there's a guy on the phone who says you told him he'd get a discount if he put his bill on Visa."

"Ridiculous."

"You come out here and tell him."

"I'm eating lunch. You tell him, or get a number and I'll call back."

Tiffany is in an especially black mood. This morning she locked her keys in her car and had to call a locksmith. In front of the whole office, in front of the whole world—at least as far as our complex is concerned—she had to admit she'd done a stupid thing.

"What is her problem!" I grouch to Bruce and Helen.

"Rumor has it when things smooth out, there'll be permanent office work for one person, not two. It's politics. You know somebody, or something. Tiff's afraid Vi'll pick you, on account of you got pull."

I put down my sandwich. "I've got pull! You gotta be kidding. Who do I know? I thought it had something to do with you. With her designs on you."

"Me!" Bruce blushes. "Designs on me? No way."

For a reason I'm not willing to analyze, this pleases me immensely. Now, if I can figure out where he stands in relation to Helen….

One day after lunch, I notice Sean "Puff Daddy" Combs is replaced with Bert Kaemphfert's schlock. Vi's voice interrupts

"Bye, Bye, Blues," pages me into the conference room. I go, filled with dread.

Vi is friendly, too friendly. She says I must have had to deal with a difficult transition, a readjustment. She asks if everything's okay now, how's my life outside the office, do I have hobbies. Am I involved with people, a support group?

I mutter something about Amy, about my neighborhood friends. I tell her about my standing date with Mr. Purdy (who's seventy-eight years old, I hastily add) to eat oyster stew every Friday night at the Soup Kettle. I tell her about Irene bringing me chrysanthemums, Frieda a piece of apricot torte. Frieda asked me if I wanted some venison, and I said no. Vi laughs with me about this. She says she's squeamish about eating game, too.

Vi compliments me on the red sweatshirt, the one Jerry liked. She says she likes my new black leggings. I tell her they're Amy's—I'm losing weight, she's gaining; we're meeting in the middle at a size 8. Vi chuckles with me.

She grows serious, invites me to pull my chair in closer. She says that men gather around when there's a single woman giving them the come-on (that's not the word she uses, but that's what she means). I feel my face flush. Who is it: Jerry, Raoul, or Sid? Or even Bruce? Am I interfering with these helpless men, me, the conniving man-hungry woman?

Vi says it would pay me to check the signals I'm sending, because women are in control, in these kinds of situations. She goes on, "We're a team here, you know. Everyone has a job and gets it done. By now that must be clear. Tiffany might seem a bit rough around the edges, but she's a jewel, sharp and smart. I was hoping you'd get close to her. She can be a friend."

I murmur something, yes, of course. I'm thinking, Aha, it's Tiffany, she's carrying stories about me back to Vi. I should get close to her? Only when I'm wearing my silver cross, my garlic wreath.

Vi goes on about crossing the line from business to personal, how undermining, irresponsible. She spreads around some pat phrases about cooperation, teamwork, something about putting the good for the whole over selfish self-satisfaction, blah, blah,

blah. I can barely listen, I'm embarrassed, insulted.

At the end of her lecture, I go into the bathroom and gaze at my flaming cheeks, and into my eyes. I've started doing them with mascara and shadow and liner, but gently, not ferociously, like Tiffany. I wonder: Why all this subterfuge, now? Surely not to impress these men. I tell myself it's because I was bored with the way I looked. I embellish for the same reason I'd redo the bedroom. There's nothing wrong with the off-white color, we used the same paint as in the hall, but a nice soft yellow (to highlight my new bedspread) would brighten things up. However, now I question my motives. "Who am I turning into?" I ask my reflection.

CHAPTER 10

Slumped at my desk in the cable office, I stare into a rain-darkened afternoon. The double glass doors are smeared and dirty. What's eating Zack, I wonder; it's his job to keep them clean and he's been extra sullen and sluggish lately. Did he and Tiff have a falling out? Everyone's edgy, perhaps due to just losing an hour, going back to standard time.

I get the Windex to wash the glass myself, then pause in mid-swipe to watch a pair of crows in the parking lot. They're cavorting in a puddle of rainwater, laughing raucously, splashing each other while sharing a bath. First rain of the season, and on Halloween, too. It's also Friday, a double holiday.

Once I'd been glad when it rained on Halloween. It dampened Amy's urge to dress up and go out sexy. When she was little, and I was still in control, her costume was no problem. I'd put together odds and ends, create a semblance of a ballerina or a fairy princess or a cowgirl, something innocent, and I got away with it. But when she was older, say around twelve, Halloween gave her an excuse to paint on gaudy makeup—glittery swaths around her eyes, heavy rouge, mascara, and lipstick. Then it would rain, and she'd have to cover her bare midriff, her attempt at décolletage, with rain gear.

However, those crows—*they're* not ambivalent about Halloween rain, flapping and shaking water from their black suits. Probably a mated pair. Crows mate for life, and they can live thirty years or more. The partnership I'm watching could last longer than mine had with Emmett. I'm doing the math—they'll outlast me by six years—when Helen comes in from the warehouse.

"You nervous about tonight?" she says.

"Nah," I lie. "Perfect timing, having a blind date on Halloween. I can use a camouflage to get out of myself."

"Atta girl. *Blind date.* Peg, you kill me."

"What would you call it?"

"I dunno…that's a toughie."

I brush this off, vaguely nettled. "How about you?" I ask to divert her. "What're you doing?"

"I've got a friend in San Francisco; we're going out for some hijinks. What are you going as?" She's joined me, is also staring at the crows.

"A China girl, I've got one of those coolie hats, a dress with a mandarin collar, sandals. I hope I can dance in them. If I can dance, period."

The truth is I *am* nervous. Tonight I'm stepping out with Frieda's cousin to a singles' party down at the Elks hall. What prompted this: Frieda's been after me to get out, get out, get out, and that phrase of Vi's, *support group,* resounds in my head. Because I don't *really* have one, apart from Helen and Bruce, my lunch partners.

They are a sort of support. One day after work when my Bronco wouldn't start, I had to ask Bruce to give me a ride home to get Mr. Purdy who seems to speak the Bronc's language. On our way across town, I was self-conscious with Bruce, sat bolt upright, hadn't been with a man in his vehicle for so long. It's a huge diesel pickup, a rig (his term, "rig") he bought when his kids were little. At Christmas, as a family, they used to go to a tree farm in the Mother Lode to cut their own silver tip, and to get it home they needed the truck.

"You bought this—what is it?"

"A one-ton Dodge Ram, biggest they make, with the dual wheels and all."

"Just to haul a Christmas tree?"

"I know it sounds silly now, but me and Jan, we did everything for the kids. I, I miss my family. I hope we—my son and me—can work something out some day, get back together. Not Jan; she's remarried." He went on to say he and his son are estranged, but he lives with his grown daughter in an apartment complex across town.

This bleak recital of his family's fracturing brought him to the brink of tears. I was embarrassed, and irritated at having to witness such unadorned pain, such abject servility. I wanted to snap, "Get a grip, fella!" Instead, I asked how long he'd been divorced.

"Four years this coming Thanksgiving. But I'm not alone, I've got Izzie, Isabel, my daughter. She's twenty-four, just finished her CPA course. Todd, he's twenty-two, he still lives with Jan and…the new guy."

"Yes, but four years—"

"I know, only four years. I'm doing okay."

It occurred to me that some people, men, might be so damaged by their personal tragedies that they never recover. I vowed it wouldn't be that way for me, that I'd rebuild myself into being tougher, more capable, than I was when Emmett died. Which, I conceded, wouldn't be hard. Lately I'd been very critical of my former caviling, indecisive self.

"There. That's my house, the beige one," which was ridiculous: all these houses are beige. A monotone street of *beige.*

"Nice neighborhood, sort of like the one Jan and me lived in. Well, she's still there." A gulp. Then he went on, "Listen, are you sure you can deal with the Bronco?"

"Mr. Purdy," I said, clambering down about eight feet from the cab, "he knows the Bronc. He's good with it, and he's home, too. His lights are on."

And I hurried away to my real support group, well, not *group,* but one person—steady, dependable Mr. Purdy, who has been more valuable than a whole bunch of Bruces and Helens.

Taking me back to the office in his rattly little pickup, though, Mr. Purdy made some smart comment I didn't like about Mad Max bringing me home…which made me think, could he be jealous? Preposterous. However, I recalled, with chagrin, my attack of possessiveness when he paid attention to Frieda at the garage sale.

In the parking lot of the cable office, he tweaked things under the Bronco's hood. While he worked, I told him I was thinking about a new car, that the Bronco needed Emmett's hand to keep it going, although he'd pretty much ignored it.

Mr. Purdy peered at me over his glasses, said I'd put my finger on the problem. Emmett had neglected routine maintenance and the chickens were coming home to roost. For him to point his accusing finger at a dead man annoyed me. But it was true. Why had Emmett let the car go so badly? Well, I knew. I was back at the beginning: Emmett expected to be driving that red Miata.

Mr. Purdy, my support group. Because I admit that Bruce is too openly wounded to count on for much. Well, I've got Helen, too. She "supports" me, as well as she is able to, which means she invites me along on some of her jaunts. We've been to Sutter Creek for Mexican food; to San Francisco for Chinese; to the Delta for seafood—Helen likes to eat.

The Delta trip sent me into a depression. The levee road twisting through the autumn mist; the peach, pear, walnut trees throwing up gnarled skeletons against the gray sky, their crops long harvested. Fields of barley, wheat and safflowers now reduced to stubble. Down through an edging of shrubbery, I saw the river flowing sluggishly, a khaki-colored avenue, uninviting.

This is Emmett country. Near here: Courtland, land of the Pear Fair. Around another bend in the road: Isleton and the Del Rio Hotel, home of the Crawdad Festival—Emmett had yearned for them while in Vietnam. And right there at the point: the Deep Water Channel emptying into the Sacramento River on its way to the Bay. I imagined Emmett aboard the *River Rat* returning from the South Tower race; I could hear his triumphant whoop as he popped the red and gold spinnaker, the prevailing west wind parachuting him home to me.

I'd wait for him at the sailing club in Stockton, where his buddy docked the *River Rat.* Emmett would arrive like Odysseus, consumed with desire for me, Penelope. But then he'd suffer a falling off in the car on the way home. He'd get moody and cross. I put it down to fatigue. The South Tower race took thirty-six to forty hours, sometimes longer.

However, in Helen's VW, I tried to jolly myself out of dejection, chattering away, filling the car up with a load of bullshit. No point in bringing Helen down, too. That's what Bruce does, and I hate it. I wonder what Helen loves, or hates. Does she burn with hidden fires, buried passions? If she does, I don't detect it. I like her well enough, but there's something missing. Almost as if she's had a lobotomy on her emotions. She's exempt from my kind of devils; can I count on her as a member of the support team? I'm not sure.

So, if I already have the feeble beginnings of a support group, although I'm lukewarm about it, why do I need to do what I'm doing? Which is checking out my pseudo-Chinese outfit in the mirror on the back of the closet door. Have I seen *An Unmarried Woman* too many times? Am I waiting for a handsome, sensitive, artistic creampuff to fall out of the sky to rescue me? Would I believe it or accept it if such a thing were to happen? I am not Jill Clayburgh, I'm not thin or beautiful—although I do think this Chinese getup is attractive. It's a shiny cranberry red sheath dress with a high collar, a diagonal line of frog closures from collar to cap sleeve. I found it in the thrift store, a bargain that pleased me. I add my pinecone earrings, the coolie hat, some perfume. I am ready for my first "date" in twenty-five years.

I hear a car door slam out front; then steps up the drive. I glance back into my own golden living room—I've left a light on for myself—and I wonder why I'm voluntarily leaving my safe cocoon. If Frieda hadn't come up with what I now consider a harebrained plan, I would stay home tonight, eat popcorn, watch TV in my sweats. Heaven.

Some of my TV people have become more real to me than

the actual people I know. I'm going to miss my Friday lineup—Jim Lehrer, Bill Moyers in his reassuring crew-necked sweater; then David Letterman, who makes me slightly uneasy with his gap-toothed sarcasm, or Jay Leno, who I *really* depend on to put me straight. Is it possible, is it *allowable,* to count your TV viewing as a "support group"? No.

A tentative knock…I take a deep breath, my hand shakes as I open the door. He's taking a deep breath, too, a random sort of fellow, an ordinary guy you'd have trouble picking out in a lineup. Square face, small pale eyes behind steel-rimmed glasses, blondish hair that is not golden like Emmett's, but washed out, the color real blond gets when it grays. Square jaw, jutting chin. He reminds me of Donald Rumsfeld, has a pugnacious, belligerent look about him. I am immediately on my guard. But that's crazy, and when he holds out what I discover to be a smooth hand, soft as a woman's, we exchange a cool shake. He introduces himself, Zack (another Zack) Phelps—even his name has a snap to it. I think I'm too harsh, too quick to judge, because we both laugh when we begin to speak at once, saying, apparently, the same thing—something about Frieda "fixing us up."

I grab my jacket, a black velvet blazer borrowed from Amy, and my purse, and we make small talk shuffling our way out to his car. It's then that I realize we are eyeball to eyeball. I am too tall for him; I catch myself reviewing my collection of flats. Ridiculous! I rephrase the situation: he is too short for me.

He says he likes my outfit, and I tell him the same. He has gone Hawaiian, a gaudy flowered shirt, strings of plastic leis. He nervously fiddles with a straw hat, obviously feeling silly about it. He opens my door and I'm ushered in, encapsulated in a deep bucket seat whose plush upholstery grabs onto my velvet jacket like Velcro. As my house recedes, as Mr. Purdy's house recedes, I throw a longing look back. Mr. Purdy has left his porch light on. He watches out for me. I should be doing the oyster stew routine instead of this foolishness. I cast a glance at this guy next to me, wondering if he has reservations, if he too has given up a customary Friday for me. I probably owe him.

He's seen me look back, and says, "You're not concerned

about being away from home tonight, about missing the trick-or-treaters? No mischief-makers'll soap your screens, throw an egg or two?"

I tell him most of the kids around here have grown and gone. The ones left are more apt to parade in a warm lighted mall than canvass the neighborhood in the wet. Merchants give out treats to these future, or current, customers, well aware of making an impression. "How about you?"

What I'm asking about are his trick-or-treaters, but he says in a stern tone, "Judy, my ex, she loves Halloween, goes all out. Lines the walk with pumpkins, big one on the porch, battery-operated with an electric eye, that gives out this phony laugh. She drapes the place with these fake spider webs you spray out of a can. Coddles the little freeloaders, treats them to caramel popcorn balls, candied apples. Costs her a fortune cooking and decorating because she allows for nothing but the best, and plenty of it." Then he realizes how he sounds, because he adds in a lighter tone, "Well, the neighborhood kids make a point of stopping to show her their costumes. I suppose it's worth it. To her."

"Child support, eh?"

To his credit, he grins sheepishly. "Yeah, but not for much longer. She's remarried, and the kids'll turn eighteen one of these days.At least you don't have *that* hassle."

For a second I wonder how and what he knows of my situation, but then Frieda will have told him. Seen from her point of view, or his, I'm not a bad deal. No kids at home, which I own free and clear, I have a job and a car that runs, sometimes. I shuffle in my seat, and cross my legs. My skirt hikes up, and I realize that this is a hard dress to sit in. I pull it down; I consider my nylons, the money I spent on this sexy pair of sandalfoot stockings. Then I see him glance over, so I tug again at myself, rearrange my hem into its lowest possible position.

Progressing across town, we make stiff small talk. The rain, which we agree we need; the lack of traffic; the early push to Christmas—some stores already have decorations out. Then he says, "How well do you know Frieda?"

"Not well at all." Then I add cautiously, "But she's a good

neighbor."

"Ole Lyle, he's a kook, that weird end-of-the-world stuff."

I am encouraged. "Really? You think so?"

"Yeah. But I play along with him. When I've had enough, I say so, and he's got the sense to back off. Lyle and me, we understand each other. I keep in good with him so I get invited for a venison roast every now and then."

Just when I'd begun to thaw, he adds this last remark, and I stiffen again. "She makes great coffee." Mentally I compliment myself for my adroit tact.

At the BPOE hall, he parks, helps me out of the deep plush seat. I take heart again when he confesses he's not much of a dancer, but he'll do his best. I say the same, and we laugh nervously. This will be okay, yeah.

The lobby reminds me of the office at Mountain Valley Cable, the splintery wood paneling, spotlighted showcase of grotesque trophies (Mountain Valley Cable's for "community service," "customer satisfaction," etc.). Tacked up around the room, the same collection of incomprehensible information/symbols—membership rosters, bulletins, pennants, certificates. The collection reminds me vaguely of Emmett's wall, which I've dismantled. The air is full of what must be ancient cigarette smoke, because no one's been allowed to smoke in here for years. It has soaked into the woodwork, like a coating of shellac.

A guy behind the counter collects from Zack whatever fee is charged. I look away in case there's a secret handshake. The dance is upstairs; the ceiling reverberates with the pulse of music. The racket of a party in full swing leaks down to us, like audible rain. I feel Zack's eyes on me, like cold little prickles through my clothes, as he follows me up the narrow wooden steps. But at the top, when I turn around, he's not looking at me. He's eyeing the dancers, sorting through them and the couples seated at tables around the dance floor. Aha! He's looking for someone, there's a history here, a former girlfriend, and I have been brought to throw in her face. Well, never mind.

There's been a perfunctory attempt at decoration. Orange and black crepe paper streamers twist from corners to fluorescent fixtures that look like shop lights suspended from the high ceiling. These lights are now off, thank heaven. Adorning the walls: cutouts of black cats with arched backs, dancing scarecrows and skeletons. Each table has its own centerpiece of an accordion-pleated pumpkin.

Big Band sounds issue from a disk jockey-type setup. *Chattanooga Choo-Choo* plays, and there's a punishing echo in the room. The people seem elderly to me, but I can't really tell how old they are. They're in costume, and it's very dark—what light there is comes from little spots in the ceiling, and a couple of wall sconces. Zack threads us through dancers to a table, then leaves me to hang up my jacket, get drinks at a bar at the end of the room. Alone, I try to arrange a pleasant expression on my face, while I study the crowd.

Something by Fleetwood Mac plays while a buccaneer swings by with Snow White; a hobo struts his stuff with a Little Bo Peep. There are some outrageous costumes that took real work to put together, and are hard to dance in: a spaceman, a robot, even a computer, the wearer staring out of an opening cut in a box. Only a man would dare wear such a getup. But most outfits are restrained and make-do, like mine and Zack's. I see a recycled bridesmaid's outfit, a Robin Hood in tunic and leggings, a clown with ruffled collar, a ghost trailing a sheet—also hard to dance in. In fact, impossible. A couple of bums, couple of hula girls. By now Zack has our drinks, but he's laughing with a group of guys at the bar, and I see his glance follow Raggedy Ann dance by with Raggedy Andy. If that's her, Zack has his work cut out for him, because she's into it enough to coordinate their costumes. Most costumes are the woman's job, although that hadn't been true with Emmett. He'd been the dress-up expert, the aficionado. The chameleon. But aren't I one, too, reinventing myself as I go along?

Zack arrives with my drink. I asked for a gin and tonic, and this one's so strong it threatens to dissolve its plastic cup. However, I gulp it, grateful for the warm steadying rush. I tell myself to slow down, but I ignore my own advice. Zack is doing the same with his Scotch and water, which is the color of tea. I begin to worry about getting home, and I express this. He says there's a midnight buffet, which will soak up the alcohol. Midnight! I sneak a peek at my watch: it's nine-thirty.

We shout more small talk over the music, postponing the inevitability of *dance.* However, when a slow number plays, good old threadbare *Star Dust*, we take to the floor. He steers me around as if I'm a boat, and we pass the island where Raggedy Ann sits anchored to her Andy. On a turn, which Zack grants me, or executes to make a point of presenting to her his indifferent back, I get a good look. She's watching us, all right, with an expression I can read. On this admittedly flimsy evidence, I confirm my suspicions that these two have a history.

Next they play Cyndi Lauper's *Time after Time*, which I happen to be fond of, but it's tricky, so we return to the table. We have new drinks, and I ask for a basket of pretzels—on our cruise around the room, I'd seen other tables with them. Zack jumps up eagerly, glad to be sent on an errand (and to be temporarily quit of me). He's gone for some time, talking to his buddies along the way. He returns, flourishes pretzels, as if they're a hard-won prize. He becomes animated, talkative, a hot glow lights his cheeks and especially his nose. He expounds on his philosophy of family life, which is a vehement statement of outrage. Women should know their places, the courts are slanted in favor of the feminists, etc. I manage to hold my tongue, which has become untrustworthy, slippery, and slurry. Then he talks about his kids, a girl and a boy in their teens. He lets on that the girl, Tami, enrages him with her whiny self-absorption, her disregard for his rules.

"How so?" I lean forward: this is familiar territory.

"Well, she has this boyfriend, I can't stand the kid, but he practically lives at our house, or at Judy's house. Judy allows them to go in Tami's bedroom, and shut the door. I tell Judy not to permit this, but she doesn't listen to me."

"Ah, but does *she* listen to *them*? See, I've been through this, and it's when they get quiet that you should worry." Amy and Matt Butterworth giggling in her room, turning up the stereo to cover their mischief. "Be glad they're at your house. Protect your daughter and hope for the best."

His jaw tightens, he aims his bullet-shaped face at me. "I will not allow any messing around, not under my roof, by God...or under what used to be my roof."

"What I'm saying is don't turn her off." But I can see that he already has. I see why, too, and how. Another old-fashioned parent with the new kid.

He frowns, then his face clears. "Now, my boy, Zack—he's named for me—Zack Junior, or Zack II, how would you say it? He's a pure pleasure. Here, I've got a picture of him." He opens his wallet, sorts through. "This is him, he's just shot his first bear. He didn't go out for bear, but this bear charged him and he brought it down. Emptied his shotgun, but he got 'em. Big guy, isn't he?"

At first I don't know if he's talking about the kid or the bear, but after squinting at the photo in the dark, then reaching for my glasses, I understand it's the bear. Because the smirking callow kid in the camouflage suit, about fifteen or so, is not big; but the bear is. Zack says, "That sucker went four hundred pounds. Here's another one of my boy holding up one of its paws, lookit the size of it! Talk about a thrill!"

I am horrified. The kid is covered with blood, which is also all over the animal, clotting its fur. It bleeds from its nose, ears, one of its eyes is jelly. The paw the boy holds up for the camera is enormous. The claws look four inches long. I seem to smell the gamy scent, the odor of blood, its mangy coat. "Terrible!" I mutter.

"What's terrible? What could have happened to my kid? Or that my kid had to kill it? Well, it was Zack or him, and it turned out to be him. What would you have done?"

"I wouldn't have been out there to begin with. Where is this place?"

"Alaska. Judy's brother lives outside of Sitka, and there's a helicopter you hire to take you into the backcountry. Expensive, but that was what Zack wanted for his birthday, and they guarantee you a kill."

"No business being there." I snap off my glasses, snap the

pictures back. He clears his throat, looks around. I tell him I have to use the john, collect my purse, and try to trot off. I'm surprised at how unsteady I am on my pins, as if I'm used to walking on the rolling deck of a ship. Once in the restroom, I sit on the toilet for a couple of flushes. I'm sifting through my situation, grasping for any debris that will keep me afloat. That man out there, I've alienated him as badly as he has me, and how will this play out? Could he refuse to take me home? I should have been more politic, but he's a jerk.

I see clearly that I've begun to enjoy my widowhood, I've begun to wallow in it. The power of being alone. I see that my support group needs *me,* and *not* the other way around. Oh, pshaw…what a thought. How arrogant…but it's true. I sense a new certainty; I've built myself a new foundation.

This is when I should be careful. I've got to cover my tracks. I've got to go back out there, and act a certain way to get what I want. And what I want is to arrive home with self-esteem, and not let this fool rob me. I practice smiling a couple of times, flush again, then take my time washing my hands. I have never washed my hands so thoroughly.

Plus, I want to give him a lengthy absence so that he can connect, or reconnect, with Raggedy Ann, or anybody else he wants to. Because I am through with him.

Reluctantly I leave my safe harbor, my refuge of the bathroom and reenter the hall. Zack is talking to another man at our table. They glance at this door I'm coming out of. They see me and draw apart, affect a casual posture, and I know that I've been discussed. But I smile when I sit down, shake hands with the new fellow. His palm is tough as a baseball mitt (later, on the dance floor, he tells me he works with sheet metal). His costume is his old army uniform, even down to the helmet, and the tunic fits him too snugly—he's put on weight since Korea, or Vietnam or wherever—so many wars to keep track of. I want to urge him to keep in shape. After all, here he is at a singles' dance. What's the matter with him?

He takes off the helmet, and I realize he'd put it on to impress me with the effect of the whole picture. He has dark curly hair sprinkled with gray, a high bulging forehead. I don't think he's going bald, he just bulges. Dark eyes under a heavy uni-brow, and his eyes are too close together. In fact, his features all crowd together in the center of his face. In the helmet he'd looked sort of cute, like a small animal peering out of a hole. Without it, he's...odd-looking. But his manner is tentative, uncertain, and I like it. The uniform becomes him. It strikes me as a true expression of who he really is. Zack, on the other hand, Zack the Ripper wears a shameless façade with his lighthearted playful Hawaiian shirt. He'd admitted, earlier, that he's a cop on the homicide squad, which had bothered me. He wouldn't have admitted it, but I asked. He got defensive, said the most common occupations represented here, at this singles' dance, are policeman, and teacher. In both occupations, you have the final say-so, and on your own turf, too.

Zack has indulged in false advertising. But what about me in my sexy Chinese dress? I, too, have engaged in a lie, because I don't feel a damned thing for any of these people, except a simmering dislike for Zack.

Jeff, the new one is Jeff something or other, Jeff asks me to dance. It's an ABBA number, smooth and slow. He is warm in his scratchy suit—I sniff a faint deodorant scent on him—and his body has a tough meaty feel under my hands. "My daughter used to play this song," I say. "She didn't believe me when I told her the group is Swedish, none of them spoke English."

"I'll be darned. I didn't know that. How old's your daughter?"

"She's twenty-four. I missed her music when she moved out and took it."

"A daughter that old?"

"That's not old. I'm twice that, well, almost."

"You don't look it."

I laugh. "You don't have to *look* it. That's not part of the requirement."

"Say, I don't know how connected you are to Zack—"

"Not at all. Just met him tonight."

"'S'pose I could get your number? I saw you come in, and I thought by George, this might not be a waste of time after all."

"Sure," and I rattle it off for him. "You can't remember that."

"You wanna bet? Thanks…Peg?"

"Yeah, Peg, that's me. Thank you, Jeff. Who'd you come with?"

"No one. I'm on my own. This number's about over, too bad for me. See you later."

He returns me to Zack and I look at my watch: almost eleven-thirty. I may live. After a bit, the lights come up, those unforgiving fluorescent lights that show us to each other exactly as we are. The fixture above our table buzzes and crackles like a bug-zapper. Zack's face ages ten years, his skin acquires a bluish pasty look; dark bags hang under his eyes. He has a surprised expression, a bemused look, as if he's taken aback at life's injustice. Well, he has suffered random hurts and pains, an ordinary man coping with what he sees as unearned tragedies. I soften my opinion, view him with a condescending sympathy. After all, I must look as old to him as he does to me.

It's not just us. Everyone in the room fades and droops; it's obscene: the clown, the movie star, the performer take off their makeup, and like magic in reverse, they turn into ordinary people. It's like seeing a candid photo in the *Enquirer* of Elizabeth Taylor, or Julia Roberts without the airbrushing, the cosmetics, the plastic surgery. We're embarrassed with and for each other. We quiet down except for an occasional self-conscious twitter. Ordinary people, tired and faded, up past our bedtimes.

Like kids on the playground, we're instructed to make a circle and parade around the room while the president of the singles' club judges us for best, most original costume. For the first time I get a full look at the other outfits. The Far East has come in for a big play. Besides me, there's a sari, a Punjabi-type outfit, the hula girls, a Crocodile Dundee in an Aussie-style hat, like the one I dreamed of on Emmett. I hear the wearer scatter "g'day, mates" around the room like tips for the caterers.

The winner in the female division: a woman done up as Glenda, the Good Witch of the West (I think that's what she is) with a sorcerer's pointed hat and luxurious long flowing sleeves. The winner in the male's: the man impersonating a computer, which should have won—the poor fellow has suffered with that box over his head. The winners make an odd pair, but that's why we're here: we've displayed this proclivity for unwieldy combinations in our outside lives, and it has landed us in a pickle. The prize: a pair of tickets for dinner and a movie, following the group's rationale that all creatures, like those crows in my parking lot, should be mated. For every pot, there's a lid.

The buffet is a nice assortment spread out on a couple of tables. Finger foods predominate: fried chicken nuggets (KFC?), riblets, which prove to be messy—the women avoid them, but not the men. Hors d'oeuvres aplenty, pickles, olives, cheeses, ham and salami, crackers, sliced veggies, which are rather universally ignored. Cakes, cookies, chips. The last time I ate a buffet was at Emmett's funeral supper, and I'm apprehensive that a rerun of that miserable experience will ruin my appetite. But it doesn't happen, and I wolf down a surprising amount of food, including the ribs. What the hell.

That night at home again, stripping off the sandalfoot nylons that I ruined early on, I think, Well, that wasn't so bad, although maybe I won't do it again soon. There's not much danger of that. Zack will not call me. Are all guys named Zack assholes full of bullshit, I wonder; and my goodness, I scold! Where does this awful language come from, although it's all in my head and not out loud, not even to PawPaw, who has waited up for me.

Zack and I were finished before we started, which shows me what a poor eye Frieda has for what's right, fitting, and proper. Good coffee, yes. Match-making, no.

The next morning I have a mild hangover—thick head full of cobwebs. Tendency to become dizzy. Scold myself for the abuse, but laugh, too. I remember an old joke of Emmett's, one he stole from W.C. Fields. A man sits next to a woman in a bar, turns to her, says, "You're ugly."

"You're drunk," she says.

He responds, "Tomorrow I'll be sober, but you'll still be ugly."

Tomorrow I'll be sober, but Zack will still be Zack, full of what I think are misplaced values, and bitter judgements about women and their proper places. None of that is going to help him get on in this new age. If Emmett had lived, I wonder if his true nature wouldn't have manifested itself and gotten in his way with Maggie Quinn. Suddenly I'm sure it would have. This ought not to make me happy, but it does.

I take a couple of aspirins, drink a gallon of water and go back to bed. Such are the pleasures of the single life.

Jeff, the guy at the dance in the army getup, did call, but I was gone. If he'd called sooner—I suspected someone else stood him up—things might have gone differently. Then again, it was already too late, because I had no control over forces that were beginning to operate in my life.

(And what a crock *that* is, to make such a statement: "*...I had no control over forces...*" blah, blah, blah, what a stuffed shirt thing to say. As if anybody has control, as if life's a checker game, there're rules, and a plan. That's a naïve, cop-out of an attitude, and I apologize...but it was what I felt at the time.)

CHAPTER 11

Helen trudges up from the warehouse where she's swamped with work. "TGIF, cubed! Let's go for a beer tonight. Oops! Sorry," she says, seeing me on the phone. Zack, fired for using cocaine on the job, has left us reeling from the fallout, agog with scandal.

I nod yes around my headset, while listening to another irate customer carp about the injustice of her cable bill. "I realize..." a quick glance at my computer screen... "Mrs. Stocker, I realize that this seems like quite a hike in your bill. It's not a hike, it's just that your introductory period has expired, and I'm sure you want to keep all those good channels....Yes, I know some of the movies on HBO are risqué, and you're not into prison dramas, or

Mafia stories, but there are so many....Yes, I know, but there's the BBC channel, have you seen the one where they come in and redo your garden? And ENCORE with all the good old shows, well, not *old* in the sense of dated, but the ones that people like. And the History Channel, the Learning Channel...oh, well, sure, I'm glad you enjoy them. Thanks for calling, Mrs...uh...Stocker."

I've been dealing with an avalanche of unhappy people. Over and over I explain the rates, I explain the difference between Basic and Expanded and Premium. I don't blame people for being shocked at how much just Basic costs. I am paying the price, too, and I don't like it, either. I have considered doing without, but I'm addicted to my TV and I don't think I can give it up. Some days I report for work with my eyes shaped like little TV sets, having sat up half the night in front of the tube. Not that TV is so good; it's that I'm having trouble sleeping again.

Staggering around at work, edgy, nervous, out of kilter. I'm not alone. We're all wiped out. Tiffany rampages around, alternating loud nastiness with cold pouts in the bathroom. While Vi was here, delivering the coup de grace to Zack, Tiffany maintained a smooth exterior, projected her usual unflinching efficiency, but as soon as Vi left, Tiffany went back to what's become her normal, which is unpredictable vindictiveness. She's taking it out on us because she thinks we snitched on Zack. I know I didn't, can't tell cocaine from baby talc; and I doubt Helen can, either. Bruce? No. Not Bruce. I see him as too timid and pussy-whipped (a phrase of Emmett's I deplored, and still do) to effect such a heroic deed as ratting on Zack. I'd put my money on one of the installers, Al or Eugene; one of them blew the whistle. They called him Zack the Jerk, my private name for him, too. In any case, as a group, we're irascible, upset, stretched thin.

Then too, people are unhappy with us because a pre-Thanksgiving Sunday storm took down cable lines. The timing couldn't have been worse: this knocked out a big football game; Emmett would have been livid. I was, too, because I had to forego my beloved ice-skating special. In general, an increasing number of people are griping about their service, are threatening to quit us. Some days I want to shout, "So, cancel the damn cable, just do it!" But such honesty I can't afford.

People don't limit themselves to phoning; they come in to personally chew me out. "Robber barons, that's what you are!" said one woman, plunking down her payment. Another one brought in her black box, the digital equipment, thumped it on the counter. "I quit! I want you out of my house. Take your stuff and shove it!" A man threatened, "I'll show you, I'll get a satellite dish." I'd had the same idea myself, but found out that signing up for all those channels would cost me the same as cable, and I'd have to buy the dish, too.

Waiting on all those angry people. Answering the phone, listening to them. Explaining, cajoling, accounting to them their charges. Nerve-wracking.

Later at the Jolly Roger, our neighborhood saloon, Helen agrees. "That place is hell these days. Did you see Raoul when he came in? I swear he rolled his eyes like a horse that smells fire…really spooked. Funniest damn thing now that I think about it." Helen lets out a belly laugh. "I mean for even Raoul, the stone man…for him to feel it."

"Yeah, Jerry didn't hang around long, either. Say, do you think Bruce—"

"What? That he ratted? Nah, he's too nice a guy, I mean, really. He's so nice his face hurts. But here's the part that gets me. Whoever would have guessed it was Zack keeping us balanced."

"What! No way."

"It's true. See, when Tiffany had Zack to jolly her around, she'd go along, do her part with customer service. But now that she spends half her time sulking in the bathroom, it's up to you and me to do the work of four people."

While I consider this idea, she adds, "Listen, you never know who's in control. In school, didn't they ever ask you to list the two people you wanted to sit next to? And the teacher makes a grid of it? And then the teacher—because we kids never saw the results—could map out ringleaders, chart classroom dynamics. See who's pushing the buttons, or who's an isolate; I forget how it works….You never did that? I guess that kind of thing came along later."

She trails off, embarrassed for me, for my aged backwardness. Young woman like her: I wonder why she never married, or if she has a boyfriend. Then I wonder whom I'd have picked to sit next to, if Emmett couldn't have been one of the choices. Or who would have picked me. Had I been an isolate? Am I still?

"Listen, Peg, it's not worth brooding over. You know the really weird part? I suspect Tiffany turned in our coke-head. Just the bitchy kind of thing she'd do."

"Whatever for? They were friends."

"Friends? Don't you think they had a thing going? And it blew up? Besides, she'd have done it just to keep us off balance, so we can't gang up on her. Divide and conquer."

"Oh, come on." But Helen has a point. The way Tiffany and Zack were always canoodling, laughing in corners. Then, too, Tiffany is smart, plays both ends against the middle.

While the beer gives me a warm rush—it's dark, heavy, and cold—I play with my glass, make an interlocking design of wet circles on the bar. We're sitting at the bar, perched on a pair of barstools. We never take a booth. Helen has explained the fine points of bar etiquette to me. You don't take up a booth unless you're a foursome, or at least a pair. You keep your eyes to yourself, and do not let your look linger on a person who is obviously already paired up. You leave your drink and your change (but not your purse) on the bar when you go to the john, or off to dance; no one will mess with your stuff. You do not talk across someone. You do not join in someone else's conversation unless invited to do so. An invitation can be delivered in a variety of delicate ways—a smile, a subtle posture, a glance, a tone of voice—and a bar patron who's mastered the code will know what he or she is about. I appreciate Helen's tutelage because I'm a raw greenhorn, although I don't plan to make a habit of this TGIF stuff. I believe Emmett had it right: the bar scene is no good. Nothing good happens in a bar.

"I'm serious," says Helen, and laughs. She's feeling the beer, too. "Tiffany could play world class chess. That convoluted thinking. Didn't Vi lay that bit on you about how messed up the kids are? That they can't even give blood because of what they've done to their bodies? But she idolizes Tiffany despite her being a poster child for exactly what Vi campaigns against. Didn't Vi preach to you that bit about thinking in ones-and-zeros bit, which, by the way, exactly personifies our Tiffany?"

"Well, yes, she did. But I don't see Tiffany as—"

I sense a presence at my elbow, and at first I think oh, shit, *Tiffany.* It could be her, because this place, the Jolly Roger, is a local watering hole, an outpost that serves the small army laboring in our industrial park. *Industrial park.* What a joke. Military intelligence. Giant shrimp. Dress loafers? Married love?

Besides the cable office, this complex houses a locksmith, a chainsaw outfit, a boat works, a flooring store, an upholstery shop, a sheet metal shop, a storage unit complex. So there's nothing "jolly" about the Jolly Roger's neighborhood, or the establishment itself. It's just another rectangle in a cinder block row of rectangles. For ambiance, for something to help it live up to its exotic name, it depends on a few faded skull and crossbones flags, a plastic "treasure chest" behind the bar, plastic treasure spilling out of it. Since it's almost Thanksgiving, the owner, a Filipino guy with a glib but unintelligible style of English, has enlivened the décor with cutouts of improbable turkeys, Pilgrim hats, and autumn leaves—although there are no trees within a half-mile of here.

There's no reason for Tiffany of the black clothes, green and white makeup, safety-pin earrings to show here. This is a blue collar, mainstream, workin'-bloke hangout, and the locals turn out, especially on Fridays. It's not Tiffany at my elbow. It's Bruce. What's he doing here?

As if to answer that, Bruce says, "Helen mentioned you guys dropping in, so, I decided to join the crowd." He shyly glances at Helen, and I get it. Bruce and Helen. Well, why not? Except doesn't this make me the odd one? The extra? But if we were to do a grid of the two people we'd want to sit next to, surely I would be their second choice. In that sense, I belong, and I make Bruce welcome, raise my beer glass to his, which the Filipino's bartending wife has already brought him: a toast to Fridays.

I laugh at their jokes. I add my own. We assemble, then dissect the office personnel. Tiffany takes her knocks; we love to hate Tiffany. Vi is a peach, we agree—cautiously. Because we don't really know Vi. The installers, Al and Eugene, I admit that I can't tell them apart; wouldn't know them if they were to come in the door right now.

The talk turns to other jobs we've worked; sour, disgusting, difficult jobs, which, in comparison, make Mountain Valley Cable a piece of cake, a slice of pie (Helen's phrase). Bruce describes working as a roofer, hot-mopping tar on a flat-topped California bungalow in the middle of August. "But it was the best I could do. Jan was expecting Isabel, I was going to be a father in a matter of weeks, we needed the money. I would have done anything for my family." Here his voice breaks, and I feel that twinge of irritation, prickle of exasperation, and I'm glad when Helen jumps in.

Helen's been on her own for a long time, and has done a lot. Early on she prepped for a house painter, thinking, what a blast, masking off woodwork, priming miles of backbreaking baseboard. She finally woke up to the raw labor, the boredom of it. Then she wandered around, clerking, waitressing, even did a stint as a hairdresser. Her worst job had been driving a school bus for special ed kids, retarded, handicapped. So depressing. Some wet their pants, or worse. They cried, they wouldn't sit still, ran up and down the aisle while the bus was moving; some didn't know their stops, or even their last names. She had to keep checking to make sure she wasn't missing any kids, or letting any off at the wrong stop—the school district could have been sued. She didn't get sued, but she did wipe out a bus bench, cut a corner too sharply and ran over it with her van, the kind with the lift for wheelchairs. She drove back to the bus barn and quit. Just recalling that afternoon when she killed a bus bench makes color mount in her cheeks, the nervous sweat pop out.

Me, I don't have those kinds of dramas to relate, because, I explain, I had Emmett to count on; I didn't have to make my own way until he died. Bruce's eyes fill with tears for me, which makes me want to act tough and reckless.

However, I dredge up a good story from my days as a Molly

Maid. "I'm on my rounds, I go in this house—I had a key—I was vacuuming away, thinking I was alone. Then the bedroom door opens, and this woman—she'd stayed home sick, had forgotten about me coming—lunges down the hall with a gun. I thought I'd had it. This wild woman, red hair, green nightgown. She about gave me a heart attack." Now that I think about it, she was a lot like Maggie Quinn. Could it have been her? The idea makes my bile rise, threatens me with indigestion. No, too long ago. Maggie would have been a child, or not born yet.

A woman standing next to Helen has been listening. She has a hard, tough appearance, bleached blond hair, rows of earrings up her lobes. She leans across Helen's shoulder (I assume she's aware of bar etiquette, has received tacit permission to do this) and adds her own bad job to our litany. She once worked in a hospital emptying bedpans, changing soiled sheets, sponging feces from smeared bottoms. It was an Alzheimer's ward, and her descriptions of their confusion, and inexplicable and frightening behaviors seems to strike a cord with Helen. The two of them split off from us, sink into their own pool of talk, like animals at a waterhole. Bruce heads for the john; I return to my pattern of wet circles on the bar.

A new person appears beside me, filling the gap Helen and Bruce left. He calls for the barkeep to bring me a new beer. I don't know this guy, but he wants to talk about gun control, and how wrong I am to tell about the woman coming down the hall at me with a pistol. Those sorts of stories give the other side more ammunition to attack our freedoms. He urges me to rethink my reaction to the situation. "What would you have done if you were alone in your own home, sick, and you heard a noise in the house? Wouldn't you have wanted to protect yourself?" he says in a silky reasonable tone.

Feeling nettled—he's undermining my best story—I slide a nervous look across his face, upon which I fancy I see a smirk. He's a distillation of the kind of guy you'd imagine hangs out in here. A bit scruffy, maybe from the work he does. He needs a shave, a bath, a scrubbing down. He's wearing the uniform: name-appliqued shirt (this one is RICK), blue jeans, baseball cap.

His cap reads *Husqvarna.* I'm about to placate him by telling him that Emmett kept guns, but instead I say, "Don't you think it's ironic that the chainsaw crowd, that staunch bunch so in love with our American freedoms, prefers a Swedish product?" His face clouds; I see the wheels turning, he's trying to put it together because that cap has become a part of his head and he's forgotten what it says.

Just then another guy, interchangeable with this one—whose name, according to his shirt, is LOU—joins us. "Hey, Rick," he says, "what's going down, man?" To me, "Don't pay any attention to him. He's full of it, right?"

Now with the two of them, I feel trapped, which is ridiculous because they are not focused on me, but on each other, and in giving each other a jokey bad time. I want my own people back, I feel let down by them, I regret the breakdown of our integrity. I search for Helen through the crowd, which has grown. A few people here are coupled, but most are floaters from the nearby shops that are closing. Finally I spot her; she's still into it with the hard-looking blond broad...yeah, I'd call her a *broad.* And Bruce...he's talking across the bar to the owner's wife—I assume that's who she is. I turn back to my two guys, smile uneasily. I didn't put in a request for them. Why aren't the international rules of bar etiquette working? Or maybe they are, and I'm sending out a signal I'm not aware of. Rick and Lou are still blithely insulting each other, playfully horsing around, although there's a real breath of belligerence, too. Bruce, looking down the bar to me, sees the guys laughing, me smiling. He returns to his conversation with the dark woman behind the bar. It's only after he looks away that I realize he'd been checking, and I could have given him the high sign for a rescue.

There's a stir at the door: the band has arrived, begins hauling in its equipment, setting up on a small dais in the back of the room. Rick tells me they are the Screw Drivers, a great combo. Lou adds that last week the Purple Enemy had been dynamite, or, as he puts it, bad. "Baaaad, man." Maybe this place *is* Tiffany's style after all.

I'm making up my own names for bands. How about the

Magenta Enema? Or the Sperm Squirts, which would fit this rag-tag bunch. To me they look like kids, seedy, too young to be out on their own, too young to live.

I'm thinking now's the time to go. I'm also thinking how I'll make Mr. Purdy laugh with their name, the *Screw Drivers*... when it hits me: I have stood him up. We were supposed to have had oyster stew at the Soup Kettle, and I have deserted him, forgotten him in the blitz of this day's events. I'm appalled, make my excuses to Rick and Lou, hurry into my coat. Bruce scuttles down to me, "You going? I thought you were having a good time."

I tell him that I've let an old man down, a lonely old man who was counting on me. I'm ashamed. I know that if Mr. Purdy were to fill out a grid, I would be numbered within his two friends to sit with.

Bruce says, "I was hoping to get a chance to talk to you."

"Okay, walk me out, talk to me as we go."

"Well," he says opening the door—the air outside is cool and fresh and I wonder again what I was doing in there. "This is awkward, but Peg...well, I thought that since you and Helen were such good friends—"

"Helen and I? I thought the two of *you* were good friends."

"We are, but not like that."

"Like what?"

"Since she's a lesbian, I thought you were, too."

"Lesbian!" Then a light goes on, and I see...I don't know what I see. I mumble some nonsense—it takes all kinds, stereotyping, hasty judgements, etc., all the while thinking what a simpleton I've been.

"Since that's not the case, I was wondering if you and I, if you and me, if we could get together, go to dinner or something."

"Bruce! You're asking me out? On a date?" My face burns in embarrassment. The antiquated term.

"Oh, no, not a date. Well, yeah, a date, although that sounds odd. Okay, how about it? You want to go to dinner some evening?"

"Sure. But not tonight. I've got to mend my fences."

"I can't make it tonight, either. Isabel and I have chores to do."

"On a Friday night?"

"Yeah, because it's a short work week coming up. Thanksgiving. But I'll call you, okay?"

I ride home with my head in a whirl. What a day. Such new influences in my life—the bar scene, hard drugs, lesbianism. Office politics. Sociological grids. A date, a real date, not a blind one, but a date with a man I know and like, I guess.

Wouldn't Emmett be amazed? I am.

I drive across town, slowly—after all, I've got beer on my breath—and I plan how I'll blitz Mr. Purdy with such a load of hardy frantic stuff. Tell him I am so sorry, please forgive me. I'll ask him to go to the Soup Kettle tomorrow night, which is chicken noodle night, somehow I'll make it up to him.

However, after I knock on his door—he's left his light for me—he is stiff with what he views as my desertion, and I see I've hurt him badly. He says he doesn't like chicken noodle soup, any fool can make chicken noodle soup. Even his Millie, who was no kind of cook, could make chicken noodle soup. It's oyster stew he wanted; oyster stew takes a fine hand, knowing just when the oysters are done, but not cooked a moment longer because that will make them tough as pieces of inner tubing.

In desperation, I invite him to share Thanksgiving dinner, I cajole him, I plead that I need him, I count on him; I promise him a lovely feast, with cheesecake from Fleischmann's Bakery on Main. I tell him Amy's coming with her friend who I've yet to meet, although I've heard a lot about him. I need his opinion about this fellow. Coolly, he accepts.

When Bruce does call, I invite him, too, because I remember that Thanksgiving is a bad anniversary for him, marking four years that he's been on his own. Or was thrown out of his house, out of his family except for the faithful Isabel, who is deserting him to eat a Thanksgiving feast with Jan. My invite is a lifesaver, he says. What the hell, I ask Helen, too. That will make six of us, a nice round number, enough to keep us off-balance, neutralized, unable to connect in a real and deep way. I'm appalled at myself for thinking this, and at the obligation I've taken on, cooking for six disparate people when I'm used to cooking for one.

Unlike Halloween, Thanksgiving was once my favorite holiday. Emmett would be home, settled in his chair with football on the TV. We'd have a fire, a glass of wine, the air full of the aroma of roasting turkey. But the air will not be full of it this year: both Amy and her friend are rampant vegetarians. Vegetarians are a pain in the ass, I think darkly as I head out to the fish store after a brief argument with the Bronco that doesn't want to start. The fish market! Whoever heard of fish instead of turkey for Thanksgiving?

However, I turn not into the fish store, but into the parking lot of the thrift shop, the one where I got the Chinese dress. I need something new, and the real stores are full of winter's dark colors, heavy fabrics. I need something light and frothy. Summer passed me by this year, and I want it back.

An hour of browsing, and then I leave Cheap Frills with an old-fashioned broomstick skirt—the kind you tie onto a broomstick to dry, to set in a million little pleats—and a drawstring blouse. Both are too young for me, and unseasonable, but they recall my hippie days and I must have them.

Then a dutiful stop at the fish market where I buy salmon. But at the real market, I defiantly lower into my cart a turkey frozen hard as stone, and I wonder if it will thaw in time, and if there is any truth to thawing a turkey in the dryer. Wouldn't that create a thunderous racket? Like Amy's heavy sneakers going round and round. Won't Amy be upset with me? Suddenly I don't care. It's my house, it's my life.

However, Amy doesn't seem upset by the fragrance of turkey in the air. What gets her is my outfit. "Mom! You look like a gypsy. Aren't you cold in that?"

"No, of course not," I snap. "Aren't you hot in that?" She wears a sweater and wool pants, and I remember that day of walking on the beach. Have we changed places? I haven't seen her for a month, not since we met for lunch at her health food café. We'd seemed wary of each other, out of touch. Or maybe I'd been adversely affected by my baked tofu with tahini sauce. Now she appears fuller and pinker, with a bloom on her.

Amy lays a hand, with decorously shellacked nails, on her guy's arm. "Mom, this is Phil, Phil Llewellen, he's a teacher, Mom. He teaches History."

I hold out my hand, but he gives me a hug. "Mom," he says.

I'm not your mom, but I try not to pull away. I also try not to stare, because she's brought home a young Emmett, blond, blue-eyed, a reincarnation. But it won't work, I think, smiling into his white grin, experiencing a flash of hostility. This time I'm wise to you; I'm on my guard, buster. Just then Mr. Purdy comes down the hall from my bedroom. Amy frowns, and in spite of myself, I hurriedly explain: he's been reprogramming my VCR (which, thanks to Mountain Valley Cable, I can do myself, but I wanted to make him feel useful).

Mr. Purdy says, "I set my specs down on that bedspread of yours. Like to never found them again on that field of daisies in there."

Amy smiles in a superior way. "You and your daisy bed-spread."

"It's wonderful and I love it. Go see how I've rearranged the bedroom, shuffled furniture around. No? Well, I'll tell you," I add defiantly, "it's great having the big TV in there." Dozing off with Brian Williams and the news; then, rousing, going on to reruns, old movies, talk shows.

I say to Mr. Purdy, "Will you pour the wine? Go in the living room, please, make yourself at home."

"Mom, you moved the furniture around. No wine for me. PawPaw!" Amy makes over the cat, but he sidles over to Mr. Purdy, who comes in with glasses for himself and Phil. No wine for me, either. I have to think to get this complex meal on the table. Salmon and turkey…am I nuts? I should have gone with one or the other.

"Yes, the furniture…you like it this way?" We survey my rearranged living room, but I still see it the way it was. Traffic patterns, furniture dents in the Berber. Emmett over there, watching football.

"Maybe it's time to rethink the rug. Otherwise, it's okay." Amy frowns.

She's frowning at either Emmett's big chair, or at Mr. Purdy sitting in it. He's wearing the brown and green combo he'd had on during the garage sale, his best outfit. In spite of myself, I feel a contemptuous familiarity, and impatience. Amy settles in my little plaid chair, Phil on the couch. I've got a fire going, I take a break from kitchen duties to perch on the hearth, admiring the fall of my skirt, the way it drapes my legs, the hippie boots I dug out for this outfit. They're suede, dark blue, with just a bit of a heel. Why haven't I worn them more often? Because Emmett had disapproved, that's why.

Amy says it's too hot in here. She frowns when I tell her to take off her sweater. "It's not that kind of a sweater," she says.

I'm on my way to open a window when the doorbell rings. "That will be Bruce," I tell them, "or maybe Helen."

It's Bruce, bringing flowers, roses from Safeway. "A Thanksgiving dinner invitation, it's so special, I can't tell you...well, I appreciate you asking me. So long since I've been invited into someone's family like this."

I laugh, try to lighten the emotional freight he insists on hauling around. "No big deal. Mr. Purdy, from next door, Amy, my daughter, and...Phil."

Amy gives Bruce a cool once-over, and I try to see him through her eyes. He's attractive with his silver iron-filings hair. Tall, thin, wiry; upright posture, good teeth and skin. Nice gray eyes with generous lashes behind wire-rimmed aviator styled glasses. What she disapproves of, and I suppose I do, too, is his outfit. He's wearing what looks like a brown leisure suit (another oxymoron, like *industrial park*). It's fuddy-duddy, and too formal. Phil, in contrast, is just right in a cashmere sweater over a button-down shirt, which reminds me of Bill Moyers. Tailored khaki pants like Docker's, no pleats.

Mr. Purdy pours more wine, leads Bruce into the living room. I escape to my dinner prep. From the kitchen, I hear them struggling with small talk.

Helen arrives in a blast of good cheer, and presents her own bottle of wine. Mr. Purdy sees to her while I try to make gravy with no lumps, no giblets. Emmett liked giblet gravy, I hate it. PawPaw will eat royally. Amy comes out to see if I need help. Yes, I tell her, and put her to work. But what she really wants is to make her report on Helen. "Mom," she breathes, "that woman, she's so butch."

"What?" I'm distracted with the damn fish, which I'm trying to poach.

"That hair, those clothes. Who is she?"

I fix Amy with a look. "She's my friend from work. Put the butter on."

I hear Mr. Purdy booming forth in the living room. He says the weather is weird, it's global warming. He complains about the cost of energy and real estate, rush hour traffic. He rattles on to Phil, Bruce, and Helen about the latest car chase through town. He'd just seen it on the news. A patrol officer tried to stop a kid in a primered pickup with no license plates. The cop cornered him out on the frontage road, in the parking lot of Allied Tool, the outfit that provided Emmett's nudie calendar almost a year ago. But the kid drove over a planter, through a barricade, and down a sidewalk, scaring the hell out of pedestrians. Then he sideswiped two cars, a van, and an SUV towing a boat. He escaped by going the wrong way down a one-way alley and disappeared. The cop had to let him go due to new restrictions against reckless pursuit.

I'm getting serving bowls out, stirring the gravy, turning the fish—and I hear him peppering them with his favorite James Bond-ish cures for reckless driving. If you start your car with alcohol on your breath, a sensor will kill the engine and activate handcuffs that pinion your wrists to the steering wheel. If you're being tailgated, you push a dash button and spray the bastard with a cloud of noxious smoke. His favorite (I've heard it before): you are not allowed to drive a car that has more horsepower than you have IQ. "Think what that will do for law enforcement!" he shouts. "The cops would know right off if they got Hannibal Lector or O.J. Simpson."

I yell from the kitchen, "But then there'd be no more car

chases. Think what that would do to your TV viewing." Mr. Purdy's favorite fare is *Cops, American Justice,* and *America's Most Wanted.* He turns the sound up so loud that in my back yard I can hear tires squealing and gunshots from his set next door.

When I call them, "People, come and eat," they arrange themselves around the table. The only seating plan I have is Mr. Purdy at its head, me at the foot. I make a last foray into the kitchen for the cranberries, and catch a glimpse of my reflection in the kitchen window. I look grand, the foxtail streak, the pinecone earrings, the eyeliner and mascara; pink in my cheeks from kitchen heat. The gypsy outfit is perfect, and I love it. Then when I approach the table to sit, Mr. Purdy stands for me. My heart is going to burst; I'm in love with this moment.

But an awkward silence follows, as we pass food. Amy says something about her dad, how she wishes he were here, and Bruce's smile freezes. I yearn to throttle her. She must know I want her to stifle this weak-kneed trip down memory lane, at least for now. But she goes on about how she misses his wall of self-congratulatory accolades, and the old way the furniture was arranged.

This kills our incipient conversation; the silence is leaden. Then Mr. Purdy tells a food joke, bless his heart. Seems this fellow went to see the doctor, with a banana stuck in one ear, a cucumber in the other, a cherry up one nostril ("that's a medical term, *nostril*") and a raspberry up the other. "Doc, I just don't feel good," says the man. "No wonder," says the doctor. "You're not eating right." We groan, then laugh dutifully.

Phil's turn to tell a doctor joke. It's about a duck that has chapped lips, a long circuitous story, too long, I think. The punch line is the duck saying, "Put it on my bill." Again a groan, then a laugh. Amy gives him a doting look.

Mr. Purdy makes a well of his mashed potatoes, fills it with peas, then floats the whole thing in gravy—Amy frowns, but I smile. Helen spreads apricot jam on garlic toast. Amy squeezes lemon on her fish, then passes the lemon segment to Phil, who finishes it off. How nice, teamwork, conservation. Bruce gazes about himself with a pleased although bemused expression, as if he doesn't quite know how he got here, and perhaps he doesn't. I myself make a barricade out of my potatoes so my salmon won't touch my turkey, am disconcerted by the amount of food I've piled on my plate. I can't eat all this. The last time I had such a dismaying plateful was at that Italian inn where Amy and I had dinner. The memory makes me turn a loving look at her. Such a good time, one I'll remember.

Phil is still talking, something about how we can control illness with a proper diet—which I don't believe—and I study him as he speaks. So like Emmett, his voice, his gestures, his sense of humor. Sure of himself, full of jaunty good humor—and emotionally stingy. Then I scold myself: I couldn't know that from our brief encounter. How judgmental I've become. To make up to him for his lack, or for mine, and to change the subject (Mr. Purdy's face has that look, he's going to argue), I praise his dedication as a leader of the youth. With the kids so distracted—the video age, instant gratification, junk food and all that—it must be hard to teach social studies. In the back of my mind, I hear Zack, the Zack at the singles' dance: *policemen and teachers: the two most represented groups among the rejects or the rejected.*

Phil frowns, and Amy says, "Mother, don't call it *social studies,* it's History. Phil teaches History."

"Amy, hon, it's okay. Yes, Peg, may I call you Peg? I'm in my third year at Washington Middle School, but what I'd like to do is write. I want to write a book for young teens about medieval England, or more precisely, Wales. I'm Welsh, see, Llewellan, that's a classic Welsh name, I feel my Welsh roots, and I think the Welsh have been overlooked. I'd like to write a Howard Pyle *Men of Iron* sort of thing. Set in Wales."

"If it's been done, why repeat it?" says Mr. Purdy rather sharply, and now I want to throttle *him.* He adds, "'Course, I haven't read it, but just the same—"

Phil purrs, "Good ideas are repeated all the time." Patient teacher with the backward stubborn student.

Around a mouthful of food, Helen says, "I read somewhere there are only four basic plots in all of literature."

"Five. Five in all of literature."

Bruce says admiringly, "Just think! To write a whole book. Say, could you pass the dressing? This is great, Peg." Then he adds, as an afterthought, "Why don't you tell us about your book?"

Helen seconds the motion, raises her wineglass, says, "Here, here!"

"See," says Phil gesturing with his fork, lecturing us, his audience of twelve-year-olds, "Pyle's book…anybody read it?" Helen says she thinkss he has, but she's not sure. "Pyle's book is about knights and kings, the élite. I want to depict the rest of society. The average people, what they were doing in those times. What it was like for them." Phil sets down his fork and smiles. I think that the little girls in his classes would develop crushes on him, the handsome teacher, until he graded them harshly. He *would* grade harshly.

Mr. Purdy snorts. "The average people, have you seen Monte Python, what was that movie? One varlet telling the other one that there goes the king. It must be the king because he doesn't have any shit on him."

Helen gives out a belly laugh. "I love Monte Python."

Bruce says, "I remember the skit about the parrot, the dead parrot."

Helen adds, "The one about Spam and eggs, what a riot. That British sense of humor, always thought I'd like to see England, Ireland, Wales."

Mr. Purdy says, "With the price of gas going up, I'll be lucky to make it to Oakland this year."

Helen says why would he want to go to Oakland, and he explains that he's got a cousin there. But on his last visit she'd annoyed him tremendously by inflicting him with a scrapbook commemorating her Caribbean cruise. There she was in her photos, red-eyed in the camera flash. A woman her age wearing a party hat, a low-cut gown that showed her wrinkled arms and chest, acting coy, kittenish. She described a flirtation she'd had with another old geezer at her dinner table. This woman, his own cousin, who'd been a widow for years, she should know better!

Helen says, "She needed one of these digital cameras—you

can cut out the red-eyed shots, these new cameras are so nifty—"

She wants to go on, but Mr. Purdy hasn't finished. The cruise line, he says, *they* should know better. They'd allowed his cousin to bring her dog on the trip. A snippy toy poodle so old it was toothless, so spoiled it demanded its food chewed up for it, which his cousin did.

Amy puts down her fork. "Disgusting."

I say, rushing in, "Little dogs lose their teeth faster than big ones. I read where—"

But Mr. Purdy still isn't finished. No, now that he thinks about it, he'll do something different this year, vacation-wise. He'll take Amtrak to Yosemite, although the mobs there bother him. But it's close, and reasonable. Enough bang for the buck.

Enough bang for the buck. His modern slang surprises me. Once, about Amy's lack of marketable skills, he said she was "between a sweat and a stink," which had annoyed me considerably at the time.

Bruce says, "Vacation's a long way off. I don't look forward to it anymore, without the family."

Helen guffaws. "I never looked forward to it *with* my family."

I want to follow up on this, because I've never heard much about her parents, her brothers, sisters—if she has any. And I want to follow up on Phil and his book idea, which Amy then brings us back to. She announces that she and Phil are thinking of going to Wales. At my startled look, she adds, "So Phil can do research. For the book. Besides, it's cheap living there. You can find a tight little cottage down a country lane, and still keep in touch through the 'Net, and e-mail, cell phones—modern technology."

This is Phil talking, not Amy. She's parroting him too soon. The subjugation of one's personality should take longer. At least put up a fight. "Well, it's a fun idea," I say. "More turkey? More…uh, salmon? Pass the rolls, Helen. Mr. Purdy, how about pouring more wine?"

"None for me, thanks," says Amy.

"No wine? But you like a nice white wine…this is good, Helen."

Phil says he and Amy are considering going overseas as soon as he can arrange with an exchange program to teach in a Welsh school. He has an uncle who'll sponsor them, and there are advantages to living in a worker-friendly environment. State-paid health insurance and leave, the pure and simple life, in an area that respects and welcomes scholars.

Amy takes up the chant. The lush value-rich lifestyle, the music, the gray-green curl of sea, the stone abbeys, the fiery sunsets. She can hardly wait. "Honey," she purrs to Phil, "bring in those pictures your uncle sent you."

By now we've finished eating, and I start clearing off dishes. Romantic nonsense, and I bang around plates in the kitchen.

Phil returns from his car with the snapshots. "See, here's my uncle, and my cousins in their garden…here's the local street fair and there's the cathedral in the background. The whole tribe of them at the breakwater in the harbor…oh, and the castle…did you see *Braveheart*? Part of that movie was filmed right here."

They are passing around photos, making the appropriate noises, but I can't concentrate, my mouth has gone dry. They really mean this. "If you go, how long would you stay?" I ask.

"*Moving,* Mother. A permanent move."

"No! You can't mean that! You'd go there to *live*?"

"You got it. Don't worry: you can visit. It's cheap to fly, if you watch for specials on the 'Net."

I have no answer. I am shaken, at a loss. I can't conceive of not having Amy nearby. True, we haven't always gotten along, especially lately. But that she would go so far away….No, this is not possible. It's a joke, a hoax, they are trying to scare me. They are chasing will-o'-the-wisps, pipe dreams, phantoms. But I look again at the set of Phil's shoulders, at his hard blue eyes; I see his square chin, and even with the dimple, I can tell he's stubborn. He's going to take Amy away from me. He already has.

I ought to be glad it's Phil, because Amy's previous boyfriends have not been exactly full of good sense, restraint, responsibility. I *am* glad, of course. Sooner or later, it had to be somebody, and it might as well be this Phil, who is an odd combination of wild fanciful dreams and stern authoritarianism. I admit it: in a sense, I am glad to be rid of her. She could still be a burden I cannot afford, that I do not want to bear. I'm suddenly teetering on the edge of depression, because I thought I had moved beyond this kind of selfishness, and I have not.

We've had lovely times together, Amy and I. And Emmett. She is a connection to him that I feel slipping away, one that I had wished to sever, but now, it's like slipping off the mooring lines, casting myself into the sea. I feel a chill…this silly outfit has let me down. I rub my arms, which have goosebumps. I get up, and reach in the hall closet and grab that embroidered denim shirt of Emmett's still in there from the garage sale. Does Amy recognize this shirt? Does she remember how I worked on it at Calavaras Big Trees? Does she remember playing in that little creek, so small it was merely a series of puddles amid rounded boulders? Does she remember the water spiders? What does she remember of growing up with Emmett and me? I try to catch her eye, to communicate with her in a sort of code, but she's intent on Phil and his plans. Although we may not have much of a present, or a future from the sounds of it, Amy and I have a past, and I don't have that with these other people here. What are they doing here, these strangers? It's time for them to go home.

But not yet. There's still dessert. By now Helen and I have cleared the table, and I present the cheesecake. It's when I put Amy's sliver down in front of her—although she objects, says she's already over-eaten—that I see a bottle of vitamin pills by her water glass. *Prenatal,* I read on the label. Amy is pregnant. The blood leaves my head, I think for a second I'll faint. Then I have to laugh at this: Amy is the one pregnant, and I'm sick. Sometimes life makes no sense.

It makes no sense that she's pregnant. She knows better, she knows how not to be. She'd allowed this to happen, perhaps to get clear of me? Or to land this guy, Phil? Is he that important to her? I yearn to ply her with questions, but cannot in front of everyone. Again I want them to leave.

Finally the company goes home, or most of it. Mr. Purdy leaves first. Helen follows him out, saying she's going to a late show with Eileen, the friend she acquired at the Jolly Roger. Despite all my bottled-up questions, I walk Amy and Phil out to their car, which is dwarfed by Bruce's rig parked behind it. It's a little economy model, a beige Ford Escort. There's a bumper sticker. It reads VEGETARIANS DO IT WITH RELISH. I suffer an evil obscene image: a long pink hotdog, throbbing with heat, spread with mustard.

Only it isn't a hotdog.

Perhaps I conjure up that obscene image because Bruce is waiting for me in the house, as the rest of my guests must have realized. Helen had left with a knowing smirk.

Bruce in his brown leisure suit. I don't know how much I want to do this, or if I'm ready for it, but I wave goodbye to Amy and Phil and then trudge back into my own kitchen. Is this any way to start a love affair?

Love affair. Another oxymoron.

Chapter 12

On Thanksgiving, the anniversary of what Bruce then began calling "his liberation," enabling him to put a new spin on his breakup (probably for my benefit), we begin our odd affair, or courtship, or romance—whatever you want to call it.

After seeing Amy and Phil off—I packed up the rest of the salmon and sent it home with them—I go back in the house to Bruce perched stiffly in my little plaid chair, deigning Emmett's La-Z-Boy. I consider, briefly, that I'd free up a lot of space by getting rid of the old recliner. But why bother? I don't spend much time out here, now that the TV's in the bedroom. Nevertheless, it dawns on me that Emmett's chair maintains a presence in the room that has become dampening, as if Emmett's disapproving ghost still hovers. At one point this sense of him would have been welcome. But no more.

"He must have been quite a guy," Bruce says, staring at Emmett's wall.

"He had consuming interests, you know, a hobby freak."

"He was good at everything."

"He did okay. You want more cheesecake?" I feel heat mount in my cheeks, because that sounds like I'm offering him a striptease, a girlie show, which maybe I am.

"No, thanks. You want me to rekindle the fire?" And now color mottles his cheeks, because of what *he's* offering.

"Sure, or do you want to watch the news?" For that, we'll have to go down to my bedroom. A blatant invitation from a sex-starved old broad?

He follows me down the hall, into my bedroom, into my bed. At first it's just homey and sweet. I am tired; the dinner wore me out. He rubs the fatigue out of my shoulders, out of my back, my feet—God, a foot massage, sexier than dinner and dancing; a soak in a hot tub, with champagne. He flops on the bed beside me, and I'm ready to open the door and let him come. In. And I do. He is gentle, patient, and slow, too slow because I reach that point and surprise myself by going off like a firecracker. "Hey, wait for me," he chuckles, but with alarm in his voice, too. However, I can double back and pick him up, because I seem to have them lined up and ready to take off, like jets at Oakland International. There's nothing here I couldn't have done alone but that foot massage loosened me up, and it's nice to share Bruce's surprisingly educated fingers.

He's the one with a problem. He is unable. It's like trying to fire a rubber gun. Finally he rolls over and says, "It's no use. It's this bed, this house—he's in here with us." I know what he means—Emmett's aura's everywhere. However, I assure him it's my fault. I'm not doing something right, I lack a sexual gift of some sort. Then I wonder why I must protect him. I don't owe him anything, not even a cover story.

I am too lazy and replete to make a really strenuous attempt, although I, too, deliver a foot massage: his feet are narrow and thin, blue-white as skim milk, nails neatly trimmed, his toes tufted with brave bits of hair. Emmett's feet had been tough as tree roots because he'd liked to go barefooted. My mother had scoffed at that. Only the poor, or the self-indulgent rich, went barefooted.

Emmett hadn't been rich, but he'd indulged himself.

"It's no use. Leave it, Peg." Bruce gets up, starts to put on his clothes.

"Wait. Don't you want to see Brian Williams and the news? He's on soon. I like to watch how his eyebrows—" I'm about to say *pump up and down,* which would be indelicate, and substitute instead, "—swivel." But Bruce goes into the bathroom. When he comes out, he's resolved to go home. I call down the hall after him, "Would you make sure the cat's in, and the door's locked? Oh, and grab that container of turkey out of the fridge. Julia Child's description of 'forever' is one person and a turkey.'" Truth to tell, I'm not sorry to see him go. Earlier I'd noticed that MYSTERY Channel is showing *Bullitt* and *Three Days of the Condor,* with my two favorite blonds. That will get me off to sleep at three, which will do. Tomorrow's an easy day, everyone in the office slow and sated with overeating.

But I never see the end of *Bullitt,* my favorite Steve McQueen movie (never did like *The Sand Pebbles).* Wake up with the TV playing to itself at five-thirty, turn it off and doze...until I'm late for work. Scramble into my clothes, into the Bronco, which doesn't want to start. However, I beat Vi who arrives from Oakland with a replacement for Zack. He's a whistle-clean kid named Timmy, who resembles, I think, a young Bruce. He catches on quickly, works hard; Helen reports good things of him at lunch, which, for all of us, is turkey sandwiches. Tiffany has called in sick, so the air in the office has extra ions, as if washed by the sea. I sail out at quitting time, looking forward to oyster stew with Mr. Purdy.

Saturday morning Bruce calls with an offer I accept. He will drive me to Sacramento to look at a VW replacement for the Bronco, if he can use the washer and dryer. Saturday is his laundry day, but everybody has the same idea in his complex, and it's hectic to get at the machines. I'm glad to have Bruce. Emmett made fun of women alone dealing with car salesman, wearing their naïveté like sandwich boards.

He arrives early, and while I'm in the house fretting over my appearance, he's been out front pulling weeds, accumulating a workman-like pile of dandelions. He tells me sternly, "If you get these now, they won't go to seed." I hang my head, yeah, I know. But he doesn't push his lecture; he merely brings in his duffel bag of clothes. Fussily, he separates whites from coloreds, gets the first batch going. We leave the machine running, which I don't like to do, but the morning is slipping away. While crossing town to get on the freeway, he says there's a home & garden show he'd like to pop in on.

"Home & garden! Do we have the time?" I'm cross—lack of sleep is catching up with me?—or is it the new person I'm changing into? I am becoming irascible as I revert into who I'd been before I met Emmett, coagulating into an obdurate boulder in my own stream of life, despite the eroding wash and roil of circumstance. I cringe when I remember all those blueberry pancakes with orange syrup that I coddled Emmett with. I don't even like orange syrup. How I kept the Sunday paper virginal, for Emmett to break open. Meatloaf—whether cracker crumbs or oatmeal, I don't bother with either one because I don't like meatloaf.

Bruce backs down. "You're right, of course. Some other time. Auto row it is. Then maybe lunch? How about Chinese?"

"Mexican?"

"How about the Food Court? Then you can choose."

"But it's not very good."

"Okay, Mexican, then."

Traffic is light, we're traveling at a good clip northeast on Highway 80 toward Sacramento. The oleander divider strip is still in bloom; I see people in shorts, tee shirts—it's summer weather, which bodes ill for our water shortage: one small Halloween rain has been it so far this year. Bruce turns onto Florin Road, drives auto row with its new and used car lots. "There, the VW dealer." He cranks the wheel over, pulls in, and parks in front of a new Jetta. Before we can climb down, several salesmen converge on us. *Mack the Knife* plays on the dealership speakers, as the alpha salesman sprints out to us, cutting off two other guys. He's a flossy fellow, with white teeth and a heavy brow ridge, like you'd see on a prehistoric skull in the museum. Dark complexion; maybe Salvadorian, Puerto Rican.

"How are you folks today," he sings out in aggressive good humor, and I begin to have second thoughts. How foolish to be here, wasting this guy's time. I should have done research in *The Kelley Blue Book* and *Consumer Report.* I should have talked to other VW drivers, like Helen. I should have looked up road tests on the Internet. In other words, I should have been doing what Emmett would have done; what he probably did do before buying Maggie Quinn's red Miata. I still need Emmett to take care of me, car-wise. I fear that Bruce isn't going to be much help when the rubber hits the road.

Nevertheless, we follow this effusive salesman, who's pressed his business card on us, around and through rows of banner-decorated Beetles precisely parked, their hoods up at the same angle—feeding time at Eidelbrok Volkswagen.

I hear the salesman, "That big rig too much for the little lady? Well, we can fix her right up, just the thing, anti-lock brakes, power-steering, dual air bags, heat and air, real leather seats." He unwinds his sticky spiel and encases Bruce, his mistaken fly. I overhear, "…makeup mirror here on the visor, for the wife…"

"…*for the wife*." Emmett's been gone almost nine months. *Wife* has an exotic ring to it. I could be Bruce's wife. We could be a pair. Why not?

Then a new thought attacks me: this is what Maggie Quinn did with Emmett. She'd followed him around rows of Miatas, a solicitous hand on his arm, beaming her green smile into his face, fantasizing, playacting the happy wife to the happy husband, the happy couple. The bottom drops out of my day, my play. I want to cry, I want to thrash around and shriek that it's not fair. At the same time I smile up at Bruce, the smile I've practiced at home.

We go into the sales office where Miguel assaults us with a glossy clutch of brochures. He staples another business card to the one on top, then covers a sheet with figures—purchase price "fully loaded," minus down payment, plus interest, blah, blah, blah. I'm not attending, partly because the showroom's décor consists of mounted animal heads—bear, deer, elk—and their glassy staring eyes disconcert me; partly because I can't afford the monthly payments, somewhere in the neighborhood of $600. What Bruce and I are playing at is charades.

We escape Miguel, Mr. Salazar, drive slowly through traffic, which is now thick, looking for Mexican food. There are a million ethnic cafés and fast-food outlets lining the road, and Bruce asks me which one I want. I point to Santiago's—it must be Mexican, done up with sombreros and cacti. Inside, pseudo adobe walls are draped with dusty serapes; the dark tables (outside is full sun) are lit with candles in yellow glass holders. The waitress, a dyed redhead with blue eyeshadow, brings us salsa and chips, and splattered plastic-coated menus. Bruce silently studies his.

"Listen, I'm sorry," I say.

"What for?"

"You wanted Chinese."

"Hey, no problem. I was just thinking that if I were you, I'd shop around. He's on the high side, but of course he'd expect you to deal."

So he's not sulking, which Emmett would have done. He's not sitting there aggrieved with the plate of goo the waitress soon slides in front of him; he's not hating me and my choices. He's tucking into his beans, rice, whatever it is that's covered with melted cheese, and he's mulling over my projected purchase of a car. I take heart, and the world seems brighter. Besides, I have ordered a better combo, a neater arrangement of distinct foods. I can recognize my items.

How lucky I am to be here with a temperate man, because he's not focused on me and my many failings, but apparently on his own bright prospect. Because he puts down his fork, which has a long string of cheese on it, and says, "Listen, how about dinner tonight? Could we get together after I do a few chores? There's always hope, you know, for a *second coming*—" He says this with a slight flush, a self-deprecating laugh.

"Sure. Your place this time."

"No, I can't. Izzie'll be home. But I've got a buddy, we can use his place. If that's okay with you."

I'm about to snap something about this being ridiculous, we're adults, but I get a look at his expression and say. "Sure, why not?" So I cast my lot with Bruce, about whom I'm lukewarm. He's a nice person, not a dreamboat, which I wouldn't have liked anyway. I've decided that handsome men are a thing of the devil.

Later, alone at home, I deal with his laundry, although he'd said not to, that he'd do it. I transfer his white load from washer to dryer, then dump it on my bed to fold. I bemoan the state of his tee shirts, a ragged collection with holes in the armpits, frayed seams. His shorts—boxers with stretched-out elastic. He needs seeing to, but not by me.

The next load, his colored clothes. I match his socks, those protectors of his delicate feet, tuck them into each other, tight little bundles. I enjoy doing this, because Emmett hadn't let me do it my way: he'd wanted this socks clipped; he always wanted something different from what I offered.

Other than a peek into his medicine cabinet, what could be more revealing than a man's laundry? I'm touched that he's tacitly permitted me to perform this intimate chore. I fold his things with a reverent hand, with none of the callous, threadbare familiarity I'd dealt with Emmett's.

His shirts, pants. They come out of the dryer exuding a familiar fragrance that goes beyond the soap powder I used. It dawns on me....Of course! Bruce deals with shipping materials, as had Emmett, and I can smell the cardboard, the paper, the indefinable something male. Almost in a swoon, I peel off my own clothes, I slip into Bruce's, still warm, a long-sleeved polo shirt and khaki pants I've seen him wear to work. The shirt hangs on me; the pants are too long—he is four or five inches taller than I—and too big around the waist. I collapse on the bed, in love with the way I feel. It's as if I am transferring some of his agreeable spirit into my increasingly hard-edged and brittle soul. After all, he pulled weeds, he spent time at the dealership; I didn't allow him to go to the home & garden show, or eat Chinese. And he doesn't hold any of it against me.

Bruce, a wash-'n-wear kind of guy. Emmett had liked his pants touched up with the iron…where is my iron? On a high shelf in the utility room, where I left it after trying to discipline the linen dress I took to the redwoods (it went to the Humane Society with the rejects from the garage sale).

But Bruce won't be fussy. No one has catered to him the way I catered to Emmett. A boil-in-a-bag, freeze-dried guy…his daughter doesn't cook; he gets along as best he can. He wouldn't expect blueberry pancakes with orange syrup.

Just the same, I'm aware of an insistent itch to please him, to astound him, to amaze him…to overwhelm him. Is this the kiss of death? I almost hope not.

His buddy's place: a shabby trailer in a motor court off the frontage road. At first I am offended by its trappings. A Formica tabletop sticky with grime and drink rings; dingy indoor/outdoor carpeting; splintered cabinets with ill-fitting catches. The bathroom: aqua fixtures and a gouged starburst linoleum countertop, uncurling at the edges.

But in a perverse manner, this environment pleases me, takes me out of myself, cancels judgmental tendencies I'm only newly aware of erecting. I'm not responsible for anything, it's out of my hands. Out of my control. This place, and what occurs here, is something I can turn my back on; I can leave here intact—it's as preposterous as a dream. Bruce evidently feels the same way, because he is willing, and he is able. He's not seized-up, is how he puts it. Not that we discuss his condition.

Afterward, while Bruce does some sprucing up, I wait at the sticky table, pushing aside a lid from a mayonnaise jar someone used as an ashtray. "Your buddy smokes?" I call down to the dark cubicle that serves as a bedroom.

"Yeah, he took it up again after his divorce. I tell him to quit, but he's at that point, he can't do it yet."

"Where is he tonight?"

"Out somewhere. He doesn't hang around here much. He's alone. Me, I'm lucky; I have Izzie." Bruce reappears with a bundle of sheets—he'd evidently changed them for our use. (Later he admitted that his afternoon "chore" had been tidying up this place for me, which I found extremely touching.)

"I'd like to meet your Izzie."

"You will. She's coming to Vi's Christmas party with me, you'll have a chance to get acquainted."

"Wonderful," I breathe, but I'm aware of a falling off, a dampening of my spirit. Had I been hoping that he'd go to the party with me? Like a date for the prom? "Wonderful," I repeat. "Can't wait to meet her."

"She's just the best kind of person, I'm so proud of her. She's got a good head on her shoulders, solid, sensible. Not like Jan at all." He frowns.

It's then that it occurs to me his talk is too full of Isabel. Don't divorced men talk about their ex-wives? Maybe Bruce is beyond that. After all, it's been four years. Four years of living with Isabel? Belatedly, an alarm sounds.

CHAPTER 13

So I ride with Helen to the Christmas party at Vi and Ed Corbet's. They live on a gently twisting tree-bordered road halfway up a hill in Oakland. An ideal location: high enough to catch the view, but low enough to escape wildfires that ravage the chaparral every summer. An exclusive neighborhood, and from the main road, curious passers-by catch only glimpses of homes tucked within luxurious grounds. "Holy cow," I breathe, awestruck.

"Yeah, Vi's husband, Ed, has money. His grandfather invented and patented some turnbuckle contraption. They use it in this prefab housing industry."

We turn down a driveway, and the house comes into view. I recognize this style of house, half-timbered, with mullioned windows, the kind that look elegant but don't let in much light due to their design, and to the second-story overhang. A bitch to clean, the whole house a bitch—I should know: I had one like this on my route as a Molly Maid.

The graveled parking area is illuminated with tiny white lights, creating a fairyland effect—a bevy of Tinkerbells run amok. Helen slides her VW in next to a beige Honda; it belongs to one of the installers, Eugene, I think. Bruce's *rig*, I find myself sneering at the enormous thing, hulks next to it, still ticking as it cools. Plenty of room in the back seat for Helen and me; again I wonder what Bruce is about…is he ashamed of us, of me?

A pair of ornamental shrubs, like bonsai plants, stands sentinel by the massive front door. It's trimmed with a wreath of straw decorated with birds and fruit, twined around with a red ribbon. The effect is Christmas, restrained and festive, yet dignified. The effect is Money.

On my own street, Frieda decreed that this year we'd carry forth a candy cane motif. To keep on her good side, I strung a few red and white lights, hung candy canes on the podocarpus Emmett planted by the entry. Emmett could have cut up sheets of plywood into giant candy canes, painted them with red and white stripes, stuck them in the lawn. Frieda would have been pleased. But then again, Emmett hadn't cottoned to Frieda's controlling tendencies; he might have retaliated with Bethlehem stars.

Actually, Emmett wouldn't have done that. He'd been repulsed by the Christmas brouhaha. If he'd lived through the attack, would he have gotten religion? He might have become churchy and pious. I'm glad he hadn't had time to develop zealotry.

Helen pushes the buzzer and we hear an echo of chimes inside. Vi appears, bringing with her noise from the party, people talking, laughing. There is Christmas music, not the usual schlock, but something classical, the muted cooing of a flock of cellos, violins; unobtrusive, a contrapuntal statement of taste, class. Vi effervesces us into the hall, which smells of pine, cedar, and food. She expresses extreme delight at finding us here, as if we've accidentally met on an obscure street in Barcelona; as if we hadn't been at work together just the day before, simmering with pre-Christmas surliness.

Vi takes our coats, exclaims over my hair, my silver dress

that I did buy after all. She exclaims over Helen in a stretchy blue velour two-piece. She herself is done up in a swishy hostess gown, in a tawny beige. "Come in," Vi sings, "come in. Make yourselves at home. Straight through you'll find the buffet in the dining room, eat, drink—help yourselves. You won't know everyone, but pretend that you do. I'll put your things in the day-room off the parlor."

I recognize the layout from my Molly Maid days. From this entry, which is low ceilinged with flat arches and dark paneling, I see the gleaming staircase with turned newels, trimmed with holiday swags. On a landing halfway to the second floor, you'll find a set of windows with stained glass inserts. Under them a mahogany table with a crocheted runner, a stand for an airplane plant throwing out a cascade of starts. I'd once hauled a vacuum cleaner up steps like those.

To my right, an arch frames the doorway into the formal living room dominated by a grand piano crowned with a still life of hothouse roses. There's a frozen-looking flocked Christmas tree trimmed with royal blue silk balls. To the left, the same archway treatment opens into the parlor/den/family room, which offers the everyday tree, a green one trimmed with plaid bows. Somewhere off this room will be a smaller room, the day-room, with a cot for naps; a place to stash the computer, its monitor showing a collage of family snaps, or a holiday-themed screensaver.

Standing between these two arches, on the cusp, so to speak, I know how this party will develop: women congregating in one room, men in the other, and in front of me the evening stretches out like a pair of queen-sized pantyhose. I feel a rush of fatigue, as if I've come here not as a guest, but as a Molly Maid whose job it is to clean, mop, and dust this monster.

I give myself a shake. Amy would not feel this way, were she here. Amy would pull it off, Amy would go in there and make friends with everyone, including the cat. Amy would kneel to rub the cat's belly, showing off her shapely bum, and her red-painted nails. Amy would serpentine a silver dress like mine with its body-hugging curves around and through the crowd clustered at the punchbowl, which will be a handsome cut-glass affair, with matching cups. Amy would knock their socks off, score big-time as the center of attention. I will use Amy as my model, I will follow Amy's lead and make this party my own. I plow ahead toward the dining room.

It's dark paneled, as is the rest of the house, a handsome room with gleaming wide oak flooring upon which are spread oriental carpets. The dining room table, with a diameter of at least eight feet, is spread with finger foods—ham and cheese rollups, platters of shrimp and smoked salmon, vegetable wedges, melon slices (in December!), a silver tray of tiny cream puffs and tartlets, with serving tongs shaped like chicken feet.

In the center of the table, on a stiff lace cloth, an arrangement of poinsettias in luxurious bloom, in pots covered with gold foil, tied with red ribbons. Clusters of mistletoe hang in doorways; holiday greenery frames the swinging doors into the kitchen (I imagine a six-burner stainless steel stove, glass-fronted cabinets, slate countertops, a circle of copper cookware suspended over an expansive oak chopping block). More greenery around French doors that lead out to a deck where I see, leaning over it, a spiny monkey puzzle tree. Indirect lighting picks out details of its prehistoric character: savage foliage, neat rows of triangular shark's teeth; bark studded with thorns. A friendlier note on the deck: built-in benches ring a fire pit. There's even a fire, for guests who want to escape the indoor party.

The thing that takes my eye, though, is a glowing Tiffany chandelier over the table. A dome decorated with red and purple grapes against a background of trees as precisely frilled as broccoli flowerets.

I wish for Helen, or Bruce. Someone to whom I can say how much I like that chandelier. I tell the man next to me. "That thing is gorgeous I wonder if it's real?"

"A real Tiffany? Sure is. You're going to ask how I know? I'm your host, Ed Corbet."

He's a tall thin drink of water, with an untidy bird's nest of sandy hair. His complexion is ruddy, freckled, dented—as if he'd had trouble with basal cell cancers. His nose is off kilter, as if broken a few times. He wears a Rudolf the Red-Nosed Reindeer tie, a trick tie that I recognize from Emmett's collection. Battery-operated, the nose will light up with the press of a button. I say to him that I know how the tie works, on account of Emmett.

"Emmett! You're Peg Malone…from the farm team."

I admit yes, it's true.

"I knew Emmett. He was a jokester. Never a dull moment."

"I've been wanting to hear about that."

"Emmett and I were in the same woodshop class at the junior college, that was how I knew him, personally. Then there were stories—"

"Stories?"

"In woodshop…move over here so we're out the traffic…okay, in woodshop we had this dork, a real dud of a teacher, Mr. Feldman, and he and Emmett clashed something fierce. Feldman drove a Mini Cooper, a tiny car, so gutless it wouldn't get out of its own way. Remember them? They're making a replica now, really cute. Anyway, after a clash with Feldman, Emmett got some guys together…well, first I should say that the shop classes had just taken delivery of some heavy equipment in these wooden crates that were out back waiting to go to the dump. Emmett got six or seven strong guys together, picked up Feldman's little car and set it on top of a wooden crate. When Feldman came out to the faculty parking lot, there was his car, two feet off the ground, he couldn't drive home, had to call the janitorial crew to lift it down. Funny as a crutch, the way Emmett told it. He was a card."

"That's funny."

"Of course Feldman found out who did it, and had Emmett suspended. But Emmett got him back, good."

"I hate to ask…tell me."

"Emmett found out where Feldman lived, and played that old trick, I was surprised Feldman went for it."

"What?"

"You never heard this? Not very nice to talk about, but what the heck. Emmett filled a shopping bag with cow manure—he had a buddy who owned a dairy somewhere—"

"That would be Tony Medeiros, I remember him."

"Emmett puts this shopping bag on Feldman's front step, sets it on fire, rings the bell and takes off. Feldman rushes out and stomps on it, on that bag of shit, it's all over him, all over everything—his steps, his porch. This steaming hot cow shit."

"The old trick."

"But that isn't what got him expelled."

"Emmett was expelled?"

"I've done it this time...you didn't know?"

"Listen, he's gone, it's over. Tell me."

"Here's what I heard—I wasn't there, but I believe it, knowing Emmett. The administration, the bigwigs, all the junior college mucky-mucks, they were celebrating getting the new auditorium built. Remember when they got that big bond issue passed? They built this beautiful new auditorium, perfect acoustics, velvet curtains, the whole nine yards. To celebrate the grand opening, to crow over this achievement, all the wheels who raised the money, plus Feldman, arranged a showing of Steve McQueen—"

"Steve McQueen movies were bad luck for Emmett."

"What?"

"Nothing...go on."

"Steve McQueen in *Papillon.* A grand opening preview for the grand opening of the auditorium. Remember that movie? McQueen's serving a life term on Devil's Island for picking his nose or for leaving the toilet seat up—something minor. This suspenseful scene where he's escaping a horror of an existence, he's floating out on the tide in the bay right under the noses of the guards. Silently slipping away without a ripple, absolutely not a sound to be heard, either in the movie or in the auditorium—you could have heard a pin drop. Well, right then, perfect timing, Emmett stood up in the dark of the back—see, the usher was his buddy, he'd let him in—and he gives out this blood-curdling shriek at the top of his lungs. Everybody in there literally jumped out of their skins, it gave them a collective heart attack—oops, sorry."

"That's okay. What happened then?"

"The dean called him in and canned him. Threw him out of school, let the Army get him."

"But he didn't yell FIRE! He didn't commit a crime. It was a joke."

"Technically, maybe. But see, the administration had it in for him, so when he ruined the party to show off that auditorium…they were out to get him, and they got him."

"He went to Vietnam."

"Have I shocked you? Let the cat out of the bag? Because he was just a kid, we all were. No worse than anybody else. He was just funnier about it, was all. You want some punch? Here, let me—"

"Thanks. I appreciate you leveling with me. I knew he'd been rebellious, of course." I stumble around with my words, at a loss, plate in one hand, cup of punch in the other. That Emmett, oh, that scamp. I want to tell Amy, amuse her with these yarns about her dad. Then again, another part of me is less than delighted with this cache of new stories.

I knew he had the ability to hold a grudge. The poor teacher. Emmett probably made his life hell. But it had been innocent, hadn't it? He'd just done what kids do, and it backfired, forced him out of whatever plans he'd had and into the Army. Still, it seemed a harsh sentence for a youthful antic.

But Emmett had been tricky. He'd had a hollowness, something amiss. He'd not rung true at times, and at times I'd been frightened, had turned back from exploring the depths in him. For example, the wedding ring fiasco.

A few months ago I took off my wedding ring, because I've lost weight and it was loose. A plain gold band, a twin to his, except mine was set with a single jewel, an emerald from his family's meager store of riches. My ring was handsome, in a stark dramatic way. Anyone could have a diamond, I told myself, a mere molecular arrangement of carbon, one of the commonest elements on earth, extracted by slave labor controlled and manipulated by a few heartless consortiums. But I had an emerald; well, slave labor involved there, too, spawning social ills, devastated landscapes and all that, but not to the same extent. My pure emerald.

An emerald? No, said the jeweler that I took it to for sizing. A nice piece of glass, but no emerald. I'd been shocked, angry;

I'd felt cheated—until I realized that Emmett's deception had been due to a deep-seated sense of his own lack of consequence. In the end, it affected me, made me feel more warmly toward him than if the stone had been real.

But there'd been other incidents highlighting his less-than-redeeming qualities. Once he'd Crazy-glued a fifty-cent piece down on the sidewalk and laughed when the paperboy stopped on his route, got off his bike, and tried to pry it up. Once he'd stolen two-by-fours from a building site, rationalizing his theft by saying anyone dumb enough to leave good wood out that close to the street deserved to lose it.

The bubble gum caper. He stuffed a wad of gum into the keyhole of a car he judged had been parked out front too long. It had a FOR SALE on it, and for someone to leave it there day in, day out, riled him. This was at the apartment complex where we lived before buying the house, thank goodness, because the sun melted the gum into a horrible mess, and the incident had caused a ruckus with the cops coming out and quizzing everybody.

So I knew Emmett had not always displayed a sterling character, but now I wonder, again, if I'd really known him. Ed says, "I've shocked you. Lemme counterbalance with something else that Emmett did. We, Emmett and I, we worked once on a building project, or reclamation project, whatever. This was years ago, right after he got home from 'Nam—you were probably dating him then. At least he wasn't married yet."

"Building project."

"Yeah, see, he was kinda mixed up, trying to find himself, but you probably know that, right?"

"Right."

"So we were involved in this program, to help people out, volunteering. What happened was this family's house burned down, they had four kids, no insurance, lost everything, so me and Emmett helped them rebuild. Worked day and night, never took a day off, or a cent of money from anybody—materials all donated, for the PR, you know. But we did the physical labor."

"Yes, non-profit." I'm remembering those lonely stretches when he left me pining by the phone. Poor me; poor Emmett, good Emmett.

"See, Peg, he was quite a guy. You want some more of this cheese? Another cracker?"

"No, I—"

Vi pushes through the swinging kitchen doors and lays a hand on Ed's arm. He's needed. While we talked, the tide has ebbed in the punchbowl, and Vi leads him off to replenish it. I'm alone, looking around. I need to go somewhere and examine these new stories about Emmett. I need to file them away under Unfinished Business, or maybe Old Business. The bathroom. Grab my purse, for cover, and head toward where I know it's located from my days of Molly Maid-ism. Once there, in an echoing high-ceilinged room done in small octagonal tiles, I contemplate myself in a little mirror on a retractable arm next to the medicine cabinet. I want to talk to someone...Amy? No, I really want to talk to Emmett, who has escaped me.

Back in the party flow, feeling terribly alone, and still longing to talk, I look around. Where's Helen? Where are Bruce and Izzie? Who do I know here? I make a circuit of the buffet, I could always eat, but I'm not hungry. At my elbow appears a youngish woman, a tiny thing with crimped, flyaway hair. She says, "I love your earrings, those pinecones are cute." I thank her, and she goes on, "Your whole outfit, the dress, the stockings, really nice. Those metallic nylons...but on me, well, I can't wear a thing like that. Too flashy."

Her remark puzzles me, but I say they're not metallic, just extra shiny. I tell her that wearing them is tricky, because, I add, as a joke on me—last year at this time, I'd been chunky—they could make your legs look fat. I tell her I like her outfit, too, although I'm not sure about that. It's a pale pink flowered print, and for my taste, it's overkill with too many bows and gathers and ruffles, sort of like Princess Di used to wear.

I spot Helen's two-piece blue sashaying into the formal Christmas tree room, and I'm about to head off when a man at my elbow says, "You must be a cable person, from Vi's side of the party." He's loading his plate with ham rollups. "At least I know you're not a Native Son of the Golden West, from Ed's."

I admit that I'm not a Native Son, and he proceeds to tell a joke, one I've heard before. The visitor to the barnyard asks the farmer why one pig has a wooden leg. The farmer relates the pig's heroics, how it scared off bandits, saved the daughter from drowning, rescued the family from the burning house, and so on. "But why the wooden leg?" asks the visitor. The farmer: "Such a good pig, we couldn't eat him all at once." I laugh dutifully while he polishes off a ham rollup. His wife appears—I guess she's his wife—she snags him, leads him away to bestow a wifely smack on his cheek under the mistletoe. I gaze out at the deck, wonder where Bruce and Izzie are, and then go back to milling around the table, grazing.

I eavesdrop on a couple of men discussing local politics, a trio of women their hairdressers. The CD of Christmas music is halted, and someone uncorks a sparkling piano piece in the formal tree room. I'm about to wander off toward it when the swinging doors to the kitchen open and Bruce comes out with a platter.

"There you are! What are you doing?" I cry out gaily.

"I'm slicing the roast for Vi," he growls, "because you're monopolizing her husband, who was supposed to do it. What are you up to!"

"Excuse me?"

"You told my daughter her legs look fat."

"What the hell! I don't even know your daughter!"

"That's her in the pink, right there," and he motions at the frizzy-haired woman in the Princess Di knockoff.

"Listen, I didn't say that at all. If she heard that I said her legs were fat, that's her problem." I shake off his hand and stomp down the hall. Glance into the formal living room, see a woman playing the piano, Helen leaning over her. Then swing into the green tree room, navigate toward an empty space on a bone and ivory brocaded couch. Apart from the couch, it's a warm friendly room done in needlepoint and books. Across from me, a pair of women discusses cookbooks; at a library table two men are looking up something in an atlas. I overhear *Dubrovnik.* One of them is going to vacation on the Adriatic Sea, has rented a villa for the month of July. How nice, I think, to get away. Just then the fellow next to me, a young guy with longish curly hair and an earring, says, "You work with Tiff, right?"

"Tiff, yeah, I'm from the cable office. Peg Malone." I hold out my hand, which is cold from cradling the punch cup, now empty.

"Jason West. I live with Tiffany. She's a controlling bitch, isn't she. You don't need to answer, but you could if you wanted to. She's off smoking a joint with the new kid, this candy-ass jerk who's got them buffaloed. Sure as shit she'll rat him out, like she did Zack."

Our new gofer, that sweet innocent kid—out smoking a joint! And it was Tiffany who blew the whistle on Zack. While I ponder that, he tells his story, unfolding it before me like a length of cloth, a table runner. "See, I'm alone, or was alone, me and my two kids. My wife left, just took off. I was going down the tube when I met Tiffany. Little Melody was three, Justin eighteen months, and there I was, I didn't know which end to feed, which to diaper. Talk about desperation… you have no idea.

"Then I met Tiff, it was at the Saturday market, I was trying to buy some tomatoes. Just buy tomatoes! Put some goddamned tomatoes in a sack and pay for them while juggling the kids around in this double stroller thing. I couldn't even do that! Well, Tiffany steps out of the blue and offers to help me. So you see, the last couple of years she'd been doing it, baggin' up my life. Organizing me and the kids. I'd be dead without her."

He turns to look at me and I see the raw panic in his eyes. "But sometimes I just want to tell her to fuck off. She must be hell on wheels to work with. She must be the bossiest bitch. She comes across so cool, all that punk junk. But I tell you she's razorblades and knives inside. Watch your back, she'll stab you. Take it from me—I live with her—but I can't get by without her.

"What I really needed, what I *wanted* was someone I could connect with. Someone who'd take time to stop and smell the roses with me, you know what I mean?" He becomes exercised and begins to jiggle his knee, drumming his fingers on his jumping leg.

I'm tempted to say there, there, and pat his head. Instead I mutter, "What happened to your wife? I mean, with you and her?"

"She met this guy, she took off."

"Where is she now?"

"How the hell should I know. I tell you, you can really screw up, you know what I mean?"

I sit there wondering if Emmett would have come to this same conclusion if he'd had the chance to leave, and if he would have wanted to come back. Probably not. We had no little children to consider; only one big one who irked him.

I begin squirming to get out of the deep couch. "Excuse me...uh, you want anything? Can I bring you something, uh, Jason?"

"Nah. I'm okay, thanks. Nice talking to you."

Where to now, I wonder. Just then the pink print outfit appears, and Izzie puts her hand on my arm. "Peg, now I know who you are—you're my daddy's new one. His project."

"What? His project?" I bristle, but then think, *no, I've got this wrong*.

"He's been telling me about this woman he's bringing around. How injured she is. He's good at that, at helping lost souls, orphans. Can we go outside and talk? We started out on the wrong foot."

I follow her out the French doors to the fire pit outside. "Let's sit here for a minute, okay? I want to tell you how sorry I am that I misunderstood you. How sorry that my dad scolded you on account of me. My dad, well, he's totally loyal and protective. You have to understand that about him."

"Oh, really? I *have* to?" I feel my cheeks burn.

"First of all, you should know that he still pines for my mom; they had one of the all-time great love stories, a classic, perfect in every way. But my mom, she went through a bad patch and things fell apart."

"She's remarried."

"That's true, but it isn't working out, and me and my brother Todd, well, we're hoping that Mom and Dad will get back together. Given time I think that might happen."

"So you want me out of the picture."

She laughs. "I can't put it like that. My dad is a great guy, but he's naïve. I can't believe that he knows yet what he wants."

"It's been four years. Time he found out."

Now she frowns. "That's exactly the kind of mean attitude I was afraid you'd have. You need to *work* with my dad, and I don't mean at Mountain Valley Cable. I mean *cooperate* with him while he figures out which way is best for him."

"*For him*? What if I decide that *I'm* the best for him, or what if *he* decides that? He's an adult."

"That's true, but then the guilt would be on you, for breaking up a family. We used to be a close family, and everything was just perfect. For example, did he tell you that he bought that truck just so we could get a twelve-foot Christmas tree, one that would touch the ceiling? Because, see, that was what we wanted. Mom would make thermoses of hot chocolate, and we'd go up to the Mother Lode, pick out the perfect tree, then eat pizza at Sutter Creek…did he tell you that?"

"As a matter of fact, he did. What do you want me to do, Isabel? Disappear from his life?"

"That's entirely up to you, but I just wanted you to know that my dad is not alone, he's got a whole family, a whole history that you'd be taking on with him."

I sit there, staring at this frilly frizzy girl, with the shadow of the monkey puzzle tree on her face. She pats my hand, mutters about how we understand each other, let's go in, join the party.

I am numb. There is something dead inside me, and I am glad it's dead because otherwise I'd be raving with anger, this little snip! I enter the dining room, gulp a cup of punch. I have never been so thirsty. I mingle. I flow with quicksilver ease, fluid with grace while the talk swirls around my silver dress, my bouncy new haircut. I am fine. Such a good party, now that I've got my bearings. Either that, or I'm heading out to sea on a life raft.

Later, in a sort of benediction—the party's winding down—a group forms around the piano, and we sing carols. Bruce and Izzie have disappeared, thank goodness, and I am in a rare good mood. I finish out the last chorus of *Deck the Halls* following Emmett's maxim: if you don't know the words, hum. Emmett had been a Pogo fan, had memorized and could sing with great gusto about decking us in Boston Charlie, and Nora's freezin' on the trolley, WallaWalla Wash and Kalamazoo, but not the real words. Typically, he could master the joke, but not the serious. I will consider this aspect, this judgement, as soon as I'm allowed to go home and mull over my Emmett stories.

Then in the dark of Helen's car on the way home, I make small talk, dissecting the party, all the while wishing for silence. Silence to assemble my pride—that damned Bruce—but more importantly, my collage of Emmetts culled from this evening. A design of good and evil? No, that's too dramatic, too black-or-white. What I have, instead, is a collection of grays, whites, and reds. Maybe some blue, because Emmett couldn't have been happy with the way his junior college capers had played out. He must have been affected by his expulsion, by the end of his career dreams, whatever they'd been.

No doubt about it, there had been several Emmetts. Emmett the cut-up, the scamp, the mischievous rascal. Emmett the devil, had Mr. Feldman done the telling. Then again Emmett the good and generous, a caring man devoting himself to helping a family in need. All that volunteering—he must have been doing his own penance, atoning for something amiss in his own life, possibly for something that happened in Vietnam. Who knows? The saddest part: it's too late to ask him.

But maybe we're all like that. Give us a twist, and our usual behavior patterns fall apart quicker than a diet, or a budget. We go to pieces and take on foreign or ill-fitting shadings or shapes that shock or surprise us. Or that please and delight—that's possible, too.

Chapter 14

I'm having a relapse. A scientific term for falling apart.

Instead of moving forward, *progressing* into my improved and promising new year, into Valentine's Day, my Presidents' Day holiday, with the added bonus of getting my taxes off early, after managing to clamp my hands around the neck of my life and throttling it into a semblance of order, I'm slipping backward.

Once I couldn't sleep; now I can't wake up. I'm a zombie going through the motions. In the bank, after waiting in line, I get up to the teller with no slip filled out, no idea if I'm after a deposit or withdrawal. In the market I wander around, since I've forgotten my list, and arrive home with useless groceries. At work, I forget what I'm doing, whose account I'm working on, or why. The central concern of my life: getting back to bed, to sleep. Sleep. The land of peace and forgetfulness. What do I want to forget? That I'm alone again after a brief flick of what passes, with me, for *sociability*? I mentioned this to Mr. Purdy, told him I was losing all the improvements I'd grafted onto my psyche. He said a leopard doesn't change its spots. It hides in the bushes, takes on a camouflage, but underneath it's still a leopard.

This is a normal development? This reverting to what must be my true nature? After all, it's been *almost* a year. Or, on the other hand, it's been not *even* a year. I don't know which applies. Again I'll mention this to Mr. Purdy. He's about the only one I talk to these days.

That's because Amy and Phil are gone, packed up and left for Wales, which might as well be the far side of the moon, although she calls (collect) every Sunday. My living room has become storage for boxes of their belongings; my garage is taken up with Amy's Mustang. Phil's Ford Escort rests, and rusts, in my side yard. I wouldn't put up with this intrusion, except keeping their things seems akin to keeping a hold on them: when they come back, and they will, they'll come to *me.*

"Is that what you want?" asks Mr. Purdy, peering at me over his bowl of oyster stew. "'Course, what do I know. I never had kids."

I'm sure he's on the cusp of peppering me with some remarks about tearing down the nest so when the birdies come flapping home, there's no place to perch; but I'm not receptive; he knows better and shuts up.

At work, my lunch group has fallen apart. Helen now goes off to eat with Eileen, her Jolly Roger friend, who works around the corner at Radio Shack. Without Helen as cover, going one-on-one with Bruce over lunch in the conference room is too intimate, too intimidating; and we drift off on our separate ways.

Besides, I'm still pissed as hell over his poor performance at Vi's Christmas party. He feels bad about it, too, and has apologized, several times, for the way he jumped to conclusions, and even for his snippy little daughter's behavior. "I'm sorry, Peg," he mumbles. "Izzie had it wrong, I know you wouldn't say her legs are fat."

I freeze him with a cold look. "No, I didn't say that, because if anything, her legs are skinny."

He gulps but manfully shoulders forward. "Whatever. I was edgy and nervous that night, and I want to forget that it ever happened. Can't we let it go at that?"

"She said you want to get back with Jan. That your ex is having problems with the new one, and you're looking to go home."

He hangs his head. "Yeah, well, I suppose I might have thought that, but it wouldn't have worked out."

"Why not?"

"Because...either she's changed, or I have. Which I should have realized. Would happen, I mean. People don't stay the same, and the way I remembered her, all sweet and funny and cute...that's not the way she is now."

I try to extinguish, or at least disguise, the warm wash of pleasure this gives me. Moreover, something in me resonates, as if I'm a bell he has just rung. If I were to meet Emmett now, would I like him? Or would I see him as an insensitive man awash in testosterone, a dinosaur of a John Wayne pursuing grotesque and overly aggressive hobbies? Would I wonder what sort of a self-effacing wife he had at home, catering to his whims, skewing the perception of both of them?

Bruce adds, "Jan, I don't know, she's got a real attitude these days, pushy and bitter, like I owe her, it's all my fault."

He could be describing me.

Apparently he's unaware of that, and goes on, "And the place is a mess, needs paint—they've let it go—and the grass, my beautiful lawn, it's all weeds. Nobody mows, not even Todd, after all

I taught him. Make a long story short, I realized you can't, you can't—"

"Go home again?"

"That's about it. You know, none of this would have happened between us—between you and me, we were doing fine—if it hadn't been for that rotten party at Vi's," he says, neatly circling back to where he came in.

Fine? I don't know about *fine,* but there'd been at least a possibility that we could have done something mutually congenial. I agree with his assessment of the party, a wretched affair, on more than one count. Because right after the New Year when we came back to work, Vi had paged me into the conference room. Uh, oh, I thought, pacing down the hall in my hippie boots—I've fallen in love with them again, and they're just the thing for this ice cave we work in—here we go, I've had it. And yes, it was more political fallout from the party. In a faux patient tone, she explained that Tiffany's had a hard time, a difficult life, for which she takes Prozac, among other medications, and the last thing she needs is people interfering in her relationships.

"What!"

"Tiff says you advised her friend—Jason?—that he ought to go back to his wife. I think that's up to Jason, and the more we stick our noses into someone else's business, the more harm we cause. Now, I suspect, Peg, that since you're older and probably consider yourself wiser—"

"Wait a minute! I never said any such thing to Jason. We sat on the couch together for five minutes, during which time he complained about Tiffany, about how hard she is to live with, how hard it is, or has been, to raise two little kids. How Tiffany…forget it! This is ridiculous."

I actually stomped out, slapping down my felt boots as hard as I could. Went to sulk in the bathroom, which was more Tiffany's style than mine. To her credit, Vi later apologized, said she hadn't had all the facts, and that perhaps she'd been out of line to speak so quickly. Please, she pleaded, let's cultivate a *professional* atmosphere wherein we do our work with a minimum of interference, of friction, blah, blah, blah.

The upshot of *that* was that I took a day off, my first one ever, and went down to the Department of Human Resources to look for a new job. A waste of time. I snagged a number from the dispenser and waited in line with fifty or sixty other people, most of them jabbering away in Spanish or Urdu or something that from the looks of them could have been Arabic. I'd visualized a cozy conference with a sympathetic professional who'd listen to me, leaning across a nice clean desk, then smile encouragingly and magically place me, a square Peg, in a nice tidy square hole. Instead, a surly clerk finally bellowed my number, then talked loudly over a counter—for all the world to hear—telling me, in sum, that I was overqualified. All they had on offer was service-oriented, motel maid, gardener, fast food. "You're employed now, right? Well, then you got no problem, right?" Shoving my paperwork back across the counter, the woman yelled, "Next! Number sixty-three! Number sixty-three!"

To cheer myself up, to form a psychic link to faraway Amy, I ate lunch at the same place where we'd last eaten, at that health food joint one block off Main in a converted Victorian trimmed with fish scales and gingerbread. I usually avoid such establishments, which intimidate me with their self-righteous purity. Macramé curtains cover windows plastered with rainbow-hued HONOR DIVERSITY stickers; tables and chairs arrogantly mismatched, overhung with creeping charlie plants; the waitresses—who give the impression they know more about my blood pressure than I do—are long-skirted women wearing Birkenstocks, their long hair in gray braids.

I ordered a sweet potato frittata, and tea (green, organic, decaf), and waited and waited…why such slow service…all they had to do was carve a square off the casserole I could see in the refrigerated display and stick it in the microwave…aha, no microwave, of course. So I had plenty of time to read from their assorted literature (smeared type, recycled paper). To chart my chakras, get in touch with my inner child (or parent), learn about the magic of macrobiotics.

Mainly, though, I reminisced, I recalled Amy's and my stay at that place in the redwoods. We'd had a jolly trip. But I realized, with my increasing ability to tolerate self-honesty, that retrospect was working its magic, that time and distance were spinning a glow that the actual event had not been blessed with—I'd done the same with vacations, with life itself, with Emmett.

However, it *had* been gratifying to spend time with Amy, walking on that beach, talking about Emmett. After all, who else could I talk to about him? No one wanted to put up with my drivel. I was even getting sick of it myself.

At last my lunch. Forking up the sweet potato thing, I wondered if the sole reason I'd ordered it was to avoid duplicating what I'd had with Amy, which I hadn't liked. No more than the food in that hifalutin inn, overpriced, over-cheesed, overdone. I was making the same mistake again and again. What was I doing here? I tossed down money for the bill and a tip—fifteen percent (no tablecloth, only a tie-dye runner), signed their petitions to save wetlands, tigers and the pandas. All the while thinking that if I hurried, I'd be able to work in a nap before bedtime. So much sleep; so little time.

Subway, that's my place. I start dropping in there for lunch, sinking into my plastic booth, wolfing down my BLT, slurping my Dr. Pepper. An angry slurp, because, between naps, I've just finished an irritating book Helen loaned me. It's about this stalwart, inventive, *plucky* babe on her own for the first time, a new version of *An Unmarried Woman.* A rich gal—she's been left by her rich husband, who decides he wants to come back after it's too late—goes to work as a temp, for the saucy thrill of it, and develops a scheme to rent out parts of her house. She makes a dizzy success of her eclectic clientele, she prospers, she engages in a warm fuzzy romance. Happiness, as far as the eye can see. I want to shriek, That's not the way it is!

Then one day Bruce rolls into the parking lot, parks his rig next to my Bronco, strides in, orders a sandwich, then plunks down across from me. How did he know I was here? Well, there's my Bronco in the parking lot. I remember Mr. Purdy remarking that Mad Max was keeping an eye on the house. Is he stalking me?

Not Bruce. I doubt he's capable of it. He takes a bite out of his sandwich, then says sternly, with mock irritation, "By the way, you owe me some Chinese."

"I *what*?" Oh, he is clever, knowing he'd get nowhere being polite, but to lay on a guilt trip, yeah, I'd go for it.

"Yes, I wanted Chinese and you forced me into Mexican. When are you going to make it up to me?"

In spite of myself, I experience a rush. He's missed me, I make a difference in his life. I manage to conceal how the pique of my iceberg is melting into a warm puddle of gratitude, of *affection* (yes, but not *love*), and snap, "Have you got Izzie's okay for that? Does she know you're eating lunch with me? You better square it with her first."

"Come on, Peg."

"Or better yet, why doesn't she fix you some chow mein at home? Open a can, throw on some noodles. That way she'll know exactly where you are."

He takes this with equanimity. "The Jade Garden this Friday night."

"Can't this Fri—"

"Mr. Purdy and the oyster stew. I forgot. How about Saturday?"

But I will not so easily give up my rich war for a threadbare capitulation. I hedge and argue, I want to rub his nose in it, back him into a corner; I want to pick a fight. After two months of sleepwalking, I am alive, alert, quivering for action. It's wonderful, but I don't want him to know it. That would give him too much power…but who am I kidding? He's got eyes in his head, he can see for himself that I have (probably) pinked up with this emotional jump-start he's delivered. I'm not dead after all.

With a philosophical shrug, he accepts the pelting I deliver—he's used to it, has, probably, gotten it from Jan, and now, probably, from Izzie. A man who's used to dealing with difficult women might just be my cup of tea. I consider this idea while I study him across from me, as he sinks his square teeth into his chicken sandwich (I think it's chicken—who can tell what the mystery meat is in these places?). He's got a slight smear of mustard on the corner of his mouth. He wipes at it, says, "How about after your soup date with Mr. Purdy? Yeah, this Friday, I'll come by, pick you up and we'll go for pie? A drink?"

When I shake my head, he says, "Well, don't say no now; think about it, let me know later."

Friday with Mr. Purdy and oyster stew. As usual, he's full of his usual indignation over the usual mess at City Hall, the usual shenanigans of the Council—which is all news to me because I've quit reading the paper. He switches over to the neighborhood skinny, tells me, with a laugh, that Lyle had something explode in his garage, was out with an extinguisher putting down a smoky blaze while Frieda ran around wringing her hands. Irene's been doing bedding plants, pansies, and he thinks it's too early. "This weather, it'll fool you. We always get a cold snap just before real spring."

I watch him slurp his oyster stew, and I think I'm in my cold snap now, this is it. I'll spend the rest of my life watching him, the high point of my week, apart from grabbing a nap, or going back to bed. Something has to change, I'm ready for a change. I can't go on like this, I have finished with one thing and I want the next thing to begin.

What I'm finished with is my grieving period. How do I know, how does anyone know, when it's over? Because it's no longer serving a useful purpose, which is emptying the well of the psyche, no longer plump with satisfying emotions. It lies down as flat as a dried out, run-over skunk in the road, deplete of juice.

One of Emmett's more dreary poems bubbles up, like an air pocket in thick soup, or a pimple in clear skin. I vow to get a paper shredder and put an end to his drivel. If only erasing them from my memory will be as easy:

There's more to me than meets the eye,
But also there's much less.
I'm deep, I'm dense, a shallow guy—
A puzzle, I confess.
Like you, I'm pure in my good life,

In oaths and vows and lies.
Deceits and dreams—with both I'm rife—
This comes as no surprise.

This world's like us, you know my dear—
No need to fret or fume.
Not much is simple, straight, or clear
Except a path from here to doom.

I'm not ready for that path yet. I want jokes and pranks and games. I want fights, and tricks, and outrage. And laughter. I want messy connections...with Bruce? Well, it's a start. Maybe more than a start.

Then Mr. Purdy says something that strikes me. "You read about that meteor shower due tonight? Whole mess of meteorites supposed to flare across the sky. I'd go out to watch it, but we got too many streetlights. You need total dark, but I don't know where you'd get it around here. Used to be dark at night, but now..." and he goes off on a reminiscence about how things used to be, back in the good old days.

I don't attend to his rant, because I know a place where I can see a meteor shower, which may be just what I'm waiting for.

At the top of my cul-de-sac I shine the light from one of Emmett's flashlights on a path through a vacant lot, one of the last vacant lots in captivity around here. This path leads to an overlook above the glow of streetlights, a place where I'll see a falling star show. I asked Mr. Purdy to come, too, but he said he was too full, too tired, hadn't felt well all day, although he put away two bowls of soup and a great quantity of garlic bread. That's fine—I really want to be alone.

This is federal land, part of an abandoned World War II ammunition arsenal, and has never been developed. The knob overlook will be a fine viewing platform. The trail up to it is rough and rocky, full of knee-high scrub that catches at my skirt. It's that foolish broomstick skirt, not practical for this trip, but I love it. I view it as a symbol, an indication of improvement—at least of change—the same way I view my boots, my earrings, even my smooth glowing teak table.

About halfway up there's a spring, but there's been no rain since that Halloween storm so there's only a bit of mud to step my felt boots around. I continue up to that wide cleared spot, the shelf-like projection. I know of this place from when Amy was a baby and Emmett and I brought her up here to watch Fourth of July fireworks—the City used to put on a show from a nearby park. Not now, of course, with the fire danger so high and the budget so low.

Later when neighborhood kids were teenagers, this fort-like projection had been a hangout and littered with debris—soda and beer cans, candy wrappers, cigarette butts, even used condoms. But our kids are grown and gone. Now the area stays fairly clean.

I can see my whole neighborhood. The lights are on at Irene's—she and her husband are fans of *Austin City Limits.* I imagine them in their den eating dessert,(for some reason it's bread pudding, or brown betty), while watching bluegrass bands, keeping time to a country banjo or guitar. I see the lights on in Frieda's garage where Lyle is probably cleaning up from his fire. I see the lights at Mr. Purdy's, at my own house, and I wish, fleetingly, that I'd brought a coat—at the last minute I'd thrown on Emmett's embroidered shirt, and it's not enough.

I spread the ground cloth I grabbed from the garage; first sit down, then lie back when my neck gets a crook in it. It's dull work. Rarely is there a brief streak of light, then it appears in exactly the area I'm not looking at. I am restless and bored. I came here to connect with Emmett in some spiritual or philosophical way. He's out there, riding a meteor through space as Slim Pickins had ridden an A-bomb in *Dr. Strangelove*. Emmett loved that movie.

But it's cold work; the smell of damp earth floods my senses, along with the realization that death is enormous, never-ending. I quail before it; and also before the inescapable fact that I've moved beyond Emmett, as he'd moved beyond me.

Dying young is best, I tell myself briskly. Emmett is frozen in time, held forever at the permanent point of perfection I grant him in my memory. On the other hand, I will age and fade—if I'm lucky. I will grow to resemble Mr. Purdy, or his cousin, wrinkled, opinionated and crotchety. Like his cousin, I'll sign up for a cruise; I'll cavort in a silly party hat, in a dress that exposes my wrinkled bosom. Maybe I'll flirt with some old codger at my dinner table. I'll tell him soft sad stories about my long-dead husband, feed him lies about investments and interesting operations, and a treacherous son-in-law—Phil will be treacherous, I already see that. I see him as tricky, devious, a problem for Amy.

Maybe I'll become a problem for Amy, too, become senile, or so tough and resilient that I develop a hide like a rhinoceros—I'm on my way now. I'll become insensitive and desperate, tiresomely buoyant. The kind of woman Emmett had found distasteful, had avoided.

I tell myself that Emmett is well out of it with wars, pollution, overpopulation, destruction as far as the eye can see. I tell myself, and I believe it, that I don't want Emmett back, or Amy, either.

Has love died for me?

Do you go on living a whole life after you admit that you are alone, and that love has died for you?

"Love is eternal."

Emmett said that once. It was early on, during his gushy period, and he'd probably had something to drink. However, I thought he meant it. Now it strikes me as nonsense. Love isn't eternal. It dies more often than it lives. Love, like fire and hate, needs fuel. I'm out of all three, and a relieved exhaustion overtakes me, sweeps through me like a clean breeze, clearing out my head. I experience a sort of wide-spreading emptiness, a peaceful acceptance, a restful apathy that verges on insensibility.

Enough! Enough! We're all a puzzle to each other, no exceptions, and I've had enough doubletalk from you, Emmett, you and your poems. I don't want anything from you. I want to drain my head and heart and not care about anybody. This business about the nature of love...nothing is more fragile, more ephemeral than love...nothing is more stubborn, obdurate, inopportune, contrary, *painful*...

I glance around, because I might even have said what I'm thinking out loud. But who would hear me? I'm absolutely alone.

I remember the time I came up here with Emmett and toddler Amy. We watched the City-sponsored fireworks bloom in the sky—bursts of chrysanthemums, pinwheels, fountains, firefalls, a real show. Amy squealed with delight, and we oohed and aahed at the man-made orchestrations of color. How ironic—that glitter-filled sky far out-performed this slow pale demonstration of the real thing.

That night I looked down at my house, as I'm doing now, and I'd felt, I'd *known,* that I had it all. Everything I needed for happiness, everything I'd ever wanted. Husband, home, family. All right there, not only in reach, but in my possession.

How lucky I'd been to have that feeling, even fleetingly…how many people ever experience such completeness, even for a short time? I have been blessed. I will quit whining about what everybody else puts up as a permanent condition. And I still have my house…I look down at it, to make sure, to comfort myself.….and I see Bruce's giant pickup trolling slowly up the block to the turnaround, then back again. It's got to be Bruce, dear Bruce. Yes, I hear it, the marbles-in-a-coffee-can diesel rattle.

Maybe I should take him on. But by the time I've navigated down off this hill in the dark, in this crazy skirt that brambles pull at, in these boots that slip, he'll have given up and gone on his way. He's not going to wait around forever; he, too, has been in limbo, and now he's waking up, coming out of it, as I am myself.

Still, just because the timing's right doesn't mean we're destined for each other, Bruce and me.

But my life is falling forward, pulling me down off my hill. The past is over, even the present—it's gone like *that,* the merest little sliver on which I can balance only for a nanosecond. Something impels me, like gravity—something not to be denied—and I gather up my ground cloth, shake it in a deliberate manner, fold it, then switch on the flashlight to begin picking my way along the scrubby trail. As I move down, back to my real life, or what has been my real life, I strike a bargain with myself: if he's still there when I arrive at my own house, we'll try to make a go of it. But if he's gone, well, it wasn't meant to be.

In any case, I'm the one who'll inflict the damage this time, because I know that Bruce is not as tough as I am, as tough as I have grown. I will not be easy on him, I am capable of dealing with him harshly. Even while I think that, I know it's a lie, a self-protective lie I tell myself to cover my vulnerability.

Nevertheless, the prospect of discovering who I am in the context of Bruce excites me, causes me to pick up my pace and I plunge along rather recklessly, skirting the mud around the spring, the brambles in the vacant lot. I can no longer see whether his truck cruises the street, because now houses loom in my view.

Please, let him be gone, let's get it over with. Ah, isn't that his truck I hear, the rattly diesel? No, it's some machine tool Lyle is using in his garage. The wild beating of my own heart almost drowns out any noise, and I can't hear clearly, I can't think clearly. I feel as if my footsteps—I'm now at the bottom of the hill and approaching the path that winds through the vacant lot—are leaving pools of regret and pain, rather than a track of mud.

Because I see now that I was happy alone, I was coming along. Oh, sure, some days were up, some down, but that's to be expected. I hear a rattle, I walk faster…isn't that his truck? Isn't he turning around, getting ready to head out? Yes, I've surely missed him, he's given up.

I break into a run, I run, but am I in time, or has he given up? I wouldn't blame him if he's given up, because he's been patient enough…and I am out of breath as I sprint into the street.